A SECRET WISH

"You are extraordinarily kind, my dear Regina," Balfour said. "I can only imagine Sir Andrew's effusive gratitude."

"Well, do not let it trouble you. I still entertain hopes for Ramsey. Something may yet be contrived."

"I have one or two notions that might help."

"Careful, Your Grace," Regina warned, looking up at him with a teasing smile. "Your image as a heartless rake is slipping."

"There are ways to rectify that," he said, his arm coming up to rest against the wall, trapping Regina between the box and the aisle. He was close enough to hear her quick intake of breath, and to see the way her lips suddenly parted. All he had to do was bend his head to taste her sweet mouth.

She gazed into his blue eyes, now filled with desire. For an instant, she longed to throw convention to the winds, longed to throw her arms about his broad shoulders and lose herself in what she was certain would be a most passionate kiss . . .

WATCH FOR THESE ZEBRA REGENCIES

LADY STEPHANIE   (0-8217-5341-X, $4.50)
by Jeanne Savery
Lady Stephanie Morris has only one true love: the family estate she has managed ever since her mother died. But then Lord Anthony Rider arrives on her estate, claiming he has plans for both the land and the woman. Stephanie soon realizes she's fallen in love with a man whose sensual caresses will plunge her into a world of peril and intrigue . . . a man as dangerous as he is irresistible.

BRIGHTON BEAUTY   (0-8217-5340-1, $4.50)
by Marilyn Clay
Chelsea Grant, pretty and poor, naively takes school friend Alayna Marchmont's place and spends a month in the country. The devastating man had sailed from Honduras to claim his promised bride, Miss Marchmont. An affair of the heart may lead to disaster . . . unless a resourceful Brighton beauty finds a way to stop a masquerade and keep a lord's love.

LORD DIABLO'S DEMISE   (0-8217-5338-X, $4.50)
by Meg-Lynn Roberts
The sinfully handsome Lord Harry Glendower was a gambler and the black sheep of his family. About to be forced into a marriage of convenience, the devilish fellow engineered his own demise, never having dreamed that faking his death would lead him to the heavenly refuge of spirited heiress Gwyn Morgan, the daughter of a physician.

A PERILOUS ATTRACTION   (0-8217-5339-8, $4.50)
by Dawn Aldridge Poore
Alissa Morgan is stunned when a frantic passenger thrusts her baby into Alissa's arms and flees, having heard rumors that a notorious highwayman posed a threat to their coach. Handsome stranger Hugh Sebastian secretly possesses the treasured necklace the highwayman seeks and volunteers to pose as Alissa's husband to save her reputation. With a lost baby and missing necklace in their care, the couple embarks on a journey into peril—and passion.

Available wherever paperbacks are sold, or order direct from the Publisher. Send cover price plus 50¢ per copy for mailing and handling to Penguin USA, P.O. Box 999, c/o Dept. 17109, Bergenfield, NJ 07621. Residents of New York and Tennessee must include sales tax. DO NOT SEND CASH.

THE DUKE
WHO CAME
TO VISIT

Carol Quinto

ZEBRA BOOKS
KENSINGTON PUBLISHING CORP.

ZEBRA BOOKS are published by

Kensington Publishing Corp.
850 Third Avenue
New York, NY 10022

First Printing: October, 1996
10 9 8 7 6 5 4 3 2 1

Printed in the United States of America

For Bebe and Pat Dalton
of Winning Spree Farm
Ocala, Florida
May all your horses be champions!

Prologue

A dense fog lay over the grove. Sir Charles Wrexmere shivered within his heavy coat. He wondered again what had possessed him to challenge the duke to a duel. Everyone knew Balfour to be a dead shot, and cold-blooded to boot. Wrexmere laid a gloved hand against his nose, but an uncontrollable sneeze shook his heavy frame.

After wiping his nose, he snapped at his second. "I hope Balfour is on time for I certainly don't intend to wait about in this damp."

"Bad for one's health it is," Mr. Foxham agreed. "But one could say the same about challenging His Grace." He laughed heartily at his own wit.

George Carlyle struggled to hide his grin and made a show of consulting his watch. "A few minutes before the hour yet. Can't say as I'd be surprised if the duke is late. I heard Balfour held the faro bank at White's last night and did not leave until three this morning."

Sir Charles felt a brief stirring of hope, quickly beaten down when Foxham pointed out a cloud of dust in the distance. "That's probably His Grace now. Timed it to the moment, he has."

The duke's black sporting curricle swung round the bend just as the church tower chimed the hour. Any hope Sir Charles had that his opponent might be impaired by the late hour he'd kept, or excessive drink, disappeared as he watched Balfour skillfully bring a pair of highbred stallions to a standstill.

"Well done, Cedric," Lord Dansford shouted, jumping down the off side of the curricle, then hurrying round to greet the others. "The doctor's coming with Houghton. They should be here in a moment. Told him he'd never keep up with Balfour's blacks. There ain't a team in all of England that can hold a candle to them."

The Duke of Balfour took his time descending from the carriage, then leisurely strolled toward the waiting group of men. Immaculately turned out, the only sign of disarray about his trim person was his hair. The dark gold curls were windblown and fell carelessly across his brow.

Sir Charles observed him closely. As was his custom, Balfour was clad in black with only a touch of white at his neck and wrists. He wore no ornaments and, although his coat was obviously tailored by Weston, it was not so tight that he needed assistance to put it on. Tall and slender, many considered the duke to be a handsome man. Sir Charles disagreed. He found Balfour's light blue eyes too cold for his taste, and considered the duke's athletic build more appropriate for a member of the ring than for a gentleman of refinement.

There was little, in fact, about Balfour to admire, at least in Wrexmere's opinion. He watched Foxham fawning over Balfour and thought that if were it not for the duke's immense wealth, he wouldn't be so catered to by certain members of the ton.

His Grace, feeling his opponent's eyes upon him, turned to glance at Wrexmere, and smiled slightly.

Sir Charles hastily turned away, cursing again his own stupidity in challenging Balfour over a game of whist. He'd regretted the words the instant they issued from his mouth. If pressed, he would have admitted that he knew the duke had not cheated, though his luck was phenomenal and the amount of money he won unconscionable. However, no one had said a word. A dead silence had fallen over the room, leaving him and the Duke of Balfour the center of attention.

Sir Charles shuddered delicately at the memory, wishing fervently that the duel was over and done with.

Foxham touched his arm indicating that it was time, then escorted him to his position. He left him with a last bit of advice. "Remember now, as soon as you see the handkerchief drop, bring your arm up. And stand sideways. No sense in giving Balfour more to aim at than necessary."

It seemed only seconds later that the handkerchief dropped. Wrexmere dutifully brought his arm up, only to gasp suddenly as a pistol ball tore through his shoulder. He staggered, then dropped to his knees, paling visibly as he saw the blood staining his coat.

Balfour, immediately after firing, turned on his heel and headed for his carriage. He had no time to waste on the likes of Sir Charles Wrexmere.

"Blast you, Cedric, must you be in such a hurry?" Dansford asked as he strode to catch up with his friend. "In all decency, you might at least wait to see what damage you've inflicted."

Balfour paused, his dark brows arching in surprise. "What, you doubt my aim? The ball went in the shoulder, I assure you. Come along. I have bespoke breakfast at the Red Lion, and as soon as we are done, I am off for Norwich."

Sir Charles, clutching his shoulder, stared after them. He cursed fluently as his second reached him. "It's little wonder they call him Devil. I swear I was hit even before the handkerchief touched the ground."

"I'd be careful what you say," Mr. Foxham admonished him. "It was a fair fight, and instead of whining about it, you should count your blessings. Devil or not, Balfour spared your life."

The weather matched the duke's black mood. Torrents of rain pelted the road, all but blinding him. His driving capes were covered with mud and so sodden they offered little protection. Balfour drove by instinct alone, though in truth, he didn't care enough for the consequences to worry over an accident. The wind shifted abruptly, the strong gust startling the horses. A deft flick of his wrist and a strong hand on the reins brought the team quickly under control.

Inside the luxurious travelling carriage, Balfour's valet, Desmond, tumbled half off his seat. He clutched Tenby's arm, certain they were about to be overturned. Normally, a most superior, almost elegant creature, he now lay pale and shivering. He pleaded with the groom, "For God's sake, can't you stop him? He'll kill us all before he's done."

Tenby glared at him. "Be more 'an my life's worth to try to stop him just because we hit a few ruts in the road. 'Course, I'm more accustomed to it, having been with His Grace so much longer 'an you."

The remark rankled, as it was intended to do. Desmond released his hold on the groom's arm. His lips worked in a silent prayer while he tried to compose himself. He had almost succeeded when a clap of thunder and a perilously close streak of lightning caused him to grab at Tenby again.

The groom was quick to sneer, "You'd best be looking for another post, Desmond, if you're going to let a little jaunt in a thunderstorm turn you inside out. This is the way His Grace likes to travel. But then, those of us who have been with him for years are used to it. I'll wager your fine Lord Drummond never had the guts to drive a team like this."

"Lord Drummond had more sense," the valet snapped in defense of his former employer. The flush of anger restored a little color to his face. He vowed not to utter another word until they stopped, or were overturned, he amended silently.

Although Tenby couldn't resist taunting Desmond, and would never own up to it, he, too, worried. He'd seen the duke in some rare moods, but never one like this. It wasn't like him to risk injuring one of the horses, pushing 'em hard in a thunderstorm. He couldn't understand what had come over his master. He knew His Grace had fought a duel early on the morning they'd left Town, but he hadn't seemed overset by it. Just a trifle out of sorts. A bit restless, was all. They had stopped to call on Lord Schilling at Bedford and passed a pleasant enough night, but the duke had insisted on leaving early in the morning, despite a threatening storm.

Then the skies had opened with a vengeance. Tenby had thought His Grace would call a halt, but instead he'd taken the reins himself. And driven like a devil ever since. Still, Tenby mused, what he'd told Desmond was true. He'd trust his fate any day of the week to the master's skill with a team. Not another whip in England could match him when it came to driving four-in-hand. Settling back against the plush cushions, Tenby pulled his cap over his eyes, and feigned sleep.

A moment later, he was jerked from his seat and tumbled roughly to the floor. He slid helplessly downward as the carriage turned over with a sickening crunch. Desmond's horrified shriek resounded in his ears, and he felt the valet's bony body slam into his own. Struggling against Desmond's weight and flailing arms, Tenby managed to pull himself up to a sitting position. He looked up to see Balfour peering down from the open carriage door.

The duke helped Desmond to climb out, with an assist from Tenby from behind, and then his groom, before hurrying to check his horses. None of the four stallions appeared to be injured and Tenby, hard on his master's heels, heaved a sigh of relief. It was short-lived, however, as he took in the damage to the front axle. "Split clear through, Your Grace! What's to do now?"

Balfour studied the wheel, then glanced at the sky. "I fear you are right, Tenby, but at least the storm is breaking. I will take one of the horses and ride back a mile or two. I believe I noticed a smallish estate just off the road. Pity we are too far from Houghton House to make it before dusk."

"You ride, Your Grace? But don't you want as I should go—"

"No. I am too restless to bide my time here. You and Desmond make yourselves as comfortable as possible. I shall send help as soon as I can."

The prospect was not pleasing to Tenby, but he knew better than to argue. Reluctantly, he unearthed Balfour's riding saddle, and got the lead horse ready for him. He gave his master a leg up, then stepped back.

Balfour, noting his sour countenance, grinned down at him. "This will give you and Desmond an excellent opportunity to become better acquainted."

With a salute of the whip, he was off.

One

Regina Westfield looked incredulously at her sister-in-law. "You cannot be serious, Beth. I know nothing of taking care of a child. What would I do with the boy for an entire summer?"

Her brother hastened to reassure her. "I promise you, Regina, he's not the least trouble. Why, you will hardly notice David is here."

"And how would you know, Andrew? You are never at home long enough to even begin to be aware of the problems a ten-year-old boy could cause. He would disrupt my entire household. Besides, I have already laid plans for the summer. There is a new brood mare that I have high hopes for—"

"Really, Regina," he interrupted. "I had quite thought you would have got over your obsession with horses by now—and may I remind you—it is hardly a fit topic for the drawing room. If nothing else, David will give your mind a more proper turn. Perhaps you might even begin to think of children of your own instead of those infernal foals."

A ready image of herself strolling across the grounds with a bevy of children tugging at her skirts, caused her to smile impishly. "Certainly, but what then, pray tell? Whom would you have me wed? Or are you proposing I should bear my children out of wedlock?"

Andrew reddened. After a concerned glance for his wife, he glared at his sister. "If you would conduct yourself with more propriety, you might find half-a-dozen gentlemen willing to wed you. You're not an ill-looking girl, but that cursed tongue of yours is enough to turn any man of breeding against you."

Beth laid a gentle hand on his arm before turning to Regina. "Forgive him, dearest. When he's not on his high ropes, you must know your brother is the first to puff off your beauty *and* your intelligence. I know he is loath to admit it, but Andrew is concerned for David's safety. That is why we must ask you to keep him here for the summer."

Regina instantly forgave her brother, and her soft green eyes reflected her concern. "What is this? Why should you fear for David? What have you been about, Andy?"

Sir Andrew Westfield, who had conducted scores of diplomatic missions for King George, and more recently for the Prince Regent, seemed to lose all his poise when it came to dealing with his sister. He could not keep a guilty flush from suffusing his face, but he stood and tried to assume an authoritative manner. It didn't help that his sister topped him by two inches and he had to look up at her. "It's really nothing for you to worry over, Regina. I am not at liberty to fully explain the circumstances which compel me to—"

His wife interrupted him again. Regina stared at her in surprise. Beth had the sweetest character, and always looked to her husband for advice and guidance. In all their years of marriage, Regina could not recall her sister-in-law interrupting Andy above a dozen times. "Twice in one day meant something serious was afoot. She gave Beth her undivided attention.

"I have already told Andrew he must tell you everything. It would be monstrously unfair if he did not, and I will have no part in leaving David here otherwise."

Andrew nodded reluctantly, then sat down next to his wife, taking her hand in his own. "The fact is, there have been a few threats on my life. The current work I'm doing is . . . not exactly popular. I have had threats before, even offers of bribes, but . . ." His words trailed off, his thoughts apparently too horrid for words, and again Beth intervened.

"This time the blackguards threatened David. We do not believe it to be serious, but you do see I cannot risk the chance. Andrew and I will be travelling far too much to take David with us, and I cannot be easy leaving him with the servants, however devoted they may be. I thought—it is so secluded here, and you have so few callers . . ."

Regina, fearful that Beth was going to cry, moved at once to sit beside her, and embraced her warmly. "Of course I shall take David. Do not give the matter another thought." Glancing at her brother, she added, "You should have told me at once, Andrew. What hornet's nest have you been stirring?"

Andrew, on his dignity again, frowned. "You do not seem to realize, Regina, that I am acting as envoy for the Prince Regent, himself, whom, I might add, reposes complete trust in my discretion. I can only tell you that he requested me to undertake a highly delicate and sensitive mission which could very well affect the future of England. I met with him personally and we talked at great length, but of course I am not at liberty to divulge the nature of our conversation."

"But it requires that you travel abroad?" she asked, watching him closely. "I suppose then that he wishes you to spy on the Princess of Wales. Is it not sufficient that he has driven her from England?"

Andrew's mouth fell open.

"Oh come, Andy. It is rather obvious. He wants to be rid of her—people have been talking about it for ages."

"Then they should not do so. There are political ramifications to his unfortunate marriage that most people do not understand."

"Perhaps, but the Regent's selfishness and extravagance is something they do understand, and do not like in the least. But I know it is futile to argue with you. Tell me instead what David will need."

More than willing to change the subject, Andrew smiled at her. "Why, nothing at all, for we shall certainly see to it that he puts you to no expense." He hesitated, then after glancing at Beth, added, "However, there is one trifling matter you might take care of for me. I promised David we would engage a tutor for him. He doesn't care where he lives, so long as he is free to study. The boy thinks of nothing but his books, so you two should be well suited."

"You sound almost disappointed in him. I should think you would be proud David is intelligent enough to wish to study."

"I am, naturally. It's just—well, it's hardly normal for a boy to always have his head stuck in a book. At least when you were his age, you rode a lot. David does not want to ride, or hunt, or fish, or anything. He needs more exercise, Gina. Even you have to admit it would be healthier for him to have other pursuits. I want you to find him a tutor who can interest him in sports."

She saw her brother was quite serious and refrained from teasing him, although she could readily sympathize with her nephew. "I shall do my best, but you have not set me an easy task. I fear it will be difficult to find someone who is not only intellectually superior, but athletically inclined, and available to begin at once."

"Nonsense. Put a notice in the *Gazette*. I'll wager you will be flooded with applicants."

Thinking of that conversation three weeks later, Regina sat at the breakfast table wondering what she could possibly do. Her brother had not been precisely wrong. She had placed the ad in the paper as he'd directed, and, indeed, there had been a flood of applicants. Unfortunately, nearly all of them were unsuitable. She had finally narrowed the possibilities to three, and after interviewing two of the young men, she was near despair. David's presence in her household for the last two weeks had convinced her that neither of the gentlemen who'd applied would be capable of asserting their will over him. She prayed her last possible choice, Mr. Jonathan Quill, would prove more satisfactory.

It was not, Regina decided, that David was in any way disobedient or disrespectful. He simply wished to be left alone to read his books. Whenever she attempted to draw him into some other activity, he peered at her in his solemn owl-like manner until she felt rather frivolous and foolish. She had yet to see him excited or animated in any way.

It only made matters worse that she felt a certain amount of empathy with him. She, too, had been an akward child, and hid from the world behind her books. Although she was frequently dubbed regal-looking now, as a child her unusual height had been cause for embarrassment and ridicule. Shamed by her inches, Regina had developed a deplorable habit of hunching over to disguise her height. Her kindly aunt frequently admonished her to stand tall and proud—and in the next breath, spoke disparagingly of her unfortunate height.

Orphaned at eleven, Regina had missed her mother sorely. Though she had been invited to live with her aunt and uncle, she'd felt uncomfortable among her petite cousins—except on horseback. Mounted, she didn't appear much taller than any of the other girls. And, certainly, she had a better seat than any of them. Regina rode easily, at one with her horse.

She recalled the number of times she'd escaped from morning callers by spending the entire afternoon riding. Fortunately, her Uncle John had shared her passion for the stables, and come to her defense whenever Aunt Sarah took her to task for wasting time in the stables. He'd been proud of her knowledge of horseflesh, and had even come to rely on her advice when selecting new brood mares. Sir John had twice taken her to the sales, over his wife's protests.

Eventually, her aunt had given up all hope of marrying her niece creditably. Between Regina's love of horses and her dreadful blue-stocking tendencies which led her to devour all manner of books, she had few of the accomplishments young ladies needed to achieve a good match. Still, it hadn't mattered in the end.

As soon as she'd turned twenty-one, Regina inherited her mother's small fortune. The settlement allowed her to live quite comfortably and indulge both her passions—much to her family's consternation. But during the last five years they had, more or less, accepted the situation and Regina lived contentedly. Only occasionally did she long for someone to share her small triumphs and commiserate with over her failures.

She hoped now, looking at her nephew across the table, that David would be equally fortunate. A pity he did not share her enthusiasm for the stables. Indeed, it seemed to her that David was uneasy on a horse, and rode out with the utmost reluctance. Andrew was a notable horseman, and Regina was beginning to understand a little of his disappointment that his only son did not ride well.

Nevertheless, she would not force David. If he rode, it had to be by his choice. Rising, she strode round the table and ruffled his dark curls. "The sun's finally coming out. Would you like to take a break from your books and join me in a gallop?"

He looked up, his large brown eyes a trifle sad. "Thank you, Aunt Regina, but I should prefer to finish this book if you do not mind terribly."

"Of course I don't. Indeed, it may even be better if you remain here. I expected Mr. Quill yesterday, but the storm probably delayed him. If he should come this morning, keep him entertained, darling. I shall be back within an hour or so."

Centering down the long drive, Regina inhaled deep breaths of the fresh air. Everything smelled so good, so clean, after a hard rain. Penrod, her powerful white stallion, pranced a little, eager to stretch his long legs.

She was about to let him have his head when she saw a lone rider turning in the lane. "Drat, it looks like our ride will have to be shortened, boy. This must be Mr. Quill." She held Penrod to an easy trot and met the rider halfway.

Regina watched him approach, reassured to see that the gentleman rode well. He held his back perfectly straight, his head high and at an angle that gave her a fleeting impression of arrogance. As he drew closer, the impression intensified and she felt a surge of annoyance. The man was late arriving and, as a consequence, she must curtail her own ride. Yet he showed no sign of remorse.

She spoke to him abruptly, her displeasure plain. "I am Miss Westfield. I suppose the storm delayed you, sir, for we quite expected you yesterday. Did you travel all the way from London by horseback?"

"No," the gentleman answered absently. His gaze appraised her, taking note of the becoming fit of her green habit, and the admirable way she handled her stallion.

Regina shivered, oddly uncomfortable beneath his scrutiny. Were he not her last hope, she would have dismissed him out of hand. Lifting her chin a fraction, she said briskly, "Well, Mr. Quill, just follow the lane around to the right, and you will see the stables. Ask for Ben. Tell him I said to see to your horse, and have someone show you to the house. My nephew, David, is in the library. You might as well make his acquaintance. I shall not be long." She nudged Penrod, maneuvered past the rider, then urged the stallion into a trot.

Balfour, left alone on the lane, stared after her. Half-affronted, half-amused, he wondered who Mr. Quill might be. It was a novel experience for him to be mistaken for a commoner, and not precisely a pleasant one. Whoever the young lady was, she needed to be taught a lesson in manners. Perhaps he would oblige her.

Following her directions, he found the stables easily

enough. The sound of hoofbeats brought a groom from the barn. Without a word, the man crossed the yard and went to the horse's head.

"Are you Ben? Your mistress said I should tell you to see to my horse, and direct me to the house."

The groom looked him over carefully. "Beggin' your pardon, sir, but just who might you be?"

"I might be any number of people, but I fail to see what concern it is of yours," Balfour replied, ice in his voice, disdain in his manner.

Ben involuntarily ducked his head and touched his cap, a mute gesture of apology. "Not meaning any disrespect, I'm sure, but Sir Andrew asked me to be especial watchful of any strangers wishing to see Miss Regina or Master David."

"Since I have already seen your mistress, it would appear your intervention is somewhat tardy. Now be so good as to direct me to the house. Apparently, Master David is expecting me."

"You can't never be the new tutor!"

Lord Balfour merely glanced at him, his golden brows lifted slightly.

"I mean . . . you don't look like no tutor I ever seen."

"Obviously, you have conversed with any number of tutors. Would you care to tell me in what manner I seem deficient?"

"Uh, no sir. I didn't mean as to . . . uh, what I meant was—"

The duke held up a hand. "I know precisely what you meant, and perhaps at some future date we will discuss it further. At present, I desire only directions to the house."

The groom nodded, apparently fearful of opening his mouth again. He managed to convey the general direction and Balfour dismounted. Following a footpath through the garden, he emerged in front of a wide terrace. The doors stood open to the fresh air, and he could see a small boy curled up on the sofa. The book he held in his hands seemed to completely engross him. Balfour stepped into the room unnoticed.

Standing quietly by the doors, he studied the lad. When Regina, if that was his mystery lady's name, had told him to see her nephew, he'd envisioned an older boy. This slim, pale waif of a lad, sitting with his shoulders hunched forward as though to block out the world and all its hurtfulness, could not be more than seven or eight. Uncomfortably reminded of himself as a boy, he watched the youngster for another moment before clearing his throat.

David, mesmerized by his book, was slow to look up. The tome was not a deep study, but an illustrated version of the *Iliad,* which told of the wondrous deeds of the Greek God, Zeus, hurler of mighty thunderbolts. An illustration depicted Zeus in all his glory—tall, muscular, blond curls falling over a noble brow and prominent nose. David gazed in open-mouthed awe at the creature before him. Zeus come to life.

"I did not mean to startle you, lad. Are you David? Your aunt suggested I talk with you until she returns."

Slowly returning from the realm of his imagination, David realized this magnificent person must be the tutor. Yet it was hard to believe. Torn between hope and fear, he asked, "Are you Mr. Quill?"

"I wonder you find it so difficult to believe. Your groom also put me through an inquisition. Pray, who else would I be?"

David grinned. "Actually, sir, for just a moment, I thought you were Zeus."

"Zeus!" A smile, such as few of his acquaintances ever saw, curved his lips, softening the harsh planes of his face. "Well, I suppose that is preferable to being thought a mere tutor. But no mere mortal could vie with Zeus—"

"I remember that bit, but I am not sure precisely what it means," David broke in, excitement burning in his eyes. "It was only that you look a bit like this picture of him." David offered up his book, indicating the plate showing the warrior god.

Balfour studied it. He realized the rain had washed the powder from his hair, causing it to curl, much like the illustration. "I believe you flatter me, lad. However, it is a pleasant change from the comparisons I usually invoke."

"I beg your pardon, sir?"

"Pay no attention. I was merely thinking out loud. You hardly look enough old to be reading Homer."

"I am ten, sir," David said apologetically, knowing he did not look his age.

Balfour laughed, though not unkindly, and took a seat next to the boy. "Then you are before me. I believe I was twelve before I read the *Iliad,* and nearly eighteen before I first saw Mount Olympus."

David stared at him, envy in his large brown eyes. "You have been to Greece, sir? Oh, please, tell me what it is like."

"It was a great many years ago," the duke began, dredging his memory for recollections which might please the boy. He thumbed through the pages of the book, hoping to stoke the fires of memory. He didn't hear the soft-footed entrance of two men, but a slight movement to his left distracted him. When he glanced up he saw the barrel of a long-nosed pistol pointed at his heart.

"We don't want no trouble, Gov'. Just stay right there nice and quiet like. You boy, get over here."

The duke rose as David obediently stood. He placed a hand on the boy's shoulder and glared with contempt at the two interlopers.

The smaller man, a scrawny fellow with a long neck and dirty, unkempt hair, peered about nervously. "Jasper! They didn't say nothing about him being here," he whined, edging towards the door.

His companion, a large man bordering on obese, possessed the air of a bully. He laughed rudely. "You scare a sight too easy, Silas. Let me handle this."

"The kid was supposed to be alone 'cepting the maids. Nothing was said 'bout no one else being here. I don't like it." A nervous tic in the man's right eye pulsated rapidly as he moved closer to the door.

"Yeah, well there's one way to take care of this dandy if he gives us any trouble. Stand away from the boy, Gov," he ordered.

The duke remained by David, intently watching the movements of both men. Nothing in his manner betrayed any fear, and when he spoke, his voice remained deadly calm. "I would think twice before you continue whatever mischief you are brewing. I am the Duke of Balfour and I warn you, you shall pay dearly for this impertinence."

"Jasper, we can't—"

"Shut up, Silas. I ain't afeared of no man, duke or else. He'll bleed just the same as any other bloke if he interferes." Keeping a wary eye on Balfour, Jasper reached out a long, hairy arm. His grip closed like a vise around the boy's neck and he yanked him closer.

David turned his head. Before the man realized what he was about, he sank his sharp little teeth into the menacing hand holding him.

Balfour saw his opportunity. With a lightning move, he kicked at the man's other hand and sent the pistol flying across the room. A second later, his right fist crashed into Jasper's jaw. The heavy-set fellow reeled backwards, falling over the low center table.

David yelled a warning as Silas lifted his pistol. The duke whirled but the bullet tore through the sleeve of his coat and he staggered back a step. "Get behind me, David," he ordered, but there was no need.

The two frightened men scrambled for the door. Balfour cursed, hating to allow them to escape, but he could not give chase—not with blood seeping through his coat. He sank wearily onto the sofa, his right hand cupping the wound.

David, his face paler than usual, and eyes round with awe, stared down at him. "Please, sir, tell me what I must do."

"Help me get this coat off," Balfour muttered. "Don't be alarmed. It is only a flesh wound, but it will bleed a great deal. Have to get it bandaged."

"Yes, sir." David tried to gently peel the tight fitting coat off but drew back the instant the duke groaned aloud.

Balfour's right arm came up to hold his own shoulder tightly beneath the coat. "Go on, David. Yank it down quickly else I shall have to cut it off."

"Let him go!" Regina's high voice rang out from the doorway, startling them both.

For the second time that morning, the duke looked up to see a pistol leveled at his heart.

Two

Regina stepped into the library, the heavy pistol trembling in her hands despite her efforts to hold it steady. She saw David struggling with Quill. Blood oozed between the boy's fingers, dropping in crimson splashes unto the sofa and floor. A feeling of suffocation nearly overpowered her.

"Aunt Regina!" David cried, whirling around at the sound of her voice. He gazed in horror at the pistol in her hands.

"Forgive me for not rising, Miss Westfield," Balfour murmured from his position on the sofa.

Two of the younger grooms crowded into the doorway behind their mistress. Ben shouldered them aside. "Careful with that peashooter, Miss Regina," he admonished. He peered at Balfour. "That's not one of the swine what tied us up, but that's not to say he ain't in league with them."

David gaped at him, then turned to his aunt, a desperate look in his large eyes. "Don't listen to Ben, Aunt Regina. This man tried to help me when those others came. They shot him in the arm. He's bleeding terribly . . ." the words trailed off as he stared down at his own bloodstained hands.

"Are you hurt, David?" Regina asked, striving to keep the terror from her voice.

"No, but he is. We must help him, Aunt."

Regina hesitated. She glanced at the dark-haired stranger sprawled on the delicate cream sofa. Certainly he did not look to be a treacherous sort—and his arm was bleeding profusely. She motioned to her nephew. "Go along to your room, David."

"No," the boy replied, defiance in every line of his slim, little body. He retreated a step toward the sofa. "Not until we get Mr. Quill—I mean the duke—not until we get his arm bandaged."

"Perhaps I should introduce myself," Balfour said dryly. "Cedric Alexander Everild, the seventh duke of Balfour, at your service." At her incredulous look, he added, "There are cards in my coat pocket if you doubt my word."

Regina, sensing he spoke the truth, stared at him curiously. His identity explained the air of superiority about the man, but it also deepened her confusion. She'd heard tales about Devil Balfour for years. He'd been abroad when she'd made her bow to Society, forced to flee to France for killing his man in a duel, or so the gossips said. But tales of his outrageous conduct had circulated swiftly in his absence until he was nearly a legend in London. Ladies whispered of his exploits behind their fans and gentlemen were careful to keep their wives and daughters out of his path. He was shunned by respectable society—and secretly envied by every young cub who came up to Town.

Andrew, of course, despised him, and had frequently described Balfour as the worst sort of rakehell, a disgrace to England. Regina remembered her brother had some sort of run-in with the duke, but she'd never known the details.

Ben nudged her. "Don't let yourself be taken in by his fancy words, Miss Regina—" he began, but halted as the duke turned deadly cold eyes in his direction.

Regina handed her groom the pistol. She crossed resolutely to the duke's side, saying over her shoulder, "Take the others and search the grounds, Ben. Make certain the intruders are not anywhere on the estate."

"They will be long gone," Balfour told her, looking up into the greenest eyes he'd ever seen. The color of new leaves, he thought. Eyes made to bewitch a man. Her long lashes swept down and he struggled to remember what he'd been about to say. "Has someone a reason to abduct your nephew, Miss Westfield?"

"Explanations can wait, Your Grace," she answered with an appearance of calm she was far from feeling. Then, kneeling in front of David, she hugged him close. "Are you quite certain you are not hurt?"

With a small boy's dislike of fuss, he pulled away from her. "They only broke the chain Father gave me and took my cross. It's the duke who is hurt."

"Very well," she said, reassured. "I shall see what I can do for him if you will go and fetch Mrs. Milligan for me. Tell her I will need some help in here."

David nodded eagerly and would have raced from the room but Regina stopped him with a hand on his shoulder. "You will not wish to scare her, so perhaps you should wash your hands first."

He looked down, somewhat astonished at the bloodstains, but agreed.

Regina, watching him leave, sighed. David was not a child one could coddle.

"He's an intelligent boy and at any other time I would be fraught with admiration for him. At the moment, however, my life's blood is slowly seeping from me. I would be deeply appreciative if you would kindly do something to staunch the flow."

Regina studied the duke as he spoke. His words would have been more effective were it not for the look of unholy amusement in his eyes. Deep blue eyes, she noticed, not green as she'd first thought, but so thickly lashed they appeared to change color at times. He returned her regard with considerable coolness, considering his present condition. She wondered if anything ever disconcerted him.

Tearing her gaze away, she stooped to retrieve a large sewing box from beside the wing chair. "Just a moment, Your

Grace," she said, while searching through her supplies. A second later she pulled out a large pair of shears.

She turned, brandishing the gleaming scissors, and thought she saw a flash of apprehension in the duke's eyes. He said nothing, however, and she sat down beside him.

"Hold still, if you please. The first thing we must do is cut away your coat and shirt."

He winced when the edge of the blade pressed against the open skin on his arm.

"I am sorry if that hurts, Your Grace, but why gentlemen must wear such tight-fitting coats is beyond my understanding. It makes baring the wound exceedingly difficult."

"I beg your pardon," he said between tightly clenched teeth. "Had I only known I would be shot this morning, I would have chosen my coat more wisely."

Regina glanced up at him for a second. Against her will, her lips twitched. She quickly ducked her head and returned to the business of tending his wound.

David appeared moments later, followed by the housekeeper. He spoke as he circled the sofa, his young body vibrating with excitement. "Aunt Regina, Mrs. Milligan was locked in the pantry with Trudy and Melchett." He grinned down at Balfour. "And Cook fainted."

Mrs. Milligan used her apron to fan her flushed face. "Lord, miss, such goings on I ain't never seen, not in all my born days! It's a blessing Miss Cornelia ain't here. Why, if she had seen those two great bandits breaking into my kitchen and forcing us all into the pantry—yes, and waving huge guns in our faces—it's a wonder any of us is still walking about to tell of it!"

"I am sorry, Mrs. Milligan," Regina said, glancing up at her. "I know it must have been quite dreadful for you, but I need your help just now. This gentleman is the Duke of Balfour and he was wounded while trying to help David."

"Gracious, Miss Regina, why ever didn't you say so?" The pudgy housekeeper dropped a sketchy curtsy in the direction of the duke, then scurried from the room. She returned a few moments later with a roll of linen, unwinding it as she chattered.

A young serving girl followed her, awkwardly cradling a basin of water in her arms. She sat it on the table, then dared a peep at the duke. Startled to encounter his gaze, she clumsily knocked against the pan. Water sloshed over the side, splattering the table and the knees of the duke's black breeches.

"I . . . I am sorry, Your Grace," she mumbled, backing away from the table. She bumped into a tall urn near the door, caught it as it wobbled on the base, and with a last frightened look at the duke, retreated to the kitchen.

Mrs. Milligan shook her head. "That Melchett has two left feet and not enough sense to keep out of her own way." She tore off a strip of linen and used it to soak up the water from the table. She looked hesitantly at the duke's breeches.

"I was already wet, madam. A little more water won't hurt."

Relief flooded the older woman's face. She dropped a quick curtsy, then hurried after the maid.

Balfour, ignoring the pain shooting up his shoulder, focused his gaze on Regina. "It appears I have disrupted your household. I pray you will accept my apologies."

"What nonsense is this, Your Grace?" she asked as she tenderly sponged his gaping wound. "You must know I am vastly indebted to you. Had it not been for your intervention—" She broke off, not wishing to put into words her terrifying thoughts. Not with David listening intently as he stood behind the sofa, staring down at the duke's wounded shoulder.

"You relieve me greatly, Miss Westfield, but I am certain you can understand my concern after your rather unique welcome. Tell me, can you fire that pistol you were waving so recklessly about?"

She spared a glance for him, her wide mouth tilting tantalizingly upwards at the corners. "Certainly, sir. Were you worried I would shoot you accidentally?"

"The thought did cross my mind," he admitted. He watched her for a moment, his eyes filled with curiosity. "If I had been a kidnapper, would you have fired?"

"Only if you'd tried to escape," Regina replied, her voice sounding serenely calm as she tightened the bandage across his arm. Her eyes met David's. She flushed, suddenly aware of the impropriety of their conversation. Quickly clipping the make-do bandage, Regina rose. "If you will remain still, I believe that will suffice for now. One of the grooms will fetch Dr. Lyons at once."

Balfour managed to grab her hand with his good arm as she turned to leave. "Hold, Miss Westfield. I hardly think a doctor is necessary. It appears you have done an admirable job, and I heal rather quickly. I promise you, I have had a great deal of experience."

He saw the flash of amusement in her eyes and the impudent smile which disappeared almost at once.

"I believe you, Your Grace. I have heard of your . . . reputation," she finished, still mindful of David listening.

"Have you, indeed?" he asked. He reluctantly released her hand. "I advise you not to believe all you hear, Miss Westfield. One must always consider one's source."

"As the source was my brother, I think I must accept his word."

"Westfield . . . I thought that name sounded familiar, but the only Westfield I am acquainted with is Sir Andrew. You could not possibly be related to that—"

"I am, Your Grace," Regina broke in quickly, sensing his words would not be flattering. "Andrew is my brother and David's father."

Balfour sat quietly for a moment, his blue eyes assessing her. "You are nothing like him, you know."

"No, but then you are not what I expected, either," she

said. Smiling enigmatically, she gathered up her supplies and left the room before he could question her further.

Regina arranged for a groom to ride to Newmarket in search of Dr. Lyons, assured Ben that the gentleman in the library was no threat to her own well-being, pacified Cook, calmed the excitable maids, and then ordered a tea tray brought to the library.

Realizing she was still wearing her riding habit, Regina hesitated before rejoining the duke. Deciding he could wait a few more moments, she hurried up to her room to change into a more suitable frock. It was not vanity, she told herself. Still, she spent several moments in front of the cheval mirror tying her wayward curls back with a silk ribbon. Returning below stairs, she stopped in the formal drawing room to fetch the brandy decanter. She felt certain the duke would require a drink stronger than tea.

A moment later, she paused in the doorway of the library, surveying the scene before her with astonishment. Her shy nephew leaned over the sofa, his high-pitched voice ringing with excitement as he questioned the duke. None of her efforts to draw David out had met with such enthused response. Amazed, she watched him chatting with a total stranger— treating the man as though he were some sort of hero. She stifled a feeling of resentment. After all, in David's eyes, the duke must seem heroic. What Andrew would say when he heard about this did not bear thinking about.

David chanced to look up and caught sight of her. "Aunt Regina, did you know the duke has been to Greece? He's seen Mount Olympus and he knows—well, he knows everything."

"Not quite, lad," Balfour corrected, rising gracefully to his feet. "I am glad you are returned, before David discovers the extent of my ignorance." His keen gaze traveled slowly from the top of her head to her slippered feet. "May I compliment you on your choice of gown, Miss Westfield. You look exceptionally lovely in blue."

Regina flushed beneath his bold scrutiny. Although there was nothing in the duke's words to take exception to, the warm intimacy in his eyes unnerved her. No man had ever looked at her in such a manner. Unsure how to handle him, she murmured her thanks. Feeling slightly foolish, she turned her attention to David.

"Come see, Aunt Regina. The duke looks just like Zeus," David insisted, holding up the illustration in his book.

Balfour ruffled his hair. "If I am Zeus come to visit, who is your aunt? The goddess Hera in disguise, Athena perhaps, or the beautiful Aphrodite?"

David considered the matter seriously, his small brow wrinkled with concentration. "Athena helped the people of Cyrene tame wild horses, and Aunt Regina is very good with horses. But wasn't she the goddess who liked needlework?" When Balfour agreed, David shook his head. "Then not Athena, for my aunt does not like to sew and such."

The duke laughed aloud and Regina, though embarrassed, hid an amused smile.

David, intent on his thoughts, never noticed. "Aphrodite was the most beautiful of the goddesses, and she had long hair like my aunt. But Hera was beautiful, too, and she ruled them all. I do think that sometimes Aunt Regina looks a little like a queen, and she is the only person who can tell my father what to do."

"That is something I should like to see," Balfour said quietly.

This conversation was decidedly improper. Ignoring the duke's impudent grin, Regina turned to her nephew. "Thank you, David. Now, would you please go find Mrs. Milligan and see what is keeping our tea?"

She waited for the boy to leave the room before facing Balfour again. It seemed odd to have to look up at a gentleman, odder still to observe the look of admiration in his dark eyes. Was he *flirting* with her? The idea was at once ridiculous and exciting. Her pulse raced and she had to fight a strong urge to return his smile. She did not indulge in light flirtations, and certainly not with a man who enjoyed a reputation like the duke's.

Looking away, she spoke to him in a manner designed to keep him at arm's length. "I see you have made a conquest of David. It's extremely kind of you to answer his questions, and I must thank you for coming to his rescue this morning."

"I vote for Hera. Definitely regal."

"Please, Your Grace, do be serious. Will you tell me how it chanced that you were in Bury St. Edmunds?" She indicated that they should both be seated, and placed the brandy decanter within easy reach of his long arms.

"Is that where I am?" he asked with a crooked smile. It did wonderful things to his mouth and his eyes. Regina struggled to concentrate on his words.

"I suppose it was fate or providence, whatever you wish to call it. I was driving to Norwich and thought I could outrun a thunderstorm when my carriage overturned. Alas, the axle was ruined, leaving me stranded. By sheer chance, I recalled passing this place. I rode back to seek assistance, which is when you mistook me—for a tutor, I believe?"

She smiled at the slight note of outrage in his voice. "A quite natural mistake, Your Grace. One which, I might add, you did nothing to correct."

"My dear Miss Westfield, were I to spend all my time correcting the mistaken impressions various people form of my character, I should be kept busy from dawn to dusk. Though I confess, I have never before been taken for someone so . . . so common."

The words were ordinary but his voice dipped low, caressing her senses. Flustered, she spoke quickly. "Yes, well I ejected Mr. Quill, you see, and you did not look precisely ducal when you arrived. No doubt due to your unfortunate accident—a most un-Zeus-like occurrence. A pity you lacked his power to control the rain."

"Sometimes even the gods must bow to fate. Perhaps the storm was only a means to an end, and I was destined to rescue your nephew."

"Perhaps," she agreed, but glanced away from his challenging look. The man was conceited, annoyingly arrogant—and impossibly attractive. She wondered how many women had fallen prey to the lazy, seductive charm of his eyes. Dozens, from what Andrew had said . . . she stole another glance at him as he refilled his glass. Well, she would not be one of them. She was past the age for such nonsense, even if the duke were so inclined. At the moment, he seemed preoccupied with other thoughts.

He looked up then, meeting her gaze. But there was nothing flirtatious in his manner now. "Since I seem to have been pitch-forked into the middle of your affairs, would you mind telling me what manner of mayhem I have wandered into?"

Regina considered how much to confide in the duke. She felt instinctively that she could trust him, but her brother would certainly disagree. Indeed, he would resent her speaking with Balfour at all.

"I gather this incident has something to do with Sir Andrew's politicking," the duke said into the silence.

Regina gestured helplessly. There was nothing she could say.

"I may not possess the all-knowing powers of Zeus, but logic is not yet beyond me. The dismay in your eyes and my own knowledge of your brother led me to that conclusion. I will not press you for details if it distresses you, but do consider that it might be wiser to confide in me, if only for the boy's safety."

"You saw to David's safety admirably, Your Grace, without any prior knowledge of the situation," she reminded him. "And as you will be leaving shortly, I do not think it would accomplish anything to divulge further information about my brother to one who is—" she broke off, realizing belatedly where her tongue was leading her.

"To one who is not precisely in charity with him?" he suggested, his lips curling in amusement. He saw her raise her hand in protest and smiled. "No, do not deny your words. I understand your feelings perfectly, although I own Sir Andrew must possess greater qualities than I had imagined to foster such loyalty."

"It would be thought very odd in me did I not feel some allegiance for my brother."

"Only because he is your brother?" he teased.

"No, of course not. Andrew has many excellent qualities which I admire. He is dedicated to serving England and sacrifices a great deal for the good of the country. He is courageous and continues to act as he feels just, regardless of threats on his life. He is a man of integrity and honor."

"A paragon, in fact?" the duke asked, a touch of humor warming his eyes. "How is it that you do not choose to make your home with such a superior being?"

A blush betrayed her. Regina stared down at her hands. Andrew was everything she'd said. Unfortunately, he could also be overbearing, opinionated, and unduly pompous—but she would never admit such a thing to Balfour. Her brother believed the duke represented everything that was wrong with England. She'd frequently heard Andrew describe him as a rakehell, libertine, wastrel, and ne'er-do-well.

But Andrew had never mentioned that Devil Balfour was unusually tall, and broad-shouldered. Or that he possessed a quick intelligence, amusing wit, and a devastatingly attractive smile. She thought again of the duke's infinite patience with David, and his courage in protecting the boy—qualities she would not have thought to find in a rake.

She looked up to find Balfour still waiting for an answer. Unable to phrase her reply diplomatically, she took refuge in a jest. "I fear I am more like Hera than you imagined, Your Grace. I value my independence too much to live beneath the rule of another woman—even one so dear as my sister-in-law."

He had no chance to question her further as David hurried in, followed by Mrs. Milligan with the tea tray.

The housekeeper sat the ornate service on the table and turned to her mistress, rattling off her messages in a rush. "Ben says to tell you, Miss Regina, that there's no trace of any of those men on the grounds, and Cook wants to know what to do about dinner."

"How is she feeling?" Regina asked, concern for the older woman edging her voice. "If she is not quite recovered, a cold meal will do fine."

"Oh, no, miss. Cook is well enough, but worrying over what to serve if, that is, . . . if His Grace is to dine here," Mrs. Milligan finally managed to get out in an agony of embarrassment.

Regina understood the dilemma at once. Meals at Whitechapel were a haphazard affair at best. She wondered if there was even sufficient food in the house to prepare a suitable dinner. She turned questioning eyes in the duke's direction, half hoping he would refuse the invitation she was duty-bound to offer. "Will you dine with us, Your Grace? We would be honored to have you as a guest."

"Thank you, Miss Westfield, but I fear I shall have to impose on your hospitality for more than a mere dinner," he said, as he glanced down at his arm. "I doubt I will be able to drive for several days. In any event, I must await repairs to my carriage. I do hope you are willing to put me up?"

Regina sat nonplussed. She was obligated to house the duke if he wished to stay and, judging from the devilish light in his eyes, that was precisely what he did desire.

David answered for her, enthusiasm spilling over in his warm-hearted assurances that nothing could be more splendid.

Regina, hiding her resentment, gave Mrs. Milligan instructions. A real gentleman would have seen she was awkwardly situated and declined the invitation. But not Balfour. When the housekeeper had left, she turned to him, remarking coolly, "We would, of course, be honored to have you stay."

"Thank you, my dear," Balfour said, hard put not to laugh aloud. He had not missed Regina's reluctance. Even had his carriage been waiting at the door, he would have found an excuse to remain. Of late, life had offered little in the way of amusement. He smiled at her lazily. "Of course, if it is a problem, I suppose I could hire some sort of conveyance to drive me to a local inn—that is, if there is such a place . . ."

"I could not allow it, Your Grace," Regina said quickly. Aware of the debt she owed him, and that her invitation had not sounded entirely sincere, she added, "We would be pleased to house you, although I must warn you the accommodations are hardly what you are accustomed to."

"I shall make allowances," he said, watching the graceful way her hands moved as she poured the tea. "Speaking of carriages, do you suppose someone could be sent to help my groom? He and my valet are stranded a few miles south of here."

"Heavens! Why did you not say so? Those poor men have been waiting there all this time?"

"They are paid to do so," Balfour said, his brows arching in surprise at the censure in her voice.

Regina ignored him. "David, run and tell Ben to send Harold at once. Tell him the duke's carriage is damaged, and to bring His Grace's servants back here."

The boy nodded and, eager to be of service to his hero, dashed out the door.

"You do realize," Balfour drawled, "that my carriage will be left unattended?"

"I hardly think it will come to any harm in Bury St. Edmunds, Your Grace. Surely, you would not wish to leave your poor men stranded there any longer? Why, they must be famished and dying of thirst."

"They are well compensated for any hardships they endure

while in my service, Miss Westfield. Servants can be easily replaced. My carriage, on the other hand, is custom-built and quite valuable."

"Really? Then I wonder at your carelessness in driving it through a thunderstorm," Regina retorted. She rose abruptly, before her tongue could utter any further indiscretions. "If you will excuse me, Your Grace?" She was gone before he could voice any objection.

Balfour, after helping himself to a liberal glass of brandy, stared bemusedly after her. He had never given the comfort or well-being of his servants much thought. They were well housed, well clothed and extremely well paid. If any were dissatisfied, they were entirely free to leave his employ, though few seldom did.

Miss Westfield, he decided, certainly had some odd notions. She hadn't flinched at the idea of shooting a man, or swooned at the sight of blood. She'd even taken the attempt to kidnap her nephew fairly calmly—but now she lost her temper over the idea of his servants' discomfort. How very strange.

Regina prudently avoided the library until Dr. Lyons's arrival. Balfour's highhanded attitude toward his servants disturbed her. Just when she was beginning to believe her brother had been harsh in his judgment of the duke, the man behaved like the boorish, arrogant peer Andy claimed he was.

Yet, she could not forget Balfour's kindness to David . . . and he had spoken most courteously to Mrs. Milligan. Her thoughts in a muddle of confusion, Regina led Dr. Lyons into the room. She observed the duke closely.

Balfour, sprawled on the sofa, was answering David's questions patiently. Regina fancied she saw pain etched in the furrows on his brow, and knew a moment's remorse. The gentleman was wounded, and she should not have allowed her nephew to pester him with questions.

She ordered David to the kitchen with the news that Cook had a lemon pie cooling. It was her nephew's favorite, but he left reluctantly, his footsteps dragging as he crossed the room.

"David," the duke called after him. "If that pie is any good, would you bring me a dish when the doctor has finished here?"

A wide grin split the boy's face. "Cook makes the best pie in England," he assured Balfour before scampering out the door.

"I can attest to that," Dr. Lyons remarked as he opened his black medical bag. "Now, then, let's have a look at your wound." After unwinding Regina's makeshift bandage, he probed at the jagged edges of the cut for several moments.

"Well, Miss Westfield has done an excellent job," he pronounced at last. "It's more of a graze than anything else, Your Grace. Change the bandage daily and nature should do the rest."

Balfour shot a triumphant look at Regina. "I told Miss Westfield there was no need to call in a doctor."

"Better not to take chances," Dr. Lyons advised as he wrapped the arm tightly again. "A wound like this could easily become inflamed. But you're in good hands, Your Grace. Miss Westfield has a level head on her shoulders, and I've reason to trust her judgment."

"Thank you, Dr. Lyons," Regina said, smiling warmly at the older man. She knew his bluff ways masked a kind heart. "Will you stay and have tea and lemon pie with us?"

"Can't," the doctor replied sourly. "Too many calls and too many people without your good sense. If ever you get tired of nursing those horses of yours, come see me. I'd take you on as an assistant any time."

"I shall remember that," she promised, then rang for the maid to show the physician out.

Balfour had remained quiet, but he'd watched her movements and listened to her words as she'd spoken with the
doctor. Regina was uncomfortably aware of his scrutiny.
Mindful of their last conversation, she felt embarrassed to
face him. He, however, appeared to have no memory of her
leaving in a temper, and smiled lazily up at her.

"Will you join me, Miss Westfield? If I cannot persuade
you to confide your troubles, perhaps you will at least explain what the good doctor meant about nursing horses."

"Thank you, Your Grace," she said, sitting down in the
chair opposite him. "I know it must seem unreasonable of
me, particularly after you saved David, but I promised Andrew I would not divulge his confidence."

"Am I permitted to ask what you intend to do about the
boy?"

"Certainly you may ask, but I am at a loss how to answer.
I would send him to his father, but I do not know precisely
where Andrew is at the moment. I have been racking my
brains to think where else David might be safe, but nothing
has occurred to me." She paused, then asked softly, "Do you
think another attempt will be made to kidnap him?"

Balfour shrugged. "Impossible to say, given my scant
knowledge of your affairs, but I should not think it likely
for the next few days. After that, anything is possible."

Regina nodded, her mind busy with the precautions she
could take to safeguard David.

"As long as I'm here, I will do whatever I can to help
you," Balfour said, watching the play of emotions on her
face. Heavy lashes swept down to hide the shadows in her
expressive green eyes, but her wide brow remained creased
with worry. He felt an irrational urge to draw her close and
kiss away her frowns. But this was no opera dancer to be
taken lightly, or one of his London ladies skilled in the art
of dalliance. He'd stake his fortune Regina Westfield was
still a virgin—a species of female he made it a point to avoid.

But she was also Westfield's sister—and he had a score

to settle with Sir Andrew. Balfour's eyes darkened as he recalled an incident at Ranleigh Gardens the previous summer.
Westfield had been present with his wife and a few of his
pompous friends, and his path had crossed that of the Duke.
Balfour had been enjoying an evening promenade with Lady
Sydney—his latest flirt. It was true the lady was of dubious
reputation, but that was no reason for Westfield to pointedly
give him the cut, sweeping his precious wife to one side as
though he feared contamination. Someone needed to teach
pious Sir Andrew a much-needed lesson. And how amusing
if it came about through a beauty like Regina Westfield, he
thought as he watched her struggling for composure. When
she glanced up, he looked suitably concerned.

"You are very kind, Your Grace," Regina replied. Then,
determined to set her own problems aside, she asked about
his arm.

"It is tolerable. However, if I am to be your guest for
several days, I suggest we dispense with the formalities. My
friends call me Cedric."

She regarded him gravely. Here was the rake, the libertine
her brother had mentioned. The duke radiated charm. His
laughing eyes and pensive smile were very nearly irresistible.
He knew it, too.

"Thank you," she said softly, then busied her hands with
the china cups. The tea had grown cold. She moved to ring
for fresh, but Balfour begged her not to.

"I've had enough tea to drown a man," he said, adding
persuasively, "Tell me about your horses instead."

She had to smile and shared the joke with him. "Most
people beg me *not* to talk about my horses. Are you truly
interested?"

"I am, indeed." He saw the spark of passion that lightened
the color of her eyes. So there was fire beneath that cool
exterior, he thought, and wondered what it would take to
ignite it.

As if in answer to his thoughts, she replied, "I warn you,

I'm extremely proud of my stable. They are mostly blood horses, bred and trained here at Whitechapel, then sold for racing."

His dark brows rose in astonishment. Breeding was a man's work. The females of his acquaintance knew very little about horses aside from where to place the saddle. "Really?" he drawled, heavy skepticism lacing his voice.

Regina smiled tolerantly. "Since I was a little girl, I've wanted nothing more than to raise horses. Their bloodlines fascinate me. Coming up with the right combination to produce stamina and speed—it's a challenge I never tire of." Her voice deepened with passion, and her eyes glistened with pride. "Just wait until tomorrow. You may watch the two-year-olds go through their paces and then tell me what you think."

"Have any of your horses actually raced?" Balfour asked with the patronizing air of one humoring a child.

"Several, but only two you might have heard of. Cavalier won the Guineas Sweepstakes at Newmarket last year, and his sister, Midnight, took the Ditch Mile. This year I have fourteen colts running."

"I thought Cavalier belonged to Lord Sayer," the duke said, no longer needing to pretend interest. One of his own horses had been entered in the Sweepstakes and run a poor second.

"He does now, but he was bred and trained at Whitechapel. You must know I would never be permitted to race Cavalier under my own name. 'Tis scandalous enough that I am involved with the breeding, to hear my family talk. I raise and train the horses, then sell them outright. Lord Sayer has bought several," she added, and though she tried, she could not quite hide the note of wistfulness in her voice.

"I saw Cavalier win that race last year—a handsome colt. You say you bred him yourself?"

She nodded. "But Andrew does not like me to speak of such matters."

"Your brother knows less than nothing about horseflesh," Balfour snorted, thinking of the mismatched grays he'd last seen Sir Andrew driving. "I, however, am an expert."

"Then I shall look forward to hearing your opinion. You will find my approach quite different from other trainers."

"Somehow, I am not surprised," Balfour said as he lifted his glass in a mock salute. "You are a most unusual lady."

"Is that intended as a compliment?"

"As you will, my dear," he said, but his attention was distracted. He turned to listen to a commotion in the hall. His voice became low, deadly. "Is your pistol at hand?"

Regina paled, but the door of the library flew open before she could move. She turned, braced for the worse.

A small, neatly dressed, elderly woman stood in the entrance. She faced them, hands on her hips, her thin lips twisted into a furious grimace, her hat sadly askew.

"Cornelia! I am so thankful you have returned," Regina said, the color flooding back into her face. "So much has happened since this morning, you will not credit it." She glanced at the duke, who had risen to stand protectively beside her. "Your Grace, allow me to present my cousin, Miss Davenport."

The duke, from his impressive height, looked down on the bony, angular, and ill-featured Miss Davenport. He'd been wondering when she'd appear, for it was inconceivable that anyone as lovely as Regina Westfield would not have a companion somewhere on the premises.

He nodded to the woman, condescension in every line of his bearing. He'd never met her before, but he knew her kind. He observed her while Regina chattered, telling the woman of his heroics.

Cornelia Davenport remained noticeably unimpressed. Her small, dark eyes narrowed with disapproval. At the first opportunity, she interrupted Regina. "I'm sure we are much indebted to His Grace, my dear, but whatever will he think of you for receiving him alone? I pray this never comes to dear Cousin Andrew's ears, or he'll rake me over the coals for not taking better care of you."

She gave a small cough of a laugh before turning to the duke. "You will have to forgive my young cousin, Your Grace. She has led a rather sheltered life and is not much in the way of entertaining gentlemen callers."

"Really?" the duke drawled, while managing to extract his snuff box with his good hand. He opened it with a deft flick of his wrist and removed a pinch. "I assure you Miss Westfield said nothing to put me to the blush. Indeed, I found her delightful company. Quite delightful," he repeated, his tongue lingering over the words as he gazed at Regina. The warmth and approval in his eyes gave an added meaning to his comment.

Miss Davenport pursed her lips at such blatant conduct. She moved between Regina and the duke at once, telling her cousin she was quite parched and would, of all things, like a cup of tea.

Balfour, seeing what she was about, would not be outmaneuvered. Instead of resuming his place on the sofa, he reclined in the large wing chair opposite. The cousin might have usurped his place opposite Regina, but he still had a clear view of her. He settled comfortably, stretching out his long legs. Devilment lightened his eyes as he looked up at Miss Davenport.

She sat down stiffly. Her eyes fell on the brandy decanter and the half-filled glass beside it. "Really, Regina! Brandy at this time of day? I cannot say I approve."

"But I do," Balfour said.

The battle lines were drawn.

Three

Dinner was an odd affair, polite conversation strained to the point where Regina wished the duke would not prolong his stay. Cornelia made no secret of her dislike for the gentleman and provoked him at every possible opportunity. She found fault with everything he said, and even his dress, remarking that most gentlemen would not sit down to dinner in their shirtsleeves. Regina had hushed her, reminding Cornelia that it was in defense of David that His Grace's coat had been ruined.

Her efforts were in vain, and Cornelia's rude behavior would have embarrassed Regina had not Balfour conducted himself in an equally offensive manner. Regina was certain that his outrageous comments were designed only to antagonize the older woman, but that did not make her own position any easier to bear.

The meal seemed interminable. Cook, in a zealous effort to impress the duke, had served up a feast fit for royalty. Far more dishes were served than usual and Cornelia, of course, made note of the fact, deploring the reprehensible waste.

At the last remove, she shook her head sadly, saying, "I can only imagine what dear Andrew would say were he to see such a prodigious amount of food set out for four people. I was privileged to stay with him and Elizabeth for a year, and I can tell you that *he* does not hold with catering to his guests, no matter what their rank. The meals at Fieldstone are sufficient to one's needs, but never ostentatious. No, not even when the Duke of Norfolk visited us. I take leave to tell you that he sat down to a dinner no different from what we enjoyed every day."

"I seem to recall Norfolk remarking on the occasion," the duke said, a devilish light in his eyes. "Very glad he was to return to London where he could get a decent meal. I believe he said he rose from the table every night with his stomach only half full, and lamented that there was not a decent drop of wine to be had in Westfield's house."

"Andrew does not imbibe alcohol—a virtue more gentlemen would do well to emulate," Cornelia snapped. She glanced contemptuously at the wineglass in Balfour's hand. "My cousin does not need to bolster his courage with spirits. He is a sober-minded gentleman."

"Oh, decidedly so," the duke replied, smiling. He leaned forward, lowering his voice to an intimate pitch. "But, tell me, Miss Davenport, do you not find such virtuous gentlemen to be rather dull dogs?"

"No, Your Grace, I do not!"

"Cornelia, pray remember where you are," Regina implored with a meaningful look in David's direction. His brown eyes had grown large as he listened with increasing interest to their exchange. She turned to Balfour, adding, "And, please, Your Grace—"

"Cedric," he interrupted, correcting her with an unrepentant grin.

"May we please speak of something more appropriate," Regina continued, ignoring him. "I know David would enjoy hearing about your trip to Greece."

"Heathenish land," Cornelia muttered.

Regina sighed. It had been a long day and the prospects for the evening were not promising. It was most unfortunate that Cornelia knew of Andrew's marked dislike for the duke, and she had willingly taken up the cudgels on his behalf. Since childhood, she'd been devoted to Andrew. Even the knowledge that they were too closely related for marriage had not mitigated her almost slavish adoration of him. Regina suspected Andy had foisted Cornelia off on her because he'd grown tired of the woman's tedious, moralizing conversations.

She looked up as Maisie tapped her on the shoulder.

The maid leaned down to whisper in her ear. "Excuse me, miss, but Ben said I should warn you that it looks like Clio will drop her foal tonight."

"Thank you. Tell him, please, that I shall be out directly," Regina said, and turned to find three pairs of eyes focused on her.

"Is anything amiss?" Balfour asked, concern showing in his blue eyes.

"Not at all," she said, trying to remain calm, but she could not quite control the smile of pleased expectation that turned up the corners of her mouth and made her expressive eyes sparkle in the candlelight. "One of my mares is about to become a mother."

"Regina! I pray you are not going to discuss such matters at the dinner table, especially not in front of David."

"It is a very natural process," the duke said, clearly amused. "And one which should be an educational experience for a young boy."

"Please, Your Grace," Regina said. "In this instance, I must agree with my cousin. Cornelia, if you are finished, would you take David into the drawing room? Perhaps you could write to Andrew for me and inform him of what has occurred."

Cornelia, certain that she had scored a point over the duke, arose with alacrity. "Come along, David. You may read one of those ponderous books of yours while I write to your father, and, if you are very good, I will allow you to add a few lines to my letter."

"A high treat," the duke murmured as she left the room.

"Will you excuse me, Your Grace?" Regina asked as she stood. "I will have Maisie bring you a glass of brandy."

"While you traipse out to the stables alone? No, I think not. Have you forgotten what occurred this morning?" He rose gracefully to his feet and extended his right arm.

Regina smiled, her dimples showing. "No, but I shall not be alone. Jeremy and Ben will be in the stable and several grooms as well."

"Then we will be well chaperoned," he said, as though that ended the discussion.

Regina, after one hesitant glance towards the drawing room, accepted his arm and moved slowly to the door. "I should doubtless leave everything in Jeremy's capable hands and remain in the house like a proper hostess, but Clio is my prize mare. If I have guessed correctly, the foal she produces tonight may well be the future winner of the Gold Cup."

"You have high aspirations, my dear," Balfour said, looking down at her. "And more than a little competition."

"I know. The Earl of Derby has put one of the descendants of Eclipse to stud and some of his offspring are outstanding. I would give anything for one of his foals."

"You do know your horses, don't you?" he asked, somewhat surprised by her mention of the famous horse that had once gone undefeated at Epsom Downs for two seasons.

"I did warn you, Your Grace," she said, as they strolled across the neat lawn.

"Can I not convince you to call me Cedric?"

"You are very kind, but I think, in light of our circumstances, it would be better if we maintained a measure of formality," she murmured, and stepped aside as she waited for him to open the door of the large stables.

"By circumstances, I apprehend you mean your cousin's presence. Why on earth do you allow that harridan in your house?"

Regina ducked under his arm and smiled at him over her shoulder. "That harridan is my cousin and a very good lady.

Oh, I know she moralizes overly much, but in general she means well."

The duke did not answer her as his gaze swept the breadth of the stables before him. He was amazed by the spaciousness of the boxes and the neatness and cleanliness of the whole. A cool, sweet breeze ruffled his shirtsleeves and he glanced up. Above every box was set a small window, most of which were open to the night air. The aroma was a definite improvement over his own dry, foul-smelling barns, but he wondered at the wisdom of such a thing. It was generally conceded that horses were healthiest when kept closely confined and guarded against treacherous breezes and ill winds.

Regina directed him to the right. As he followed her down the aisle, he noticed her horses did not seem to be suffering any ill effects from their exposure to the night air. Indeed, he had seldom seen healthier-looking cattle. Regina stopped several times to pat a silky head poked over the box door or to whisper a few caressing words to one of the horses.

"We have thirty-two boxes and, if this season is as good as I hope it will be, I plan to double that next year. Several of my mares are with foal now."

"Very impressive, but tell me—are you not taking a risk exposing your horses to so much fresh air? My grooms would be appalled at such an arrangement."

"I was, too, when Jeremy first proposed the idea. He brought the notion back with him from America and swore it worked wonders there. I changed over the stables two years ago and have not had cause to regret it. You can see for yourself how fit the horses are."

"My horse!" a high metallic voice echoed.

Regina grinned mischievously as they rounded the corner to the far side of the barn where the mares were housed.

"My horse, my horse!"

Balfour looked startled for a moment. Then he spotted the large green and blue parrot perched on a miniature set of steps within a huge and elaborately worked cage.

"My kingdom for a horse!" the bird squawked, standing on one foot and tilting his head. His bright eyes watched their approach.

"What have we here?" Balfour asked, laughing as the parrot spread his wings for their admiration.

"Your Grace, may I present Jake?" Regina asked as she reached her hand into the cage, and the bird stepped boldly onto her arm. She drew him out slowly and held him up for the duke's inspection. "He belongs to my trainer. Jeremy found him on board ship when he returned to England two years ago, and became so attached to him, he bought him. Jake stays here in the stable, and though he belongs to Jeremy, I believe he thinks we are all here merely to serve him."

"A handsome specimen."

"Hail fellow, well met," the bird chirped, fluttering his wings.

"And one with a notable vocabulary," the duke laughed. Regina started to return the parrot to his cage, but Balfour stopped her.

"May I?" he asked, holding out his good arm.

Jake eyed him dubiously for a moment, then stepped tentatively onto his arm and squawked, "Who's master, who's man?"

"A good question, my feathery friend, and one more people would do well to ask. What other tidbits do you know?" The duke lifted his arm higher so the bird was on a level with his eyes.

Regina saw Jake ruffle his feathers in a particular movement that heralded a warning, but there was not time to alert the duke. The white linen sleeve of his shirt was stained before she could say a word. Balfour sighed. He lowered his arm and Jake obligingly stepped back into his cage.

The duke took out his handkerchief, wiping at his sleeve, but as Regina could have told him, such stains did not come off easily. He shrugged his broad shoulders. "Well, that is the second shirt I have ruined today. I fear my valet will not look with favor upon an extended visit here."

Regina apologized for the bird's manners, adding, "He meant no disrespect, you know."

"Oh, certainly. I infer that this is, in fact, a mark of high distinction."

"Farewell!" Jake called after their retreating figures.

Regina stopped at the first box to pet a pretty gray filly with velvety eyes and a gentle manner, but the sounds of a horse kicking mightily against the wall stayed her hand.

"That's Clio," she explained with a sigh, then hurried ahead of Balfour to the large corner box where it seemed the mare was trying to kick down the walls. A groom stepped out of the box at their approach.

"How is she doing, Ben?" Regina asked, leaning against the lower half of the box. Her eyes intently studied the huge chestnut mare as the horse kicked out at the man examining her.

"Jeremy is looking her over now, Miss Regina, but he thinks tonight for sure," the groom replied. He, too, watched the slight man moving about the clean, straw-filled box, carefully avoiding the mare's deadly hooves. Ben glanced up then and noticed the duke standing behind his mistress and begrudgingly nodded. "Evening, Your Grace. I put your groom up with me but he's outside now, kind of keeping an eye on things."

"Thank you," the duke murmured but his attention was on Regina who, astonishingly enough, seemed to have forgotten his presence.

Regina was oblivious to everything but her prize horse. Her gaze travelled lovingly over the mare moving restlessly about the box and pawing at the floor. She watched Jeremy and prayed he was right in his prediction. By her calculations, Clio was already ten days late and Regina wanted no trouble with this foal. The mare had been mated with Lord Ashford's stallion, and transporting her to and from Canterbury had posed major problems. It was not a trip Regina wanted to undertake again.

The young man finished his examination and crossed to the door, moving lightly on his feet. Bone thin, he exuded an air of strength and capability that bespoke endurance. Perhaps it was his face, deeply browned and lined from long days spent outdoors, or the deft way he moved his large, capable hands. He lifted one to his cap, a reassuring gesture.

Regina introduced the man as her trainer, Jeremy Davies, and spoke glowingly of his talents.

Jeremy seemed embarrassed by her praise and directed their attention to the mare. "She looks fine, Miss Regina. Been up and down half a dozen times, but no problems that I can see. In truth, I'm more worried about old Calliope than Clio here."

"You stay with Calliope then, Jeremy, and Ben can keep an eye on Clio. As soon as her water breaks, have him send one of the lads for me and I'll see her through."

The young man nodded, taking her participation as much for granted as he did Ben's. The only one surprised was the duke, and he did not say a word until they were on their way back to the house.

"Do you seriously intend to birth that mare yourself?" he asked as they crossed the lawn.

Regina looked up, but she could barely make out his features in the dusty light of early evening. "I intend to be there, yes, but Clio will do all the work," she said, laughing. "Tell me, Your Grace, have you ever seen a mare give birth?"

"I have people who attend to that sort of thing."

"And yet you told David it was a natural process and an educational experience."

"You know I only said that to put your cousin in her place. I had no notion that you would actually . . . actually help in the birth yourself."

Regina chuckled. The duke was not quite as sophisticated as he would have the world believe. "Well, it is the natural order of things and something most women go through without giving it much thought. Surely you would not think it amiss of me if I attended my mother or my sister when they were lying-in?"

"That is entirely different," he replied, keeping his voice low as they entered the hall.

"I see that in your own way you are as prudish and conventional as my brother. Perhaps you and Andrew have more in common than you believe," Regina said, her voice as low as his but lacking in any censure. If anything, there was only the faintest trace of disappointment underlying her words.

She left the duke in the hall, and once more he stared after her retreating form, wondering at her very odd notions.

Regina did not join the others in the drawing room. Under the pretext of work, she remained in her small office at the end of the first-floor hall. Here she poured over the pages of *The Stud Book,* seeking that elusive combination which would make her horses true champions. This evening, however, the allure of lady luck and blood horses failed to capture her complete attention.

Regina blamed her inability to concentrate on the long, tiring day. Of course, the attempt to kidnap David weighed heavily on her mind, but with innate honesty, she admitted the duke was proving a formidable distraction. An image of his dark blond curls and clear blue eyes came compellingly to mind, and it took all of her willpower not to close her books and hurry up to the drawing room. She smiled to herself, thinking of how startled Cornelia would be were she suddenly to appear on time. Normally Regina was so engrossed in her work, her cousin had to send a maid to fetch her for tea.

They had established the routine when Cornelia first came to live at Whitechapel. Her cousin, accustomed to a busier household, needed someone to talk with at the end of the day. Regina considered it her duty to sit with the older woman for at least an hour or so, and she had trained her mind to listen to Cornelia's chatter while considering other matters. It was a tedious hour but not unendurable, and, of late, with David's arrival, had become almost a pleasant interlude—but not to the extent that Regina really looked forward to it. She still left her office with reluctance when Maisie or Trudy came to remind her of the hour. Tonight, however, she needed no reminder. Her eyes kept straying to the mantel clock. The hands seemed to be barely moving, and it still lacked five minutes to the hour.

A low rumble of thunder in the distance drew her to the windows. Pushing aside the curtains, Regina stared with dismay at the dark sky. Not a star in sight. She opened the window and leaned out. One could almost feel the storm brewing. The rising wind whistled as it whipped through the trees. She saw the smaller branches bend beneath its force and felt the coolness in the air. A roll of thunder drowned out the sound of the wind and seconds later a brilliant flash of lightning lit up the yard as the first large drops of rain fell. Trust Clio to wait until the middle of a thunderstorm to drop her foal.

A tap on the door reminded her of the hour. Regina drew the window shut and latched it securely as Maisie looked in. Nodding at the girl, she said, "Please tell my cousin I shall be there directly." The maid nodded and when her curly head had disappeared round the door, Regina stepped to the looking glass and ran her fingers through her own blond locks. The breeze had blown several tendrils free from her usually neat coiffure, and they refused to be brushed back into place. There was not time to return to her room. Making a face, she decided His Grace would have to add untidiness to her other faults.

If the Duke of Balfour found Regina's appearance less than appealing, it was not apparent when he looked up at her entrance into the drawing room. He stood at once, a warm smile on his lips. "Ah, Hera returns. I quite thought you had deserted me for the stables."

"And did the mighty hurler of thunderbolts conjure up this storm to keep me inside?" she asked as lightning lit up the windows behind them.

"Stormy weather seems to follow His Grace," Cornelia observed from her chair near the fireplace. Her thin lips twitched nervously as a gust of wind shook the panes in the long windows. "Perhaps it is an omen."

"Indeed, I believe so," Regina said, accepting the chair the duke drew out for her. "A good one," she added softly, smiling up at him. "We would be in dire straits if there were never any storms to clear the air or water the land."

Cornelia sniffed audibly. She poured out a cup of tea for her niece, ignoring the duke.

"Are you not having tea with us, Your Grace?" Regina asked, accepting the delicate porcelain cup.

"He prefers brandy and has consumed the better part of a bottle already," Cornelia informed her with a dark look.

"My wound, you know," Balfour replied with a grin. Lifting his glass in a mock salute, he added, "It helps to deaden the pain."

He did not appear to be in any pain, Regina thought, but she did not know him well enough to be certain. Still, were it not for the bulge of bandages beneath the white linen shirt, and the way his left arm hung limply at his side, one would not guess he was wounded at all. He moved like a cat, she thought, as she watched him return to his own chair with a light-footed, supple movement.

When the duke winked at her, Regina realized she had been staring. She glanced hastily away, and it was only then that she noticed her nephew was not in the room. Alarmed, she turned to her cousin. "Where is David?"

"I sent him to bed," Cornelia replied placidly, her eyes intent on the needlepoint in her hands. "The boy needs his rest."

"But he always takes tea with us first. Surely—"

"I believe Miss Davenport fears I may be contagious," Balfour drawled, casually refilling his glass.

Cornelia ignored him. "David has had a great deal of excitement today, and I thought he looked a trifle feverish," she explained to Regina. Then, her small eyes narrowed in disapproval, she turned to the duke. "I am quite aware, Your Grace, that your wound is not contagious. However, I must point out to you that Andrew's son is not accustomed to seeing gentlemen partake of stimulants as freely as seems to be your habit. I would certainly be remiss in my duty to Andrew were I to allow his son to be unduly influenced by your conduct."

"That would be dreadful, would it not?" Balfour replied sarcastically before Regina could intervene. "One sees what a perfect specimen of boyhood young David is. Pale, rather sickly-looking, and with no interests outside his books. Ah, yes, how appalling were he to come under the influence of a normal man and learn something of the world."

Cornelia colored up. His words were irrefutable for she knew that even Andrew wished that his son was more inclined towards masculine sports.

Regina, her patience wearing thin, set her cup down with a snap. "You overstep yourself, Cornelia. Andrew left David in my charge, and, in the future, I shall decide what is best for him. I believe you meant well, but please bear in mind that were it not for His Grace's intervention, David would now be in the hands of kidnappers."

Cornelia drew in a deep breath at the sharp words. Apparently her cousin was so besotted by the duke that she was unable to think clearly. A soft chuckle from Balfour did nothing to soothe her feelings. Angrily, she cast her sewing aside and stood. "Well! I must say, Regina, that I never looked to see you so taken in by anyone. You might bear in mind that mere rank does not a gentleman make, and before you allow your gratitude to completely overcome your good sense, I

suggest you consider how *convenient* was the duke's arrival!"
With those ominous words, she swept out of the room.

Regina closed her eyes for a brief moment. When she
opened them again, she saw the duke had moved to the side-
board and was pouring a glass of sherry from the decanter.
He carried it across to her.

"I think, under the circumstances, this will do you more
good than a cup of tea."

Regina accepted the glass, observing him over the brim
as she took a sip. "Thank you. I must apologize for my
cousin's rudeness."

He shrugged. "I have heard it all before. People like your
cousin do not trouble me in the least."

"How agreeable that must be," she said, smiling. "But she
was partially in the right, you know."

His brows rose in slight surprise as he leaned against the
mantel of the fireplace. "In what way? I fail to see what
concern it is of Miss Davenport's, or that of anyone else, if
I choose to indulge in a few drinks."

Regina smiled. "If the amount of alcohol you have consumed today is anything near your normal consumption, I
believe you rather understate the matter."

"I still fail to see that it concerns anyone other than myself.
I do not get disguised, my dear Regina, nor fall over the
furniture, or chase the chambermaids."

"Oh, you may drink yourself to oblivion and I would not
say a word—that is, as long as you do not do so in the presence of a very impressionable little boy who regards you as
some sort of hero."

He appeared astonished for a brief moment, caught off
balance by her words, and Regina took advantage of it.

"You may, of course, do as you please while you are a
guest here, but I would consider it a personal favor if you
would refrain from drinking quite so heavily while David is
present. Children do notice things, you know. After he retires,
I would not object if you wished to drink yourself under the

table. Every man must seek his own means of escape when the cares of the world are too much to bear."

"Escape? Are you not taking a bit much on assumption?" he asked, a lazy grin on his lips that did little to offset the sudden cold hardness in his eyes.

"Am I, Your Grace? What other reason is there for a gentleman to deliberately addle his senses? It has been my experience that most gentlemen who drink to excess do so for very definite reasons." Her eyes darkened with a shadow of sadness and she glanced down at her hands before adding quietly, "When my mother died, my father found it . . . difficult to go on without her. He drowned his sorrow in drink. Barely a year later, he was killed in a carriage accident—they said he was too intoxicated to control his horses."

The ice in his eyes melted. "My dear Regina, I had no idea—"

She waved a hand to halt his apology, giving him a tremulous smile. "I was very young at the time and did not half realize what had occurred. It affected my brother much more deeply, which is why Andrew does not allow spirits in his home. And, of course, Cornelia has always been his shadow. Anything that Andrew disapproves of, she does, too."

Balfour swirled the brandy in his glass. He never allowed anyone to dictate to him, but he suddenly found it difficult to drink with impunity in front of her after what she had confided.

Regina saw his confusion and smiled. "Pray, finish your drink. Truly, I do not hold spirits to be some sort of evil. You will find we have an excellent wine cellar, tolerable sherry, and the brandy is, so I am told, quite exceptional."

"I wonder why you allow drink in your home at all. One would expect you to follow your brother's example."

"I hope that I am capable of thinking for myself, Your Grace. In truth, I enjoy a glass of wine with dinner and find an occasional glass of sherry to be beneficial. It was not spirits which killed my father, but his inability to handle them. He used drink to excess. It is a weakness which I do not believe I inherited."

"I cannot conceive that anyone would ever describe you as weak, my dear," he responded, wondering silently if that was how she saw him. He had never thought of it before, but he supposed he did use alcohol to escape from a life he found intolerably boring. But it was well within his control.

"Thank you," she said softly and stood. "Now, I pray you will excuse me. It has been rather a long day. If you have need of anything, I am certain one of the maids will be along in a minute or two. You may have routed Cornelia, but I doubt she retired defeated."

As if to confirm her words, Maisie tapped on the open door and looked in. "Miss Cornelia said as how I should see if you be needing anything, Miss?"

Balfour grinned at Regina in sudden understanding, and this time, the amusement reached his eyes.

She returned his smile. When he looked at her like that, she found it impossible to do otherwise, but she kept her word and crossed to the door. "Thank you, Maisie. I am retiring for the evening, but you may see if His Grace requires anything else."

Regina left them and hurried upstairs. She paused at David's room. Shielding the light of her candle, she tiptoed in. She need not have worried. The young boy slept curled in a ball, undisturbed by the thunderstorm. She sat the candle down, gently pulled the covers over his shoulders, and kissed him lightly on the forehead.

Her own bedchamber lay at the rear of the house. It was a large, commodious room and its long windows overlooked the yard and the stables. The rain continued to pour down heavily, streaking the panes. The light coming from the barn was little more than a blurry halo in the wet darkness. It was only half past ten, and she judged she had several hours to wait before Ben summoned her. Most of the foals were born between midnight and two in the morning.

Regina settled comfortably in her chair. The fire Trudy had built up provided a reassuring coziness, and the rat-a-tat of the rain beating against the house was somehow comforting. She tried to concentrate on a new novel her aunt had sent her from London, but her gaze kept straying to the windows. She saw a movement near the barn and sat up abruptly, straining to see through the stormy night.

A moment later she relaxed as she recognized Tenby, the duke's groom. She remembered Balfour saying he would have his man patrol during the night. Poor fellow, she thought. He was undoubtedly cold and wet, but the duke did not seem to care for that. Well, when she went down, she would make certain that Tenby had something hot to drink and a bite to eat. By that time, the duke should be fast asleep.

Regina sorely underestimated Balfour's capacity for brandy. Far from being under the table, he remained wide-awake, bored beyond belief, and already regretting the impulse that had prompted him to stay on at Whitechapel. He'd retired to the guest chamber not long after Regina left him, but be was unaccustomed to sleeping so early, and an hour later still restlessly paced the confines of the room. There was no one with whom to talk, no one to challenge to a game of cards, or to share a drink. He glanced idly out the window. The light shining from the stables reminded him of the groom's prediction that the mare would drop her foal this evening.

Why not see for himself, he thought suddenly. He was a man who prided himself on his knowledge of horseflesh, yet it seemed Regina Westfield knew more about the animals than he did. That could be remedied. He rang for Desmond and seconds later the valet stepped into the room.

"Help me get my boots on, Desmond."

"Your boots? But . . . 'tis raining out, Your Grace! A nasty thunderstorm. Surely, you do not intend—"

"My boots, Desmond, if you please."

The voice brooked no argument, and the valet hastily pulled out the black Hessians he had just restored to their usual lustrous shine. Kneeling before the duke, he held one tenderly to his master's foot. It was a thousand pities if His Grace meant to traipse about the yard in them. It would surely ruin the finish, but he knew it was useless to protest.

"Where's my cape? Did it dry out?"

"Yes, Your Grace. Here you are," the valet said, standing on his toes to stretch the voluminous coat over the broad shoulders.

"That will be all, Desmond. No need to wait up for me."

The valet kept his thoughts to himself, discreetly retiring, but there would be no sleep for him until the duke returned. His Grace might not care if his boots were ruined, but Desmond would die of mortification were anyone to see the duke turned out less than perfectly attired. No self-respecting valet would think of retiring under such conditions. No, he would have to get his hands on the boots and the driving coat as soon as possible or they would be utterly ruined. He shut the door of his room with more force than usual, but the duke was already half way down the long hall.

Balfour crossed the yard in long strides but even so he was nearly drenched by the time he reached the stable door and flung it open. He startled Ben, who was on his way out.

"Your Grace! Is there trouble?"

"No, everything seems quiet—too bloody quiet! I came back out to see about those mares. Have they dropped their foals yet?"

"They are near," Ben said, a wry grin twisting his mouth. "I was just on my way to fetch Miss Regina."

"Leave her sleep, man. Surely I can do whatever needs to be done."

"Beggin' your pardon, Your Grace, but it would be more than my life's worth did I not call her," Ben replied, slipping past the duke before he could protest further.

Balfour let the groom go. Regina would more than likely think better of venturing out when she saw how the storm was blowing. He shrugged out of the heavy cape and tossed it carelessly against a bale of straw before making his way to Clio's box. The mare was lying on her side and turned a baleful eye in his direction as she kicked out.

The box was clean, brightly lit and Balfour could see the mare clearly. Her tail was wrapped in some sort of gauze and a sheen of sweat glistened on her coat. As he watched, the mare suddenly gave a great heave and a stream of clear water gushed out of her.

"Damn!" he cried, alarmed. Where in the hell was the groom or the trainer? "Jeremy! Ben! Where are you?" he demanded loudly, while keeping an eye on Clio. "Damn it man, there's something wrong with this mare!" His voice echoed loudly through the empty stable.

Four

As Regina crossed the yard beneath the large umbrella Ben held over her, she felt her boots sink into the mud. It hardly mattered. The excitement of a new foal overshadowed everything else. What was a soaking and muddy boots compared to seeing a new life emerge?

Pulling open the barn door, she heard Balfour's shout. The urgent, strident call for help alarmed her. She rushed down the wide aisle, fear propelling her steps. Near breathless, her heart feeling as though it had plummeted to her boots, Regina turned the corner. She saw Balfour at the same moment she heard Jeremy shout. Calliope's foal was coming and the trainer could not leave her.

"I'll see to Clio," she called as she passed, willing herself not to panic.

"Thank God you're here," Balfour said when he saw her. His face was pale and sweating. "I don't know what to do for her. She seemed fine and then all of a sudden this geyser of water spurted out. Will she lose the foal?"

Regina looked over the door at Clio and felt a wave of incredibly sweet relief. Her water had burst and the mare was obviously in labor, but everything looked to be progressing as nature intended. She spared a glance for the duke, touched by his concern. "She's fine, Your Grace. There's nothing to worry about yet."

"But all that water—"

"Quite normal. Clio's telling us she's ready. If you care

to stay, her foal should appear fairly soon, but for now would you tell Ben I need him?" Regina said, stripped off her gloves, then opened the door to the box.

She quickly cleared away the sodden straw and replaced it with fresh, carefully staying out of reach of the mare's hind legs. All the while, she whispered softly, encouragingly, to Clio. This was the moment she'd been waiting for. The miracle of birth never failed to move her and she exulted each time a new foal was born.

Matching her favorite mares to stallions challenged her intellect, challenged her instincts for picking the best of each, but it never seemed quite real until she saw the tiny nose of a newborn foal emerging from its mother's womb.

She heard Ben's footsteps as he opened the box door and moved towards her. In the same instant, she saw the bubble of white sack emerging beneath the mare's tail.

"You're just in time, Ben. She's starting," Regina said softly, not bothering to look around.

"Ben said to tell you he's with Erato," the duke said. "It appears all of your mares have chosen tonight to drop their foals. Is there something I can do to help?"

She glanced up at him then. He could not wear a coat because of the heavy bandage on his arm, but he nevertheless appeared immaculate in a gleaming white linen shirt, tight-fitting black knee breeches, and glossy black boots. He looked like the pampered, elegant duke that he was. Regina shook her head, turning away. With unconscious condescension in her voice, she replied, "Thank you, but unless you wish to ruin another shirt, I suggest you watch from outside the box."

"I had not thought you to be so narrow-minded, Miss Westfield. I offered you my assistance and I imagine I can be just as capable as your groom if you will only tell me what needs to be done."

Regina did not hear him. She stared with fearful intensity at the almost transparent bubble that enveloped the emerging foal. She could see one of the foal's long legs and its small dark nose. She breathed a prayer, but knew with a dreadful certainty that the other leg must be twisted behind the foal's head.

"Oh, God, we must get her up at once," Regina cried, rising with an urgency that the duke did not fully understand. "The foal's twisted! Grab hold of the mare's head collar and try to get her up," she ordered, forgetting in her terror that it was not Ben she addressed.

"I beg your pardon," the duke murmured, his poise for once shaken.

"Oh, damn! Where is Ben? I am sorry, Your Grace, but I don't have time for polite conversation. The foal will die if we don't get Clio on her feet."

Balfour moved with deceptive speed.

"Watch out for her legs," Regina warned, knowing the mare would likely kick out.

The duke stood above the mare's head and grasped the collar firmly in his right hand, urging her to her feet. "Come on, old girl. Regina said you have to stand and I doubt she will take no for an answer."

Regina, holding the tail high enough so that she could watch, pushed at Clio's hindquarters, praying the mare would contract her muscles and pull the sack back inside of her. Then the foal might have a chance of turning. Its only chance.

Pulling and shoving, they got Clio to her feet, but it wasn't working. Tears of helplessness and frustration nearly blinded Regina. She wanted this foal. "Talk to her," she urged Balfour as she gently began pushing the sack with its fragile life back into the womb. The mare's muscles contracted suddenly and the foal was in. Regina reached her arm up, delicately probing inside the womb. Her sensitive fingers could feel the head and the soft nose. She stretched her hand and gently tugged at the foreleg twisted behind the foal's head, and felt it dislodge. She withdrew her arm, oblivious to the blood and mucus saturating her sleeve.

"Let her go," she called to Balfour and watched as he released the mare, stepping swiftly out of the way. Clio kicked out, seemed to be trying to kick at her own stomach, then the huge bulk of her went down again. This time she lay on her left side. Regina blinked back the tears in her eyes. Now the foal should be able to turn.

"What do I do? Is she all right?" Balfour called, backing up against the far wall of the box.

Regina nearly laughed, the relief she felt making her light-headed, but she contained her amusement and smiled at him over the mare. "It's up to Clio now. Would you like to come and watch? You'll have a better view from here, and you deserve that for your efforts."

He made his way gingerly round the mare to where Regina knelt in the straw. She made no move to tidy her hair or clean her coat, and yet when Balfour looked down at the excitement shimmering in her clear green eyes, he thought her the most beautiful woman he'd ever seen.

"Come," she said quietly. "All these years you have been cheating yourself out of the best part of owning a horse. I never miss a birth if I can help it."

Balfour knelt beside her, keeping his doubts to himself. He wanted to ask her how she ever became involved in such an unladylike occupation, but she was pointing to Clio.

Regina held her breath, her fingers tightly crossed as the white sack emerged once again from beneath the mare's tail.

Balfour watched. Through the near-transparent sack, he could see the two front forelegs of a dark foal, and then, amazingly, a tiny head appeared between the legs.

"The shoulders are out now," Regina whispered, her voice taking on a joyous note.

"Shouldn't we be doing something?" he asked nervously as matters seemed to come to a halt.

"No, not unless she has a problem again. Nature designed the process extremely well. Clio will do better without our help. All we have to do is sit here and watch."

The head and the forelegs of the fragile foal lay on the straw with a deathlike stillness. The mare was not moving either. Balfour thought Regina's optimism a trifle early. It looked to him as though the foal was stillborn.

"It's just resting for a few moments," Regina explained softly. "Then its mother will give one last shove—"

She broke off her words as Clio contracted her muscles and the rest of the foal suddenly emerged. Regina moved quickly then, slitting open the thin transparent sack just above the foal's head.

Balfour stared. When the mare had moved, it was as though she'd shot a surge of life into her foal. The tiny head came up and the foal was now breathing lustily. He was fascinated and had he not seen it with his own eyes, he would not have believed it.

Regina watched, too, reverence in her eyes. That moment, that one single instant when a twinkle of life stirred the foal, always convinced her that there was a god in the heavens and a divine pattern to life.

The mare kicked out as she struggled to her feet. Regina motioned the duke to move towards the door of the box. "Either the foal or the mare has to break the cord," she told him, keeping a wary eye on Clio. A moment later, the mare's backing movement snapped the cord of life between her and her foal. Blood gushed out, but Regina did not seem to notice. She stood silently, nodding her head in satisfaction.

"Clio will clean him up now," she said. Then, for the first time since she'd entered the stables, she gave Balfour her full attention. A blush of pink tinged her cheeks. Lord, what had she been thinking of? Treating the duke as though he were a mere stable hand. She averted her gaze and awkwardly slipped out of her coat, conscious now of her bloodstained appearance. Head down, she murmured, "I have to stay here for a while, Your Grace, but there is no reason for you to remain—"

"Obviously, my education has been lacking," he replied.

When her surprised glance met his, he smiled warmly. "I should very much like to stay, if you don't object to my presence."

"Not in the least." Pleased with him, she gestured towards the straw. "We may have to wait for an hour or so. Would you care to be seated, Your Grace?"

"After you, Miss Westfield," he said, executing an elaborate bow. When she was seated, he folded his long legs beneath him. "Now—what, precisely, are we waiting to see?"

"As soon as the colt gathers enough strength, he'll try to stand."

"The colt?" he asked, a teasing note in his voice, but his brows rose a little in surprise at her knowledge.

Regina blushed. She would *not* explain that! "He will have to nurse," she said, determined to ignore the amusement in the duke's eyes. "Occasionally it takes a foal some time to find his legs and then make his way to his mother."

As she spoke, the colt managed to get his long forelegs stretched out in front of him and sat shakily on his haunches.

"Get up, boy. Come on!"

The duke heard Regina softly urging the foal and turned his head to watch the colt's struggle to stand. His trembling legs looked impossibly long and fragile. Balfour sucked in his breath as the colt lost his balance and toppled. He instinctively reached out, but Regina stopped him, laying her hand on his.

"It is better if we do not interfere. If the colt stands on his own within the first hour of his birth, we know he's healthy. If he cannot manage it . . . well, we shall try to help him up and see that he finds his mother. But if he doesn't nurse within five or six hours—" she broke off, shrugging. "We send for the veterinarian then, but there is small hope the colt will survive."

The sleek, dark brown colt tried again to stand. He managed to get his front legs up first, then seemed to boost himself up on his rear legs. His entire little body trembled with the effort.

Balfour bit his lip, but as the colt remained standing on wobbly legs, his hand tightened over Regina's in silent celebration. Together, they watched the foal take one quivering step and then another.

"He will do now," Regina said, laughing happily as the tension left her. Her eyes met Balfour's and, abruptly aware of the intimacy, she freed her hand from his.

The duke let her go without comment, watching as the colt staggered towards him. Bright, large brown eyes regarded him curiously and Balfour extended his hand as he would to a puppy. The newborn foal sucked on his fingers and the duke laughed, absurdly pleased.

"It may take him a while to find his mother," Regina explained, smiling foolishly at the colt. "He may try to nurse on your fingers or your shirt, or the wooden railings in the box."

"Not my shirt! I shudder to think of what poor Desmond would say. Your mother is over there, fellow. See, she's the big one making all the noise."

Clio was up and stamping her feet. The fragile-looking colt turned in her direction and, after a couple of shaky steps, nuzzled her. It took him a couple of tries, but he finally found the udder he sought.

Reluctant to leave, Regina sighed with contentment. She could watch a newborn foal with its mother for hours, but she knew it was unconscionable of her to keep the duke out here. Still, she sat quietly for another moment, listening to the sound of rain falling. She could hear it striking the roof, but it was no longer the torrential downpour that had soaked them earlier. Now, it seemed a comforting sound, shutting them off from the rest of the world.

"He will be fine," she said at last, making a move to rise.

Balfour stood and extended his right hand, helping her to her feet. She knew she must look a fright and half expected a derisive comment from the duke. She glanced up at him, but his blue eyes held only understanding. Regina remained still, her hand warm in his, feeling a bond forging between them. The moment abruptly shattered as the stable erupted with life and noise.

Ben rounded the corner, excitedly calling her name. "You won't believe it," he said, almost crowing in triumph. "But we sure outdid ourselves tonight, Miss Regina. Erato's done dropped the most perfect-looking filly I ever set eyes on, and Jeremy said to tell you old Calliope's come up to the mark, too. Two foals in one night! How are you doing here?"

Regina stepped aside and Ben saw the new colt, a little skittish now and still unsure on his long legs.

"Well, I'll be! Three in one night. Appears like the storm must have shaken up the mares and blown Lady Luck our way," he said, swinging his lantern higher for a better look.

Regina laughed and turned to the duke. "I do believe this calls for a toast. I've been saving a rather special wine, Your Grace—oh, good heavens! Your arm is bleeding again!"

"Is it?" he asked, glancing down at his sleeve where the blood had soaked through the bandages and stained his shirt a dark burgundy. "I thought it kind of pinched earlier when I shoved the mare to her feet. The wound must have opened again, but it's probably stopped bleeding by now. It feels fine."

"Why did you not say something?" she demanded, exasperated by his air of unconcern. Giving him no time to answer, she swung around. "Ben, keep an eye on Clio, please, while I get His Grace back to the house. We must change that bandage at once."

"It is nothing, Regina," the duke said, trying to reassure her, but he addressed only her back. After a commiserate look from Ben, he followed her docilely from the box and back to the house.

* * *

Regina awakened with a groan the following morning. Her head ached abominably and her mouth felt as dry as straw. She stumbled to the window and pulled the curtains aside. It must be nearly noon, she realized. Muttering words no lady should ever allow on her lips, she rang for Trudy.

Her maid appeared a few moments later, a tray bearing a steaming pot of tea in her hands, and a sunny smile ready for her mistress.

Regina waved the tea aside, ignored the smile, and demanded, "Why did you allow me to sleep so late? I have above a dozen things to attend to this morning. Egad, the day is half gone and I am not even dressed yet."

"His Grace said as how we were to allow you to sleep, Miss Regina. He told us about the new foals and how you was up so late."

"Oh, he did, did he? Since when is the duke running this household? You know I never like to rise past nine."

"It was only—"

"Never mind, Trudy. Lay out my riding habit and then you may tell His Grace that—no, on second thought, I shall tell him myself. Where is he?"

"Out in the stables, Miss. Perhaps if you was to have a cup of tea, you would—"

"Just get my habit, if you please," Regina snapped, undoing the ties of her dressing gown with unnecessary force.

Trudy nodded and turned away with a crestfallen face. She'd thought they was doing something nice for the mistress. Pulling the blue habit out of the wardrobe, she laid it on the bed without a word. Then, with downcast eyes, dropped a curtsey. "Will there be anything else, Miss?"

Regina, about to issue a curt order, bit back the words. She took a deep, calming breath. "I must sound like a shrew this morning and can only wonder how you bear with me. Thank you for the tea, Trudy, and I promise you I shall drink it before I come down."

Regina was rewarded with a quick smile before the maid

left, and felt somewhat better. The tea, which she drank only as a means of apology, was hot, strong, and sweet. It helped to clear her head and wash away the dry taste in her mouth. She felt immeasurably better by the time she went below stairs, and was even able to greet her cousin with tolerable composure.

Cornelia, still sitting at the breakfast table, sniffed audibly. "Good afternoon, Regina. I trust you slept well." She did not look up but continued to sort through the correspondence spread about the table.

"All too well, I fear. I could not believe the time when I finally awoke. Where is David?"

"In the stables with His Grace, and I only hope no harm will come of it. I told the duke that David should be kept inside in view of what occurred yesterday, but of course my opinions are of no account here."

"You know that is not true," Regina said, reluctantly drawing out a chair. No matter how much she had to do, placating Cornelia must be at the top of the list if they were to have any peace in the household.

"Tell that to His Grace, then. Had I known how late you retired, I would not have sent Trudy to wake you at nine, but for *him* to countermand my orders, and without a word to me, well—it is outside of enough."

"I wish he had not done so," Regina replied truthfully. "Losing a few hours sleep has never hurt me and, indeed, I feel worse for so long a sleep."

"I knew how it would be," her cousin said, sounding a trifle less aggrieved. "But that is not the least of it. Just when I had it all arranged for David to sit in the drawing room with me, that *person* insisted on dragging him off to the stables to see the new foals."

"I am surprised David would forsake his books long enough to even take a look," Regina said, mindful of her own futile attempts to interest her nephew in horses.

"Hmmph. All the duke has to do is crook his finger and

the boy comes running. Mark my words, Regina, no good will come of this. The association is highly regrettable, and what Andrew will have to say when he learns his only son has chosen to idolize a man that he considers to be beyond the pale—well, I am sure you know how your brother will feel. I must say I am surprised that under the circumstances, you continue to positively encourage the man."

"I understand how you feel, Cornelia, but are you not exaggerating? Do consider the enormous gratitude we owe the duke. I am certain Andrew would wish us to extend extraordinary civility to any gentleman who rescued David, regardless of his personal opinion of the man."

"Perhaps," she conceded, pursing her lips in a moue of disapproval. "But to allow the Duke of Balfour to run tame in your house goes beyond mere civility." She held up a hand as Regina started to protest. "Pray, allow me to finish. I know you think me unduly harsh, my dear, but I am several years older than you and you would be wise to allow yourself to be guided by my experience—experience which clearly tells me that permitting the duke to remain here is inviting trouble to walk in the door. Send him on his way, before we all have cause to regret it."

Regina sighed as she stood, forsaking any hope that in the calm light of day her cousin would be more amendable. "You must see that I cannot, Cornelia. Not only is the duke wounded, but he must wait for repairs to his carriage to be completed. Would you have me turn him out?"

Her cousin ignored her, concentrating on the letter in her hand.

Regina took a step towards her, placing her hand on the older woman's shoulder. "Perhaps my brother has misjudged the duke," she suggested softly. "They are not, after all, well acquainted, and it is possible that were Andy to know the duke better, he would change his opinion. I think we should at least accord His Grace the benefit of the doubt."

"There, you see!" Cornelia cried, throwing down the letter

and turning to face Regina. "He is getting round you just as I feared he would. You may be taken in by his sly ways, but I will not be, and I have already written to warn Andrew of his presence here. I only hope my letter reaches him before it is too late."

Regina's head was beginning to ache again. Above all things, she hated arguments of any sort. It was one of the reasons she preferred living alone. She turned away, knowing it was useless to try to reason with Cornelia in her present mood. "We shall discuss it later," she promised before retreating to the stables.

She felt better the instant she stepped into the yard and felt the warmth of the sun and smelled the freshness of the grass after the night's rain. A horse nickered as she pulled open the heavy doors and, despite her preoccupation, Regina could not help smiling at the reproachful look in the stallion's eyes. Penrod nickered again as she approached and she paused for a moment to soothe him. He should have been turned out into the field to work off some of his energy, she thought, avoiding the sharp teeth nipping at her jacket. He would be a handful if she rode him now.

She heard a low murmur coming from Calliope's box and thought she recognized David's voice. She drew nearer, listening to the soft, crooning words, unable to believe what she was hearing.

"So who cares if one of your legs is turned out," David murmured. "I don't. Jeremy said you didn't breed true and you'll never be able to race, but that's not important, not really. Papa says the race is not always to the swift."

Regina tiptoed closer, peering over the box door. Calliope was contentedly munching her hay, occasionally turning a baleful eye in the direction of her foal. The colt, a dark, long-legged foal with threads of gray in his coat, butted against David. Regina ran knowing eyes over the foal. He looked to be unusually small, but would soon have the coloring of his sire, a magnificent dark gray stallion. Then she saw the right foreleg and realized what her nephew was saying.

She would take a loss on this colt. No knowledgeable trainer would buy a foal with a foreleg turned out, and she would not risk the prestige of her stable by selling him to an unsuspecting buyer. It was unlikely the colt would ever see a race. Too much pressure on the knee with his leg turned like that would snap it. Time, nature, and sunlight would do much to strengthen the leg, and possibly the blacksmith could help, but as far as the stable was concerned, the colt was a loss. She would have to give him away or use him for a pleasure horse.

David rubbed the foal on its head, just above the dark, velvety eyes. "I'm not like my father or mother either, you know. Papa said I'm a throwback and that's what you are, too. But it doesn't matter to me if you're not perfect. I like you just the way you are. I think you are beautiful and if Aunt Regina does not want you, well, I have saved some money and perhaps she will let me buy you. Papa always said I should have my own horse, but I never wanted one—not before I saw you."

Regina stepped quietly back. David would be embarrassed to know she'd listened to his conversation, but what she wanted to do was rush in and throw her arms about the small boy. She wanted to hug him and tell him that she thought he was perfect, perfect just the way he was.

She heard voices approaching and hurried round the corner to intercept Jeremy. The duke was with him and Regina motioned for them to be quiet. For the time being, it would be best to leave David alone with Calliope's new foal.

Balfour smiled at her. "Regina, did you—"

"Sssh. Come with me," she whispered and led the way outside the barn. When they stepped out into the bright afternoon sunlight, she turned to the duke. "What made you bring David out here with you?"

Surprised by her question, he shrugged. "A mere impulse,

I suppose. You'd said the boy needed to get out more, and I thought it unkind to leave him locked in the house with your cousin. Why? Is something wrong?"

"No, not at all," she answered, smiling enigmatically. "Indeed, I believe I owe you a double debt of gratitude." She turned to Jeremy and asked, "Did you tell David that Calliope's foal was no good?"

"David? Why, no—well, at least not directly. I suppose he may have heard me explaining to His Grace that the colt's foreleg is turned. Did you see the foal? He's useless, I'm afraid."

"I saw him and I think it may be the best thing that could have happened—almost as good as winning the Gold Cup," she answered, her eyes bright with the joy she felt.

Jeremy looked at her as though she'd lost her mind.

Balfour was quicker and chuckled aloud. "Has that poor misbegot colt found a champion, then?"

Regina laughed happily. "He has that. I overheard David telling the colt that if I did not want him, he would buy him. And I plan to let him do just that. Or Andrew. Yes, now that I think of it, it would be morally just for Andrew to buy that colt for David."

"You are going to keep the foal here?" Jeremy asked, aghast. He'd heard Regina say a dozen times or more that breeding farms did not keep horses they could neither sell nor race. If a stable was to be profitable, one could not afford sentiment.

"Not forever," she assured him. "Only until my brother returns to claim David. He will take the colt then." She would see to that. She glanced at Balfour, but he was no longer paying attention. His gaze seemed fixed on the road that ran north of the house. Regina turned in that direction, and drew in a sharp breath.

Two men riding that fast could only mean trouble.

Balfour, ready to shove Regina into the stable, relaxed perceptibly as the riders drew near. He recognized Tenby mounted on one of his own stallions, and no doubt that was Ben just behind him. The duke had ordered the grooms to patrol the grounds as a precaution—one that was apparently warranted.

The pair raced into the yard, their horses lathered from the hot ride and unrelenting pace. Tenby shouted something unintelligible, struggling to control the high-strung stallion.

Ben slid to the ground with practiced ease, but he, too, had difficulty speaking and gasped for breath. "It's old Ramsey. We found him tied and gagged in his cottage," he wheezed.

"Half-dead, he is," Tenby added, bringing the skittish horse to a halt and dismounting.

"Oh, no! Merciful heavens, what is happening?" Regina cried.

The duke, seeing the color drain from her face, and half-fearful she would faint, reached out and encircled her shoulders with his good arm, drawing her protectively towards him.

Regina was not aware of the way she naturally leaned against Balfour, but she took comfort from his presence. First David, and now Ramsey. What evil had Andy brought down on them?

"Who is this man and where is his cottage?" Balfour demanded.

All three men tried to answer him, but Jeremy won out. "Old Ramsey was the kennel master for Lord Snow—him that owned Whitechapel before Miss Regina bought it. He pensioned off Ramsey and gave him a small cottage up near the woods. Sometimes the old man helps out with the horses—he's got a way with animals. But Ramsey's just an old man, Your Grace. Never bothers no one. Why would anyone want to harm him?"

Five

The Duke of Balfour took charge of the situation and no one questioned his authority to do so. Regina, nearly numb with shock, listened as he ordered Jeremy to ride for the doctor and bring him as quickly as possible to the old man's cottage. Tenby received terse instructions to remain at Whitechapel, standing guard over the house and stables.

"Ben, as soon as you're rested, you can guide me to the cottage. Have one of the boys saddle us some fresh horses and see if they can find some rifles or pistols." When the groom nodded, Balfour turned to Regina. "Stay in the house while we are gone and tell the maids to admit no one. Keep the doors locked, and if you can use that gun you waved at me, keep it at hand."

"I am coming with you."

The words were quiet, her voice as soft as ever, but Balfour had no doubt of her determination. He could see it in her eyes, and in the stubborn stance she assumed as she stepped away from him.

Still, he tried to convince her otherwise. "Regina, be rational about this. If the men who did this are the same ones who tried to kidnap David, I do not want you anywhere near them. They are louts—the sort of bully boys who take pleasure in tormenting children or old men. Or women. You would place yourself in considerable danger, and for what purpose?"

"Those men attempted to kidnap my nephew. They abused one of my people. I am coming with you."

A sardonic smile curled his lips. "I suppose that if I insisted you remain here, you would ride after us as soon as my back was turned?"

She raised her chin half an inch. It was answer enough.

"As you will then," Balfour said, silently condemning her willfulness even while he admired her courage. "Do you wish to ride or follow us in the carriage?"

"I shall ride Penrod, but perhaps you should let Ben drive you in the carriage. Your arm—"

"Will not prevent me from riding," he interrupted curtly. His rudeness stemmed out of concern for her. He knew with a certainty that, had he not been there, Regina would have ridden off into the Lord only knew what sort of danger. His opinion of Sir Andrew had never been high, but it reached a new low as an image of Regina in the hands of the thugs he'd seen, assailed him. Her brother had no business placing her in so much danger. The man was an abysmal fool.

Regina, covertly watching him, saw the muscle in his jaw tighten and his blue eyes turn icy cold. She wondered at his anger. She had not meant to insult him and was about to proffer an apology when Balfour looked down at her.

His anger evaporated and he lifted a hand to lightly touch her on the cheek. "It's only a graze, Regina, and my left arm at that. I might have trouble with a team, but I can certainly handle one horse."

Ben stepped out of the barn, drinking thirstily from a water jug. One of the younger lads followed him, leading two fresh mounts. Balfour started to order a horse saddled for Regina, when another boy appeared leading her stallion.

The duke glanced at Ben, then down at Regina. "Perceptive of him."

"He would expect nothing less," she said as she accepted a leg up from the groom. Penrod pranced sideways, threw his head back, then reared up. Regina drew on the reins, forcing him to canter once around the stable yard. She held him under control, but she could feel the surging energy in the stallion. The sheer power of him and the warmth of the sun raised her spirits. She sent the duke a mischievous smile. "I hope you will be able to keep up, Your Grace."

"We shall put it to the test one day, but for the present, remember that this is no pleasure jaunt. Stay beside me, Regina. If we are fired upon, I don't want to be distracted, worrying about where you are."

His grim reminder sobered her abruptly. For a moment, with the bright sunlight glinting against Penrod's satin coat, none of it had seemed real. She'd almost forgot the attempt to kidnap David. Forgot that a helpless old man had been savagely beaten and left tied to a chair.

Somberly, she followed Ben as he led the way out of the yard. She held Penrod to a steady trot apace with the duke's horse. They travelled slowly along the trail that twisted and meandered through the home woods. Twice, where the path narrowed to a point that only one horse could pass, Balfour dropped back, letting her ride ahead of him.

The duke had said little since they'd left the yard, but Regina was aware of his keen eyes scanning the area, and knew he listened intently for any sound foreign to the woods. Nothing seemed amiss. She could hear the rush of the creek winding its way down to the River Lark, and the chattering of birds scolding the newcomers. There was nothing out of the ordinary.

She turned her head for an instant, just a second, but long enough to miss seeing the brown rabbit bolt across the path. Penrod shied, rearing up and nearly unseating her. Balfour cursed and grabbed at the stallion's reins, but missed as Penrod sidestepped. He plunged away and brushed against a tree, but by then Regina had control again. She halted the stallion and leaned forward to whisper a few words in his ear before giving him the lead again.

"I am sorry, Your Grace," she murmured, drawing near to

where the duke waited. "Penrod has an unreasonable fear of rabbits that I have not yet been able to break."

"Perhaps you should choose a more suitable mount for a lady," he replied, masking the sudden fear he'd felt behind biting sarcasm. "I should loathe being the one to pick up the pieces after that stallion tramples you."

"I shall remember that, Your Grace, and endeavor not to be trampled in your presence," she shot back.

"Thank you, my dear. In as much as I am rapidly running out of shirts, I do appreciate your consideration."

She saw the amusement that lightened his eyes and the way his lips twitched as he tried not to smile, but she was miffed that he thought her incapable of controlling her mount. Any sort of criticism went straight to her heart, and she retaliated with a taunt. "Tell me, Your Grace, have you never had a horse try to bolt with you?"

"Never," he said emphatically, putting his own well-mannered stallion to the trot again.

"Oh, how stupid of me. No horse would dare to bolt with the great Duke of Balfour on his back. But how boring for you. No challenge to speak of, unless, of course, you prefer a tame ride on animals with no life in them?"

"My dear Regina, I thought on first meeting you that you needed someone to teach you manners. I have not revised that opinion, and I warn you that if you do not behave yourself, I shall put you over my knee and administer a spanking that is obviously long overdue. And that, my girl, should prove challenge enough for any man."

"I should not advise trying it, Your Grace," Regina said, smiling impudently. "Only consider how devastating it would be to your self-esteem when you failed." She had succeeded in getting past his guard and with her good humor restored, she dared to laugh at him.

"Do not be so certain I would fail," he warned softly, allowing his gaze to drop to her breasts and then her waist in a suggestive leer. "It might prove . . . interesting."

"You would not dare!" Regina tossed her head, but she was not as certain as she sounded. The idea was outrageous. No man had ever lifted a hand to her, not even Andrew. She stole a look at the duke and felt a shiver run down her spine.

"We goes left here, Your Grace," Ben called, turning in his saddle to warn the duke. "Just a little ways ahead there's a clearing and the cottage is just on the right."

The duke nodded. He would have preferred to order Regina to wait where she was, but he knew she'd refuse, and perhaps it was better to have her where he could keep an eye on her. They slowed the horses to a walk and halted just inside the woods.

The tiny timber-framed cottage was an old one, built before brick had become so popular. The once bright-painted facade had faded with the years, and the front was nearly covered with a riotous ivy that curled over the window and doors. Weeds and scrubby bushes had taken over the small yard, slowly choking the straggly roses and wildflowers. A neglected red geranium sat wilted in its pot by the door.

They watched in silence for several moments, but there was no sign of life about the house. The duke waved to Ben to go ahead. He would have preferred to investigate himself, but he doubted Regina would wait patiently with Ben. He watched the young groom dismount and run in a low crouch to the side of the house, where he peered in the window. After a moment, he motioned for the others to join him.

"It's just like we left it, Your Grace, excepting Old Ramsey's resting on the bed instead of tied to the chair," Ben said when the others drew near. He led the way round to the door, and held it open for the duke and Regina.

Balfour had to duck his head to enter and it took a few seconds for his eyes to adjust to the dimness of the cottage. There was not much to it—one large room, starkly furnished with a cot on the far wall, an old table and chairs stood beneath the window, and a rounded arch that led to a smaller storage room. He strode through it, motioning Regina to wait where she stood.

She ignored him, ignored the clutter and the stench that pervaded the room. She'd heard the old man groan and hurried to his side, kneeling in the dust to take his gnarled hand in hers. The rough, calloused hand jerked beneath hers and Ramsey muttered furiously. She could not understand the words, but she sensed the fear her touch had aroused.

"Mr. Ramsey, please do not be alarmed. I am Regina Westfield from Whitechapel. Do you remember me?"

His eyes opened, brown orbs beneath heavily lined lids and bushy brows. There was a flash of recognition, then a look which Regina was hard put to describe. She knew only that he was silently imploring her to help him.

"What is it, Mr. Ramsey? What do you wish me to do?" she asked, searching his face for answers in the dim light. A large bruise discolored his face above the right eye, and she thought there were dried traces of blood on his swollen lips.

"Abby," the old man moaned thickly, his hand tightening on hers, his eyes silently begging. "Find Abby."

Regina had leaned close to catch the faint words, but she was puzzled. Ramsey had lived in the cottage alone, had done so for years. He had no family that she knew of, and had been content with only the company of an old brown and white collie. "Do you mean your dog?"

"Find her. Find Abby," he repeated, the words taking all his strength. The lids closed over his eyes, and his labored breathing softened as did his grip on her hand.

Regina rose slowly. The old man was resting easier, but he would not be content until they found Abby. The duke and Ben had stepped outside for another look about the cottage, and she hoped they had found some trace of the dog. She stepped to the window and opened it, taking a deep breath of fresh air. The putrid odor in the room and about Ramsey was abominable. She remembered Ben saying that he had been tied to a chair for at least a day, possibly two.

What kind of beast would do such a thing to an old man, and why?

She saw the duke and Ben conferring in the shadows of a huge chestnut tree and hurried out.

Balfour saw her coming and crossed the small yard to meet her. "I think it would be best if you wait inside for the doctor. How is the old man?"

"He is resting for the moment, but he was beaten horridly, and now the poor soul is worried about his dog. She's an old collie—have you seen any sign of her?"

Regina glanced towards the rear of the cottage, searching for a glimpse of the dog, and missed the flare of anger in Balfour's eyes.

He placed his good arm about her shoulders, urging her back to the house. "The dog is dead."

"Where is she?" Regina demanded, refusing to move. She stared up at him with disbelieving eyes.

"I . . . 'tis better if you do not see her," Balfour said gently. He saw the stubborn set of her mouth and added, "Regina, trust me on this. Someone slashed the collie's throat. There is nothing you can do. Nothing anyone can do, save bury the creature, and Ben is tending to that."

She went with him then, unresisting, and unable to comprehend what was happening in her well-ordered world. Dr. Lyons arrived with Jeremy just as they reached the door. Regina left Balfour to tell him what had occurred and stepped inside to see what she could for Ramsey.

They brought the old man to Whitechapel late on Monday afternoon, and it took four days of continuous nursing and care to bring Ramsey back to the point of lucidity. Dr. Lyons said the old man had been beaten severely, half-starved, and was near to dying of thirst when they had rescued him. The shock and the humiliation of the condition he'd been in when found, had taken their toll. Ramsey had been delirious for the first three days.

Cornelia, to everyone's astonishment, had insisted on taking charge of the sick room. Regina was allowed to sit with Ramsey for a few hours during the day while her cousin rested, but it was Cornelia who did the bulk of the nursing. She ordered the maids about, had Mrs. Milligan prepare a special broth made to her order, and in general enjoyed herself more than she had in years. In the sick room, she reigned supreme and became so engrossed with her patient that she quite forgot to worry about the Duke of Balfour's presence in the house.

For his part, the duke was in a quandary. Tenby had informed him on Tuesday that the carriage had been repaired, and they could leave whenever he wished. Therein lay the problem. For the first time in his life, Cedric Alexander Everild felt personally responsible for the well-being of others. He could not simply walk away and leave Regina and David alone at Whitechapel.

He smiled wryly. Regina would be the first to tell him that she was not his responsibility, and, of course, she was not—at least not legally. As for morally, the notion was sufficient to make him laugh aloud. Not a soul in all of London would believe he possessed any morals, particularly when it came to a beautiful young woman. And yet, he could not leave her to fend for herself.

David interrupted his reverie, tapping softly on the library door before peering in. At the duke's nod, he entered hesitantly.

Balfour wondered what was amiss. Usually, David eagerly sought out his company, and had shown no shyness. "What is it, lad?" he asked, with unaccustomed gentleness.

"Could I ask you a question, Your Grace?"

"Not if you persist in being so formal," Balfour replied, smiling. "I thought we'd come to an agreement on that head." He had, in his careless way, given the boy leave to address him as Cedric. David, with a touch of his father's innate sense of propriety, had protested it was too presumptuous, but he had agreed to address the duke as Uncle Cedric. Now he stood before Balfour looking stricken.

"It was most kind of you to allow it, but Aunt Cornelia said I must not address you so. She told me it is not at all proper, and quite disrespectful," he said, unconsciously mimicking his aunt, and added, "And she said that if Father ever heard me, he would be most displeased."

"Ah, that would explain it. Is Cornelia out of the sick room then?"

"Just for a bit," David answered. He kept his head down and was plainly embarrassed. "Dr. Lyons is here and he said Mr. Ramsey is beginning to make some sense. Aunt Regina thinks that maybe now we shall learn what happened to him."

"Well, that is something I should like to know, but first things first. Come here to me."

David came round the desk and stood shyly near Balfour's chair. He was a sensitive lad and any sort of rebuke tended to make him withdraw into his shell. Until Cornelia's interference, David had not regarded the duke as a gentleman of high rank, or even as an adult male. He saw in Balfour a mythical hero come to life, worshiping him with a boy's natural adoration for an idol. The realization that he had behaved improperly, and to someone he so much admired, made him feel wretched.

Balfour, though unaccustomed to dealing with small boys, knew intuitively something of what David was feeling. He held out his hand. "We are friends, are we not?"

At David's shy nod, he drew the boy into the circle of his arm. "Then, just between friends, let me tell you that your Aunt Cornelia is right about some things and wrong about others. You were not behaving disrespectfully by addressing me as Uncle Cedric, because I granted you permission to do so. On the other hand, she is undoubtedly right that your father would not approve. He is a very formal person. So let us do this. When we are alone, or just with your Aunt Regina, we will be informal and you may call me Uncle Cedric. When Cornelia or others are present, you will use my title and it will be sort of a joke between us. Agreed?"

"Agreed," David said, grinning widely.

"Good. Now what was it you wished to ask me?"

"Is it true that you are leaving us? Aunt Cornelia said you would be now that your carriage is fixed. She heard Ben and your groom discussing it, and said there was no reason for you to stay any longer."

"She did, did she?" Balfour murmured, motioning to David to allow him to rise. "Your aunt has been very busy. Well, let us go take a look at my carriage, and then we shall see."

David trotted by the duke's side as they crossed the sweep of lawn, passed the stables, and entered the carriage house. An undergroom, lounging near the door, was sent scurrying to fetch Tenby.

The duke's groom appeared a few moments later. "Afternoon, Your Grace. Was you wanting to take one of the carriages out?"

"I understand my own carriage has been repaired, Tenby."

"Yes, Your Grace. Don't you recollect I told you on Tuesday—"

"I wish to inspect it. Bring it out, if you please," Balfour interrupted, at his most imperious.

"Yes, Your Grace. Right away," Tenby muttered, backing away. He didn't know what Balfour was up to, but he misliked the look in his eyes. It boded ill for someone. With the assistance of one of the stable lads, Tenby rolled the duke's private travelling carriage into the yard.

Balfour strolled round it, arms folded across his chest. He paused to study the axle that had been replaced, and one hand came up to stroke his chin. He stood immobile for a moment before he spoke. "It is unacceptable, Tenby. Send it back, and this time have it repaired properly."

"I beg your pardon, Your Grace?"

"Did I stutter, Tenby, or slur my words? I believe I spoke quite clearly. The repairs to my carriage are not acceptable. The workmanship is shoddy and the paint does not match. I would not be seen in such a carriage. Send it back."

"Yes, Your Grace. At once, Your Grace."

The duke nodded and turned his back. Only David saw him close one eye in a broad wink. "It appears I shall be forced to remain here for a few more days. Now, let us go see what Mr. Ramsey has to say."

The old man had been given the long room at the end of the first-floor hall. A large, airy chamber, its convenient situation made it ideal for nursing an invalid. The duke, having no experience with a sick room, and even less desire for Cornelia's company, had thus far avoided the chamber, though he had received daily reports on Ramsey's progress from Regina. Now, however, he strode down the long hall with David at his heels. Reaching the door, he knocked authoritatively.

Cornelia opened it and stood blocking the entrance. "Oh, 'tis you, Your Grace. If you are seeking my cousin, I am afraid she is busy conferring with the doctor at the moment."

"Excellent. It is the doctor I wish to speak with, and Ramsey, too, if he is, as I understand, now coherent."

"Well, I really do not think—"

"Good afternoon, Your Grace," Regina interrupted as she came up behind Cornelia. "Do come in. I know you will be interested in what Mr. Ramsey has to say, and Dr. Lyons is here, too."

Cornelia had little choice but to step aside. She did so reluctantly, warning Regina, "Too much excitement in one morning will likely set Mr. Ramsey back. He needs to rest, and I am certain Dr. Lyons will agree with me."

No one paid her any heed, and she did not fail to observe

the intimate look which passed between the duke and her cousin. David made to follow his hero in, but Cornelia angrily grabbed the boy's shoulder, venting her frustration on him. "Where do you think you are going, young man? This is not a drawing room, and what Mr. Ramsey has to say is not for young ears. Run along now."

The duke heard her and spoke quietly to Regina. "It is your decision, of course, but perhaps it would be wiser to permit David to stay. He will be more on his guard if he hears for himself what Ramsey has endured."

Regina agreed with him and turned to her cousin with a conciliatory smile. "Surely, it cannot do any harm for David to remain, and as this concerns him directly, I think it would be best. He will be more aware that there is danger about."

Cornelia pressed her thin lips together. Knowing it was useless to protest further, she released the boy. He hurried across the room before she could change her mind, standing as close to the duke as he could.

The doctor finished his examination of the patient, and after greeting Balfour politely, addressed Regina. "It appears medical skills run in your family, Miss Westfield. Your cousin has done an excellent job of nursing Ramsey, and I suspect a few days more of such care and the old man will be on his feet again. I am rather pressed for time, but I would appreciate a word with you in private. Will you walk out with me?"

"Certainly, sir," Regina said. Excusing herself to the others, she followed the doctor into the hall.

"I did not want to say anything in front of Ramsey, but I am gravely concerned about him," Lyons explained. "He's recovering well enough from his physical injuries, but I am not certain he has the will to live."

"I do not understand, sir."

"Miss Davenport told him his dog is dead. He asked about the animal this morning, and I suppose your cousin thought it better not to deceive him, but I do wish she'd waited until he was stronger. The dog apparently meant a great deal to him, and he is taking her death hard."

Regina nodded. "I know he was most attached to Abby, and I believe he raised her from a pup. But what can we do?"

"Unfortunately, I don't know that you can do anything, but try to interest him in something. He needs a reason to live, something to care about. It is often the case with older, lonely people. Without a purpose to their lives, without anything to give life meaning, they just pine away. With Ramsey, it was the collie that kept him going. Without her . . ." he shrugged.

Regina sighed. "I will try to think of something. Thank you for telling me."

"I only wish the news was better. Keep him on soups and broths for a few more days, and then, if he feels like it, he may have something more substantial to eat. By then he should be able to get up, perhaps spend a little time in the garden. I shall call on Saturday unless I hear from you before then."

Regina saw him out and remained at the door watching his carriage until it was out of sight. Dr. Lyons was a dear, one of the sweetest gentlemen that she knew, but what on earth did he think she could do to revive Mr. Ramsey's interest? She walked back to the sick room slowly, her mind preoccupied with the problem.

Nothing inspired her, however, and she set the troubling matter aside as she entered the room. Ramsey sat propped up, resting against several large feather pillows. David occupied a stool near the bed and the duke had drawn up a comfortable chair. Cornelia was nowhere to be seen.

"What have you done with my cousin, Your Grace?" she asked with an amused smile.

"I? How very suspicious you are, my dear," the duke said, rising. "And unjust. Mr. Ramsey thought he could eat a little soup and Miss Davenport went off to see that it is prepared."

"Indeed," she murmured, accepting the chair he offered. "And you did not even put the notion in his head?"

"Perhaps, but he must eat if he is to keep up his strength, and he shall need that to tell us what occurred. We were just waiting for you to return."

The old man, who had been resting, opened his eyes and looked imploringly at Regina. His distress was plain, and she reached out a hand to comfort him.

"I didn't tell them men nothing, Miss Westfield," he said.

"I know you did not," Regina assured him, unable to believe how weak the old man's grip was. "If it won't tire you, too much, would you tell us what happened at the cottage?"

He nodded, closing his eyes for a moment and his other hand twitched against the covers. Pain clouded his eyes when he looked at her again. "There was two of them. One was a big fellow, fat as an old sow and just as dirty . . . the other one, skinny as a bean pole, called him Jasper. I heard him when they thought I wasn't . . . wasn't—" His words were choked off as a fit of coughing racked his body.

It was a wretched sound and the poor man seemed unable to stop heaving. The duke handed him a handkerchief and Regina had to glance away when she saw the blood on the cloth.

"Pour him a glass of water," Balfour directed David. It was the duke who supported the old man's slender shoulders as he sipped from the glass. It seemed to help and, when he had recovered a bit, Balfour eased him back on the pillows. "Take your time, Ramsey. If this is too painful for you, we can wait to hear—"

"No!" A shaky, gnarled hand reached out to clutch at the duke's sleeve. "Miss Westfield must know . . ."

"All right, then. Just take it slow and easy. We will stay as long as it takes. Do not strain yourself."

The old man nodded and visibly relaxed a little. He took a deep breath and his eyes focused on Regina. "I knew they was up to no good, and I tried to chase 'em off. Abby . . .

she went after them. I thought they'd gone for good. Then I heard her barking just after sunset. I went out to see but I couldn't find her and she'd . . . she'd quit barking then. The big one, he came up behind me. He . . . he held a pistol at my head."

Silence filled the room as the old man paused. His words were quiet, but the image he conjured up was frightening. His listeners waited patiently, their eyes intent on his face. The only sound in the room was Ramsey's raspy breathing and the ticking of the bracket clock on the mantelpiece.

"They forced me inside and tied me to a chair," Ramsey continued at last. He gazed at the ceiling, speaking in a low drone. "They wanted to know about Whitechapel. Who was here . . . how many men you had working for you. I wouldn't tell them nothing—that's when they hit me."

"Oh, Mr. Ramsey, I am so sorry," Regina cried.

"They asked about the boy," he continued, seeming not to have heard her. He turned his head so he could see David. "I didn't know you had a lad here. The big one—he didn't believe me. He just kept asking . . . and hitting."

"How long were they at the cottage?" Balfour inquired softly.

Confused, the old man shook his head. "I think . . . I think they left the next morning. They stuck a rag in my mouth and tied me to a chair. I . . . my stomach hurt where they'd hit me. I think . . . I must have passed out a time or two. I know they came back twice, but then it got dark. I don't 'member them coming after that. Then Ben came."

Regina breathed a silent prayer that the duke had thought to send someone to search the grounds. If Ben had not found the old man, he might have died tied to that chair. Waves of anger washed over her. She stood and crossed the room to the window. Regina bit her tongue, afraid to say a word. Afraid her voice would betray the rage she felt.

She heard the duke telling Ramsey to rest. He thanked the old man for the warning and assured him that they would be on guard. Balfour sounded so calm, as though nothing out of the ordinary had occurred, that she swung about to stare at him. He adjusted the pillows so Ramsey could sleep, and she watched as the duke drew the covers gently up to the old man's chin. How could he behave so placidly when she longed to throw something, to beat her fists against the wall in protest of such brutality to a harmless old man. Were she able, she'd strangle the pair that had performed such unspeakable acts.

Ramsey struggled to speak again, but his body shook with another fit of coughing. His face was ashen when he regained his breath, and his hand trembled as he gestured to the duke to come closer. "Abby? My collie—is she . . . is she still out there?"

"Ben buried her a few days ago. In the garden at the back of your cottage," Balfour told him gently.

The old man turned his head away, his eyes glistening with tears.

The duke stood quietly, staring down at Ramsey, staring at the wasted, battered body of an old man whose dignity and desire to live had been cruelly wrested from him. When he spoke his voice was soft, barely above a whisper, but loud enough for Ramsey to hear. "On my word of honor, the men who did this shall pay dearly for it."

Balfour turned and walked out of the room without another word.

Regina wanted to run after him. She had thought she'd seen the duke angry before, when she or Cornelia provoked him beyond bearing, but that was nothing to the fury she'd just seen in his eyes. She glanced at David. He was naturally upset and she swiftly hugged him to her. After a moment, she tilted up his small chin. "Would you stay with Mr. Ramsey until Cornelia returns?"

David nodded and as Regina left the room, she heard him asking in his solemn little voice, "Is there anything you would like, sir?"

Regina went in search of Balfour. He was not in the library or the drawing room. Puzzled, she walked down to the stables and asked Tenby if he had seen the duke.

The groom nodded reluctantly. "He's out riding, Miss. I expect he'll be back in an hour or two."

"Which way did he head?"

"If you was to ask my advice, Miss, I'd leave him be. It 'pears like he's in one of his black moods, and when His Grace gets that way, he's not fit company for no one. I seen him this way a spell of times. Best thing to do is to leave him be."

"Very well, then, but if he is not back in an hour or so, would you please let me know?"

The groom promised and she returned to the house. Dozens of tasks awaited her attention, but Regina found it impossible to concentrate on any of them. She finally settled in the library with a book to occupy her mind, but her attention wandered. Thoughts of Balfour kept intruding. She laid her book aside and rested her head against the cushions, allowing her mind to drift.

Her world seemed to have turned upside down since the duke's arrival. First, there had been the frightening attempt to kidnap David, and then the horrible attack on Ramsey. And yet, for hours at a time, she'd forgotten everything in her enjoyment of Balfour's company. Regina admitted she was dangerously close to falling in love with him.

She smiled, imagining Andrew would have a stroke if he knew. But she doubted such a notion would ever occur to her brother. While he would be absolutely livid that she'd been forced to house so notorious and scandalous a gentleman, the notion that she might actually form a tendre for such a man would never enter his mind.

The duke, while having wealth and rank, was decidedly not the sort of suitor Andrew would select for his sister. She recalled the vast number of gentlemen her brother had introduced to her. All very proper and very well-behaved men with political leanings that marched with his own. Perfectly nice, well-bred young men who had proved incapable of arousing in her any feeling stronger than amusement. Her unwillingness to allow any of the gentlemen to court her had infuriated Andrew. Her brother had declared that he washed his hands of her, but she knew full well that did not mean he would ever countenance a marriage with someone of Balfour's stamp.

Marriage? The word had crept into her mind unbidden. What in heaven's name was she thinking of? She had no desire to marry anyone, even if Balfour could be brought to make such a proposal. She had her house and her stables, everything ordered precisely as she liked it. She needed no man to order her about or restrain her freedom. Not even a man like Balfour, she thought.

On the verge of falling asleep in her chair, she wondered idly what it would be like to be kissed by a man whose reputation as a rake was so well known. Surely, he would be skillful . . . he would not paw at her like Lord Bottomly had done with his clammy, wet hands . . . or reign sloppy kisses on her shoulders like Mr. Allendale that night he'd had a bit much to drink. The duke, she thought, would make a proper job of it . . .

Balfour found her there an hour later, sound asleep, but with a smile on her lips that sorely tempted him.

Six

"Are you not finished yet, Aunt Regina?" David asked, peering round the door of her office.

Regina sighed and laid down the papers she'd been working on. It was annoying to be interrupted every hour and yet she could not be angry with her nephew. The childish appeal in his eyes and the eagerness in his voice effectively cancelled any aggravation she felt.

"No, David, I am not finished," she said with mock sternness as she rose to her feet behind the heavy desk. "However, it is obvious that you will not allow me to work in peace until I have looked at that colt of yours. We will do so now, but on one condition, young man. When we return to the house, you will read your book while I work. Agreed?"

David promised so readily, Regina laughed. He would have agreed to anything that would get him out to the stables. The last week had wrought a tremendous change in her nephew, one that Andrew would have difficulty believing when he returned. Far from having to drag David away from his studies, she now had to practically force him to stay in the house. The boy spent every moment possible with his new colt.

It would have been wonderful except that Regina was afraid to leave him alone. The time she spent with him took her away from her own work, and her evenings were now spent in the drawing room instead of her office. She reasoned it was her obligation as a hostess to entertain the duke, but the truth was she enjoyed the long, cozy hours of amusing games and stimulating conversations. Balfour had proved to be a master of chess, a wizard at whist, and knowledgeable on every subject she or her nephew broached.

Now, she watched David skip down the long hall and heard him shouting for the duke. Balfour strolled out of the library, a book tucked beneath his elbow. Regina shot him a reproachful look. *He* could have accompanied David down to the pasture, but David told her the duke refused to go without her.

"Immersed in some deep study, Your Grace?"

"Mythology, my dear, in a vain attempt to stay one step ahead of your nephew's countless questions."

David, already waiting at the door in a fret of impatience, called back, begging them to hurry.

Balfour laid his book on the hall table and walked leisurely down the corridor beside Regina. When he reached the door, he grinned down at David and ruffled the boy's hair in an affectionate manner. "Restrain yourself, my lad. Young gentlemen do *not* race down the hall or beseech their elders to move so rapidly as to be unseemly."

"Now you sound just like Father," David complained.

"Egad, how low have I sunk? Regina, I implore you, tell me 'tis not so."

"I believe David has paid you a rare compliment, Your Grace, and you should be honored," she said, but could not help smiling at his feigned look of horror. "If you truly wish to redeem yourself in David's eyes, you may rush down to the paddock with him instead of walking tamely beside me."

"Nothing would induce me to do so," he replied, keeping an eye on David as the boy easily outdistanced them. "Is it not sufficient that I am abroad at this unseemly hour of the morning? And, pray tell me, what is so vastly important that we must all traipse to the paddock before the dew is dry on the grass?"

"I fear 'tis later than you imagine, my friend. The dew

dried several hours ago," Regina said, laughing. "And David would not confide in me. He said he wished to surprise us."

"One can only hope that his surprise is not the sort I devised at his age. My father was quite unappreciative of my efforts and, as I recall, I received a tanning on more than one occasion."

"Deservedly, I expect."

"My dear girl, has anyone ever mentioned that you are supremely lacking in sympathy?"

"Only my brother."

"Really?" he drawled. "I had not thought Sir Andrew so perceptive. Perhaps I have been overly hasty in my estimation of your brother's character. Betwixt you and David, it is little wonder the man behaves so pompously. Obviously, 'tis a measure of defense against the extremes his family exercises. Tell me, is his wife a problem as well?"

"My sister-in-law is the dearest soul imaginable, and you, Your Grace, are completely unprincipled. Your father should have employed the rod much more frequently," she retorted as they approached the paddock. She removed her hand from his arm and leaned against the fence beside David.

She smiled happily, partly in response to Balfour's nonsense, and partly at the vista spread before her. Five mares with their foals roamed the enclosure. Three colts and two fillies, and except for the problem with David's colt, they were all healthy and good prospects for the coming season. Each had excellent bloodlines and if not sold privately, she knew they would bring a handsome price at auction. The foals were developing well and she watched them frolicking with a great deal of pride mixed with pleasure.

"Do you see, Aunt Regina?" David asked, tugging at her sleeve. "Watch Boreas!" He moved a few feet down the fence line and whistled shrilly. The gangly colt trotted to the fence, his nose quivering as he sniffed the air.

"What an outlandish name to choose for a colt," Regina commented.

"Boreas? I thought it rather appropriate. He was the god of the north wind and changed himself into a stallion to mate with Erichthonius. Legend has it that they produced twelve young mares so light of foot 'they ran across the fields of standing corn without bruising an ear of grain, and over the crests of the sea without wetting their feet.' Very apt, and surely no worse than naming all one's mares after the muses."

She glanced up at him, smiling ruefully. "I thought that had escaped your notice. I should have known better."

"Yes, you should have, my dear. There is little about you that escapes my attention. But tell me, is it merely my imagination or has that colt of David's grown amazingly?"

"He has certainly grown, but no more than is normal," Regina replied. She gazed at the colt but her mind was on Balfour. Had there been a compliment hidden somewhere beneath his words? He had an annoying habit of slipping in a flattering thought or bit of praise amidst a flurry of commonplace chatter.

She had little chance to dwell on her thoughts. David beckoned them urgently and demanded she take a closer look at Boreas.

"Do you not think his leg is stronger, Aunt Regina? See, it is not nearly so turned as before, and I've been watching him run with the others. He doesn't have a bit of trouble."

"He is coming along splendidly, David, and you may be right," she said. The colt's leg did seem to show some slight signs of improvement. "It happens now and then. Nature and sunlight may very well undo the damage."

"Would you . . . do you want him back, Aunt Regina? I mean, I know you only said I might buy him because of his leg—"

"I never go back on my word, David. He is yours, for better or worse."

"Sounds like a marriage made in heaven," the duke said, then groaned aloud as he saw David reach into his coat pocket for a handful of oats to feed his colt. "Do not tell me you are in the habit of carrying grain in your clothing."

David grinned unabashed. "That's why Boreas comes running when he sees me. My aunt said I might."

Balfour raised his brows in Regina's direction. "You will have much to answer for, my dear, when your brother collects his son. He left a well-mannered, studious boy in your care, and will retrieve a sunburned urchin positively reeking of the stables."

"It does not trouble me," she said, giving him a sunny smile. "I shall simply lay all the blame at your door."

Balfour watched her for a moment, enjoying the way her eyes sparkled when she thought she'd bested him. "For that, Miss Westfield, you must forfeit the rest of the afternoon. What say you to a ride? My stallion grows restive penned up for so long."

"Penrod, too," she said, half-tempted, but then shook her head. "No, I really cannot. I should be at my desk even now tending to the accounts."

"The accounts will keep, Regina, but how often do days like this come along?" He took her arm in his, turning her gently towards the stables, adding persuasively, "Come ride with me and then you may face your musty accounts with a fresh, clear mind."

"But David—we cannot leave him here alone."

"If I can persuade him to ride with us, will you come?"

Regina nodded, unable to resist Balfour's smile and knowing her nephew would undoubtedly refuse to ride.

The duke grinned triumphantly for a second, then lifted his voice. "David, come along! I have persuaded your aunt to go for a ride if you will agree to join us."

David fed his colt the last handful of oats before running back to them. "Are we going to begin my lessons today, Uncle Cedric?" he asked, a flush of excitement coloring his cheeks.

"Lessons?" Regina turned a puzzled look on her nephew. "What lessons, David?"

"Uncle Cedric promised to teach me to ride so that when Boreas is old enough, I can break him myself. Is it not a splendid idea, Aunt Regina?"

"Splendid, indeed," she said dryly. She tilted her head to look up at Balfour. "But perhaps if you are to instruct David, it would be better if I were not present. I can work on my—"

"Forget your accounts, Regina," he interrupted ruthlessly. "You said you never go back on a bargain and you promised to ride with us if David would come along. I fully intend to hold you to your word. Now, go put on your habit while we get the horses saddled, and if you are not back out here in twenty minutes, I will come and carry you out."

"Definitely unprincipled," she said, as she turned dutifully towards the house, but with much less reluctance than she pretended. She glanced back over her shoulder. Balfour stood there, hands on hips, watching her, an amused smile on his lips. She chuckled softly. There were times when the Duke of Balfour was definitely, undeniably, irresistible.

It was several hours before the truants returned. Regina had been aghast when she realized the time, having intended to ride for only an hour or so. But she'd enjoyed the afternoon so much, and the time had sped so swiftly, she had not realized how late it was until she noticed the sun riding low in the west.

Regina left Balfour and David to tend to the horses and hurried up to the house. She entered quietly from the garden door, hoping to reach her room and change her habit before she came under Cornelia's scrutiny. The duke, mocking her concern over her windblown appearance, had assured her she looked quite lovely with her curls escaping her hat and a natural blush from the sun on her cheeks. He made her sound wonderful, but Regina knew her cousin was unlikely to regard her appearance in the same light, or approve of the long afternoon spent in Balfour's company.

She supposed it was cowardly of her, but the duke did not understand how very much she loathed scenes. Hated contention of any sort. If creeping up the stairs of her own house would help her avoid a confrontation with Cornelia, then creep she would. She had just reached the landing when she heard her name called. The voice of martyrdom, Regina thought, turning reluctantly to face her cousin.

"So, you are returned at last," Cornelia said. "I was just about to send Jeremy out to search the fields for you, as I was certain you would not be so thoughtless to disappear for so long without a word to me. Obviously my concern was misplaced."

"Come, Cousin, Jeremy must have told you that I rode out with the duke and David. There was no reason for you to worry."

"No reason? Have you completely lost your senses, Regina? Why, just look at you. Your hair is tangled disgracefully and there are grass stains on your skirt. I am mortified that a relative of mine could behave so shamelessly. Frolicking all afternoon with a man known to be a rake, and with no better chaperon than a small boy."

"Need I remind you that Ben was also with us?" Regina asked as she straightened her shoulders and lifted her chin. It was an unconscious gesture but one which Andrew would have recognized as a signal that his sister was near the end of her patience. A prudent person would have retreated, but Cornelia had never seen Regina truly angry.

"If you are referring to your groom, I pray you save your breath. The duke won him over quickly enough, and no doubt he could be bribed to look the other way if—"

"That is quite enough, Cornelia," Regina interrupted furiously. "I am sorry if you find my behavior offensive, but it is completely innocent, and I very much resent your insinuations to the contrary. I may have allowed Andrew to install you here as my companion to placate his notions of propriety, but I will not allow you to disparage me or those with whom I choose to associate." With each sentence, Regina had advanced down the stairs until she stood towering over her cousin.

Cornelia took two steps backwards. "I did not mean—that is to say, I know of course that you are above reproach. You must forgive me, Regina, if I spoke out of turn. 'Tis only that I was so mortified when Dr. Lyons asked for you and you seemed to have disappeared. I did not know what to say to him, and he waited above an hour for you to return."

"Dr. Lyons? Heavens, why did you not say so? What has happened? Is the doctor still here?"

"No, he said he could wait no longer, but he would call back this evening. It is Mr. Ramsey. The poor man has taken a turn for the worse, and Dr. Lyons fears he may not recover. Oh dear, this has all been so upsetting. I feel rather faint."

Regina did not think it merely a ploy for sympathy. Cornelia, with her white face and pinched lips, did look as though she might faint. Her own anger fading quickly, Regina helped her cousin to a chair in the drawing room and fetched a cool glass of water.

When her cousin showed some signs of improvement, she asked gently, "Are you feeling better now, Cornelia? Can you tell me what occurred?"

"Thank you, my dear. I shall be better directly, I am sure. It has been such a dreadful day, and that poor, sweet man. I cannot bear it, if after all my nursing, he should . . . should depart us."

"I thought Ramsey was recovering," Regina said, prompting her. "Did not Dr. Lyons say he could walk out into the gardens a bit?"

"Yes, dear, and he did so yesterday, but today he refused to get out of bed. Said there was no point in going on, and he would not even take a bite of the nuncheon Mrs. Milligan brought in. I tried to find you and when I could not, I thought it best to send for the doctor."

"I am glad you did, Cornelia, but I do not wish Dr. Lyons to have two patients here. You look overly tired, Cousin. I think you should retire to your room and rest until dinner. As soon as I have changed, I will look in on Ramsey."

Cornelia nodded. She was feeling much recovered but thought it strategic to elicit Regina's sympathy. The harsh words between them still hung in the air. They could not be unsaid, but perhaps they might be forgot. She allowed Regina to help her up and then walked slowly from the room.

David, running ahead of the duke, nearly collided with her in the hall, but for once she did not scold him.

Cornelia never noticed the boy. Her attention was focused on Balfour and she gave him a venomous glare. *He* was the cause of the rift between her and Regina. They had gotten along quite well until his arrival at the house.

"Good afternoon, Miss Davenport," the duke murmured politely.

She looked him straight in the eye, longing to wipe the insolent grin from his face. Quite deliberately, she turned her head. Gathering her skirts about her to avoid even the hem of her dress touching the loathsome creature, she walked round him and hurried up the stairs.

The duke's brows rose at the direct cut, but he said nothing. Smiling lazily at David, he told the boy, "Run along and change. I believe we may have time for a game of chess before dinner if you do not tarry." He almost laughed at the speed with which David disappeared and envied the boy his energy. But his mind was on Regina. He caught a glimpse of her in the drawing room.

Leaning casually against the open door, he said, "I gather the she-dragon caught you before you had time to change."

Regina, resting in a chair near the window, glanced up and smiled ruefully. "She did, and scolded me royally."

"Odd. She did not look pleased with herself when I encountered her in the hall."

"Did she say something uncivil? I pray you will not pay her any heed. She is not herself at present."

"She said nothing uncivil," Balfour replied, evading the issue. Regina looked distressed enough without him adding to her worries, and he sensed something had occurred to overturn her composure. "I hope you are not sitting in here berating yourself for playing hooky this afternoon? It would quite spoil my enjoyment of the day."

"How kind of you, after browbeating me into neglecting my duties! But you need not be concerned. In truth I thoroughly enjoyed the day and do not regret it in the least."

"Then what is troubling you?" he asked as he crossed the room. He sat in the chair opposite her and held out his hand. "Can you not confide in me?"

The kindness and concern in his voice brought Regina to the edge of tears. Ridiculous, she thought, to be undone by a few gentle words, but she accepted the warm comfort of his hand. The news about poor Ramsey coming on top of the scene with her cousin had unraveled her nerves. It was a moment before she felt sufficiently in control to speak, then she said quietly, "I am worried about Ramsey. Cornelia told me he took a turn for the worse while we were gone. She sent for Dr. Lyons, but there does not seem to be anything the doctor can do to help him. My cousin said he refuses to get out of bed, and would not eat this morning."

"Regina, there are some things we cannot change however much we might desire to do so. You have tended to his physical injuries—the rest is up to him."

"I know. I just . . . I feel so responsible. If he dies—" She could not get the rest of the words past the lump in her throat, and the tears brimming her eyes threatened to overflow.

"Well, sitting there like a watering pot will not accomplish anything," Balfour admonished roughly. He watched her reaction closely. He'd guessed right. Sympathy might have brought on a deluge of tears, and had he been kinder she would be sobbing in his arms. The thought was not unpleasant, even tempting in a rather reprehensible way, and he had not been above such devious behaviour in the past. Regina, however, was an extraordinary woman and if he ever held her in his arms, he did not want it to be because she needed a shoulder to cry on.

"It is foolish, is it not?" she said, wiping at her eyes.

"No, little one. Not foolish but merely futile. Come, let us take a look at the old man and see if there is any way we can be of help." He tugged at her hand as he rose to his feet.

"Little? Now, it is you who are being foolish," she chided, rising and looking into his blue eyes. "My dear sir, no one has ever called me little."

"Then I shall be the first," he said. With one hand beneath her chin, he tilted up her head. "For all your inches, I suspect you are feeling rather small and vulnerable just now. But you need not fret. Only a cad would take advantage of such a situation."

Regina stood motionless. He was so close she could feel his breath upon her cheek and the touch of his hand as he pushed back a stray curl set her pulse racing. "Are you . . . very certain you are not a cad?" she asked, her voice barely above a whisper.

"I'm ready for our game, Uncle Cedric."

Balfour quickly stepped away from her, greeting David with his usual nonsense. If he was annoyed or irritated by the interruption, he gave no indication of it. She felt her own disappointment must show plainly, and feeling foolish, hastened towards the door.

"Regina, wait!" the duke called. He saw her pause in the hall and spoke quickly to David. "You are too fast, lad. Your aunt and I must see to Ramsey before we have our game, and we both must change yet." Then he stooped and whispered in the boy's ear.

David's small face lit up like a candle suddenly flaring, and he nodded eagerly. "I will, Uncle Cedric."

"Take your time. There is no need for all this rushing about," the duke called after him, but David was already racing down the long hallway. Balfour followed more slowly. Regina stood waiting, her back to him. He knew he should say something to her, but for once, words failed him.

"Whatever did you say to David?" she asked nonchalantly. She'd regained a measure of composure, and felt pleased that she at least sounded calm, but she was still shaken by her own brash behavior. She'd practically invited Balfour to kiss her, and been out of reason disappointed when he did not. She really must control her curiosity about the duke's kisses, she thought.

"I merely sent him on an errand," Balfour was saying. "A pity it did not occur to me sooner."

Regina continued walking though it took all of her willpower not to look at the duke, and she couldn't help wondering if he meant he was as regretful as she that they were interrupted. Aloud, she said, "You are very good with him. David will miss you greatly when you leave."

"I hope he is not the only one, but as I am not planning on leaving for some time, we need not discuss that. Or are you planning to throw me out? Has the she-dragon finally convinced you that I am beyond redemption?"

"No one could convince me of that," she replied. The words came swiftly and without thought, but she realized their truth and bit her lip. It seemed she was bent on making a fool of herself.

"Your faith is touching, my dear, but I am not at all certain that it is deserved."

Gone was the teasing, bantering tone she was accustomed to hearing from him. Regina glanced up and the tenderness she saw reflected in his eyes was sufficient to make her feel light-headed. Confused, she looked away.

"Your brother is not the only one who is capable of behaving like a gentleman. Oh, I admit it is not a habit with me, but then, few ladies have ever honored me with their trust. I hope you will believe me, Regina, when I say that I would never do anything to hurt you."

She did not know how to answer him and was relieved that they had reached the door to Ben's room. She tapped on it, but before she opened it, she said softly, "I never doubted it."

She hurried inside then, thankful that the dimness of the room hid her blushes. "Mr. Ramsey? May we come in, sir?"

The old man lay stretched out on the bed, appearing shrunken and lost in the middle of the huge four-poster. He did not answer her, and as they approached the bed, he turned his head to face the opposite window.

"Come now, Ramsey, is that any way to greet your hostess?" Balfour scolded.

If he heard the duke at all, the only indication was the flicker of the old man's lashes as he closed his eyes.

Balfour tried again. "If we catch the men who beat you, you will be needed to identify them. Are you just going to give up and allow them to go free?"

Ramsey might as well have been unconscious. He gave no sign that he'd heard the question, and his breathing was so slight the sheet covering his chest barely moved.

The duke watched him for a moment and when he was sure the old man was listening, said, "Forget what they did to you then, but can you really forgive what they did to your dog? Do you not owe it to her to see them punished?"

Regina gasped. She thought it cruel to taunt Ramsey and she pulled at Balfour's arm to indicate that they should leave. Let the old man find whatever peace he could.

"Can you find them?" the raspy whisper came from the bed, just loud enough to bring the duke closer.

"I am trying. We think it likely they will return here, and this time we shall be ready for them."

Ramsey closed his eyes again as though the effort to speak

had taken all his strength. His breathing was harsh and, for an instant, Balfour worried that he'd pushed too hard.

"Don't . . . don't take too long," the old man said.

Balfour drew a deep breath, more relieved than anyone would ever know as the old man's mouth actually curved upwards in what might be taken for a smile. "I shall do my best," he promised, and stepped back allowing Regina to take his place. He watched her kneel beside the bed and heard her speak softly to Ramsey, urging him to try to eat. The duke left them then, slipping quietly into the hall and then through the library and out into the garden.

Regina found him there later. He sat on a wrought iron bench, his long legs stretched in front of him, his head tilted back. Smoke spiraled upwards from his cigar, and his gaze seemed focused on the setting sun.

"Thank you," she said, coming up behind him and lightly touching him on the shoulder.

"For what, my dear? Giving an old man false hope?"

He did not look at her and the despair in his voice disturbed her. Regina circled round the bench and sat down beside him. "You have given Ramsey the will to live again."

"Temporarily, perhaps. It seemed expedient at the time," Balfour replied, knocking the ashes off his cigar. "But now what? We've seen no sign of the louts who beat him. I was so certain they would have made another attempt by now . . ."

"You sound almost disappointed."

"Perhaps I am. I made a promise to a dying man—a promise that I am not at all sure I can keep—and I am finding that such a responsibility weighs heavily on one." He shrugged. "You must know that I am unaccustomed to anyone depending on me."

She sat still, not knowing what to say. She'd never seen Balfour in this sort of mood. He reminded her of a small boy in need of comfort, like David when she'd heard him say he was a throwback. The notion was ludicrous, of course.

The great Duke of Balfour in need of comfort? Absurd to even think it.

"Ramsey aside, there is something else which worries me, Regina. It occurred to me that this pair who tried to abduct David were strangely well informed. They knew the boy was here, which is certainly information most people would not be privy to. How many people even know Sir Andrew has a sister who lives in this remote area? I have been on the Town for years and have never heard even a whisper of your name."

"No, you would not. I had only one Season and have not visited London since. But if, as you suspect, someone is trying to use David to force Andrew into some sort of compromise, surely they would have learned what they could of his family? I do not imagine it would be difficult to learn of my existence or of this farm. It was never intended to be a secret."

"Granted, but what then? Suppose they had succeeded in kidnapping David? What good would it do unless they could get word to Sir Andrew at once? He has apparently gone to great lengths to keep his whereabouts a secret. Even you do not know how to reach him."

"We have only a general address to post letters to and a courier is supposed to send them on, but there is no saying when they will reach my brother. Is that important?" she asked, half-afraid to hear his answer.

"Someone very close to Sir Andrew is likely behind this abduction attempt. Someone who knows where he is and who can reach him quickly if need be."

"Oh, Lord! I pray you are wrong," she said fervently, her eyes growing dark with concern. "If it is someone in Andrew's entourage, then he and Elizabeth may be in danger."

He threw his cigar aside and took both her cold hands in his own. "Gad, but I am growing clumsy in my old age. I never meant to frighten you, and I swear I don't believe you need fear for your brother or his wife. Whatever is afoot, they must need both Sir Andrew and his wife to lend credence to the scheme. I think David is the key. What puzzles me is why they have not made another attempt to abduct him."

"But those men disappeared. Perhaps your presence here frightened them off."

"I hope you may be right," he said, and knew an urge to kiss away the worry he saw reflected in her eyes. He leaned towards her. Regina lifted her head slightly, her lips were parted and her gaze was warm and inviting. And trusting, he thought. He dropped a gentle kiss on her brow before releasing her hands. "Let us talk of something else. Tell me, did you persuade Ramsey to eat something?"

She nodded, confused by the change in him. "He agreed to try some soup and Mrs. Milligan is with him now."

"Good. I suggest we do the same, then. I vow I am near starving." Balfour rose easily to his feet and helped her up. "I promised David a game of chess before dinner. Have we time?"

"Yes, of course. I must still change and I should look in on Cornelia."

"Give her a sleeping draught," he advised.

"Is that a considered prescription gleaned from your vast medical experience, Your Grace?"

"No, my dear. It is an entirely selfish notion gleaned from my desire for an intimate meal with you minus the presence of your sharp-tongued duenna."

"You are forgetting David," Regina teased.

"Not at all. I shall ply him with brandy during our game and he will fall asleep before the first course is served," Balfour replied and managed a credible imitation of a leer as he opened the library door.

David was waiting for him. "There you are, Uncle Cedric! I was looking everywhere for you. I have the board set up for our game."

Balfour put an arm about the boy's shoulder. "Tell me, David, have you ever tasted brandy?"

Seven

When Regina came downstairs the following morning, she found the house unusually quiet. Trudy informed her that Mrs. Davenport was in the garden with Mr. Ramsey, and young David was out at the paddock with the duke.

Regina, pleased to have the parlor to herself, accepted the cup of tea the maid poured for her, and prepared to enjoy a quiet, peaceful breakfast. What with the duke and Cornelia constantly sniping at each other, and David's endless questions, it had been weeks since she had eaten a meal in solitude. Dining alone did not depress Regina as it did some people. She knew her brother and Elizabeth hated eating alone, and her Aunt Sarah was like that, too. She, however, luxuriated in the blessed silence and always saw the absence of company as an opportunity to prop up whatever book she chose next to her plate.

Regina fetched the novel she was currently reading and settled quite contentedly in the nook of the breakfast room where the morning sun bathed the table in sunlight. She read two pages before she realized she'd not understood a word, then began again. But her attention wandered, and too frequently her gaze lifted to the window. From her seat, she could see the path leading through the rear garden and down to the stables. She glanced up several times, imagining she heard voices, but no one appeared to distract her and she resolutely returned to her book. An incredibly boring novel,

We'd Like to Invite You to Subscribe to Zebra's Regency Romance Book Club and Give You a Gift of 4 Free Books as Your Introduction! (Worth $18.49!)

If you're a Regency lover, imagine the joy of getting 4 FREE Zebra Regency Romances and then the chance to have these lovely stories delivered to your home each month at the lowest prices available! Well, that's our offer to you and here's how you benefit by becoming a Zebra Home Subscription Service subscriber:

- 4 FREE Introductory Regency Romances are delivered to your doorstep
- 4 BRAND NEW Regencies are then delivered each month (usually before they're available in bookstores)
- Subscribers save almost $4.00 every month
- Home delivery is always FREE
- You also receive a FREE monthly newsletter, *Zebra/ Pinnacle Romance News* which features author profiles, contests, subscriber benefits, book previews and more
- No risks or obligations...in other words you can cancel whenever you wish with no questions asked

Join the thousands of readers who enjoy the savings and convenience offered to Regency Romance subscribers. After your initial introductory shipment, you receive 4 brand-new Zebra Regency Romances each month to examine for 10 days. Then, if you decide to keep the books, you'll pay the preferred subscriber's price of just $3.65 per title. That's only $14.60 for all 4 books and there's never an extra charge for shipping and handling.

It's a no-lose proposition, so return the FREE BOOK CERTIFICATE today!

she'd begun to think, when David's high-pitched voice sounded clearly from the garden.

Regina looked out the window again and chuckled at the sight of him scampering ahead of "Uncle Cedric." Her nephew turned and walked backwards for a few steps, waving his hands as he talked. She imagined he was pleading with the duke for some privilege or promised treat. Balfour was amazingly good with David, willing to spend an inordinate amount of time with the boy, and she doubted that it was merely because he had nothing better to do. That was what he'd said when she'd mentioned his patience with her nephew. Children had a way of seeing through adults who patronized them, and David plainly worshiped the ground Balfour trod upon.

The duke saw her watching and waved. Regina returned the salute and laid aside her book without regret. She ordered Trudy to bring a pot of coffee for His Grace and hot chocolate for her nephew.

The small breakfast room suddenly seemed crowded and the peaceful tranquillity of the morning was forever destroyed as David greeted her exuberantly, and the duke with more restrained amusement. Regina discovered she did not mind in the least, and invited both of them to join her.

"Slug-a-bed," the duke accused her, laughing. "We had breakfast hours ago. David has been practicing his riding and now, if you will grant us permission, we are off on an expedition."

"Please, Aunt Regina. I have been waiting forever for you to come down that we might ask you."

"Gracious, and it is only just nine. You must have been up since daybreak."

"So it seems," Balfour said, accepting the cup of coffee she handed him. "However, there is something to be said for rising early. I saw the most spectacular sunrise while sitting here—a truly incredible sight. Are they all so stunning? I don't recall ever seeing one before."

"Now that I do believe," Regina replied. "Undoubtedly, you are much more accustomed to retiring just as the sun is coming up."

"That, too, has a certain appeal, but much depends on the company one is keeping," he said, his voice low and intimate.

"Please say yes, Aunt Regina," David interrupted, impatient with the adults' banter.

"What is this expedition that has you so excited? Where are you planning on going?"

"I cannot tell you, but it is going to be a splendid surprise," her nephew assured her, his round eyes bright with fervor.

The duke met Regina's glance of enquiry with an amused smile. "If you do not object, I plan to drive David into Bury St. Edmunds. I promise you I shall keep a close eye on him, and we should not be gone above two or three hours."

"I see no harm in that, for I know you will guard him carefully, but why Bury St. Edmunds? Are you driving in to see about your carriage? Tenby told me you were not satisfied with the repairs."

He leaned forward and lowered his voice to a whisper, like a conspirator. "The repairs were fine. In fact, I could find no fault with the work and sent the carriage back only to quiet your cousin. The she-dragon seemed to feel that as my equipage was restored, I should take my leave." Balfour expected Regina to laugh. When she frowned instead, he said, "What is it, my dear? Never tell me you are concerned over such a harmless deception?"

"No . . . not really—at least not in the manner you assume. I was merely thinking of poor Mr. Swansea."

"Who is Mr. Swansea and what has he to say to anything?"

"He is the poor man who worked so diligently to repair your carriage. He must have felt mortified when you sent it back."

"Nonsense. Tenby will have recompensed him handsomely.

In fact, your Swansea will be paid twice over and shall see a handsome profit."

Regina shook her head sadly. "Mr. Swansea takes a great deal of pride in his work, and when you sent the carriage back, I am sure he was devastated. Do you not see that he would have considered it an insult? Is that beyond your understanding?"

Balfour sighed heavily. "What is beyond my understanding is why you care a twopence what a blacksmith in the village thinks, but if it pleases you, Miss Westfield, I shall stop and tell the blasted man what an excellent job he did."

"It would indeed, but it would please me far more, Your Grace, if you were not so careless of other people's feelings. Swansea may be a poor blacksmith who cannot say nay to you, but that is no reason to treat him shabbily."

"Shabbily?" The duke's mobile brows rose in real astonishment. Surely, you are jesting? I would hardly call it shabby to pay a man double for a job he performed only once, and will tip him handsomely besides."

"Money is not the issue, Your Grace, but I suggest we continue this conversation at another time," Regina replied coolly, and glanced at her nephew to remind the Duke of the boy's wide-eyed presence. "Run up to your room, David. You must change your clothes if you are going into the village. Hurry, now. I should not like you to keep His Grace waiting. We must remember what is due to a gentleman of his rank."

"That was unworthy of you, Regina," Balfour said softly as the boy left the room. "I have never stood on ceremony with either you or David."

"Oh, did I wound your sensibility, Your Grace? How very careless of me to behave so inconsiderately, when you have done nothing to warrant such ill-treatment. But then, perhaps, you will understand, if only in small measure, how Mr. Swansea must be feeling."

The duke looked startled for an instant. Then he threw his head back and laughed aloud. "Touché, my dear. You have driven your point home. Will it help if I tell the smith how much I admire his work?"

"Only if you are truly sincere," she answered, but this time a smile accompanied her words. "Do you really comprehend what I am saying?"

"I have some notion, Regina, though I confess it is foreign to my nature. I do not abuse my servants, but nor do I extend to them any extraordinary consideration. I do pay them extremely well and, if that is not adequate compensation for whatever they endure, they are always free to leave my service. In return, I demand neither their loyalty nor their allegiance, but only that they perform their duties well. These odd notions of yours are alien to my way of thinking. Egad, I can only imagine how outraged my father would have been had someone told him he must consider the sensitive feelings of the second footman. I doubt he ever knew the man's name."

"I suppose your views are common with the aristocracy, and if you are at fault, you have a great deal of company. Even my brother does not always treat his servants as well as I would expect." She sighed, looking down at the cup of tea she was aimlessly stirring and confessed, "Perhaps I am the one who is wrong. When I was a child, my feelings were hurt a great deal by the thoughtlessness of others. I suppose it has made me overly sensitive."

When Balfour remained silent, Regina glanced up to meet his eyes. She wished she knew what he was thinking, but it was impossible to tell. She laughed ruefully, trying to make light of the conversation. "I must warn you, my friend, my nature is not something I can change."

"Nor would I wish you to," he said, reaching out impulsively to cover her hand with his own. "There is nothing about you I would change."

The tenderness Regina saw reflected in his eyes touched

her deeply and warmed her heart, but the gentle moment of harmony between them was shattered as David raced into the room.

"Nothing, that is, save your relatives," Balfour amended.

During the duke's absence, Regina tried to concentrate on the long list of chores which had accumulated during the week. She knew she'd neglected both the house and stables, her business journals, and even Cornelia and their patient. She shook her head as she tallied up all that had to be done. Balfour was proving a most distracting influence and it behooved her to guard against her own growing feelings for the man. He would leave soon to resume the dissolute, sophisticated life he normally led in London. In all probability, he would forget her within the space of a few days. The thought depressed her—all the more so because she realized it would be a long, long time before she would forget the Duke of Balfour.

Regina determinedly set to work, poring diligently over her journals for an hour before she allowed herself to visit the stables. After she'd made certain the mares and foals were progressing as they should, she watched Jeremy put a few of the two-year-olds through their paces. A black colt, dubbed Commander, showed particular promise and she made a note to write to Lord Sayer. His success with two other foals from Whitechapel made him eager to acquire more, and he would be willing to pay top price.

Jeremy agreed with her and enthused happily over the speed the colt had shown during the workout. "This one's the best yet, Miss Regina. Did you see the way he moved? A winner for certain."

Regina nodded. "He is first-rate, Jeremy, and you have done an excellent job with him. Lord Sayer will be most pleased."

"A pity you cannot race Commander under your own

name. A colt with this much promise would have all the toffs clamoring for your stock."

"I know," she said wistfully, her eyes still focused on the black colt. "But his breeding is recorded in *The Stud Book* and word will spread eventually."

"I intend to do what I can to help it along," Jeremy said, grinning. "I thought I would drive to Newmarket tomorrow for the opening of the Second Spring Meet. Lord Sayer's running Cavalier in a sweepstakes race and Daylight in a special for three-year-old fillies. If they both do well, a few words to the grooms will help spread the news that Whitechapel is the best place to buy bloodstock."

Regina envied him, half wishing she could go as well. She loved the races, although she had not attended any in years. Uncle John had taken her to Newmarket a few times—over the protests of her aunt—and she still remembered the thrill of it all. She had loved the excitement, the vivid colors, the sheer power of the horses as they thundered over the turf to the roar of the crowd. Races were magical—the aristocracy mingled with the commoners and the only thing that mattered to anyone was the outcome of the race.

She turned reluctantly away from the paddock and the tempting thought of Newmarket, mindful of duties yet to be performed. Next on her list was a visit to Mr. Ramsey. She found him still sitting in the garden with Cornelia. Her cousin was reading to him, some sort of improving work by the sound of it, though the old man did not seem to be paying much heed.

Regina had approached silently, and she stood watching for a moment, unobserved. Ramsey's color was better, his face no longer a deathly white, but there was a listlessness about him she found worrisome. He sat motionless, his gaze trained on the distant hills.

"Good morning," she called, entering the garden through the small gate near the rose bushes.

Mr. Ramsey nodded in her direction, his thin lips forming what might be the semblance of a smile.

"Regina, my dear," Cornelia said, carefully marking the passage in her book as she rose. "Do join us. I was just reading to Mr. Ramsey from *Christian Morals,* and I must say it seems to have done him a world of good. We are feeling better this morning, are we not, Mr. Ramsey?"

The brown eyes flickered and Regina hid a smile. If the old man felt better, she thought it much more likely due to the duke's rather crude intervention the night before than to anything Hannah More might have written. But peace was her priority and she did not mention the matter to her cousin.

"You really should read this book, Regina. I find it truly enlightening. Miss More writes that this is a time of testing for all of us. She believes that the two classes of character are more decided now than they ever were. The wicked seem more wicked, she writes, and the good, more saintly. I am much inclined to agree with her."

"I have read some of her earlier works, Cousin, and I will agree that Miss More writes with much good sense."

"Indeed yes, my dear, and it would be well for us to take her words to heart. The wicked seem more wicked . . . there is a warning there, I believe."

"And most appropriate," Regina said with a smile. "Especially in view of what Mr. Ramsey had endured." She turned away as she spoke, knowing that was not the reference which Cornelia had intended. Seating herself near the old man, Regina asked, "Are you truly feeling better today, sir?"

"Yes, Miss," he said, but his eyes continued to scan the horizon. He seemed almost unaware of her presence and the only sign of life he evinced was his hand, slowly clenching and unclenching as it hung by his side.

Regina searched her mind for some topic to interest him. "The duke has ridden into the village with my nephew, but they should return soon. Perhaps, he will have some news for us."

The brown eyes flickered again, but there was no other response and Regina rose, feeling helpless.

"I do not believe Mr. Ramsey feels like conversing," Cornelia said. "That is why I have been reading to him, but it is just as well. He needs to conserve his strength. Dr. Lyons quite agrees with me. He thinks, with a few more days of good food and rest, our patient will be much improved."

Balfour overheard her as he stepped into the garden from the house. "By all means, do continue to read to him, Miss Davenport. I am certain that would spur anyone to a rapid recovery."

"Well it does seem to soothe him," Cornelia said, kneeling to adjust the blanket over Ramsey's legs.

Regina, under the pretext of snipping a wilted rose, moved closer to the duke and whispered, "If you do not behave, I will suggest she read to us every evening!"

He threw up his hands in mock surrender and for Cornelia's benefit, said, "Your cousin is doing a remarkable job of nursing, but I did think of something that might help. We brought Ramsey something back from the village."

"Really?" Cornelia asked, turning. "Another book, perhaps?"

"No, nothing like that. David selected it and he is bringing it round. Ah, here he comes now."

David, laughing and giggling, tried to open the garden gate while the ball of fur in his arms wiggled and licked at his face.

"A puppy! Really, Your Grace, that is the last thing Mr. Ramsey has need of. Tell David to take it away."

Balfour ignored Cornelia. His attention was on Ramsey, who had not said a word. He was not even sure if the old man understood what was afoot. Certainly, he did not look at the boy or the small collie.

David stood in front of Ramsey's chair, holding out his offering, a tan and white squirming, panting puppy. "I know another dog can't replace Abby, sir, but we thought you might like a pup to keep you company when you go back to your cottage."

When the old man continued to ignore him, David looked helplessly up at the duke.

"Put him down, lad."

David tried to place the pup in the old man's lap, but Ramsey's hand came up, nearly knocking the animal off. "I don't want it," he said clearly, his voice low and furious.

"Put the dog on the ground, David," Balfour suggested and watched as the pup scurried round, sniffing at everyone's shoes. Perhaps it was the scent of Abby lingering on the old man's boots, or perhaps it was instinctive on the dog's part, but after a moment, he settled down at Ramsey's feet. David sat down beside the pup, scratching its ears.

Regina broke the silence. "Well, Mr. Ramsey, it was very kind of His Grace to think of you, but if you do not wish to keep the collie, I am very sure David would be glad to have him."

"Andrew would not approve," Cornelia was quick to protest. "He does not believe in keeping dogs as pets and I agree with him completely. They are messy creatures, leaving their hair everywhere and digging up the flower beds. Really, Regina, you must know your brother will not permit David to keep that animal."

"Indeed, I do not know any such thing. It is true, we were not permitted to have any dogs as children, but if you'll remember, that was only because Aunt Sarah had a tremendous fear of them. Andrew certainly doesn't and he likes dogs—that much I do know. I do, too, for that matter, and it simply never occurred to me to acquire one as a pet. That may well be the case with my brother, but I cannot say."

"Well, I can, and I am telling you that Andrew will never allow it! And I hardly think he will appreciate you encouraging his son to think otherwise!"

David, from his seat on the ground, followed the discussion with interest, and the duke with a certain amount of amusement. The puppy, the cause of the dissension, remained unaware of the problem and crawled round the chair. Ramsey's arm still dangled temptingly over the side. The small dog rubbed his head against the old man's hand, then licked his fingers. Whatever Ramsey's feelings, he could not help caressing the silky head beneath his hand. Balfour saw the motion, but said nothing. He knew it would take time.

"The question is moot, Cornelia, so let us please not argue about it," Regina was saying. "For the time being, the pup may remain. If Mr. Ramsey does not wish another dog, I may decide to keep it for myself. I am sure David will take care of it while he is here."

"I will, Aunt Regina! I'll make sure he's not a bit of trouble."

"Thank you, David. I suggest you start by retrieving him from wherever he has crawled. I do not know much about dogs, but I believe they must be properly taught good habits if they are to reside in the house. Perhaps His Grace will help you to train him."

Fury goaded Cornelia into protesting. "You will never allow that dog in the house—"

"I should like a word with you in private, Cousin," Regina interrupted. "Will you step into the library?"

Mindful of their last discussion, Cornelia nodded meekly and followed Regina through the tall windows and down the hall to the library where they were closeted for some time.

"Whatever did you say to your cousin?" Balfour asked later that evening as they made the rounds of the stable, David trailing along behind them. "She was very nearly cordial at dinner."

"Cornelia can be very pleasant when she chooses," Regina said, avoiding the question. "And if you would only refrain from provoking her at every opportunity—"

"I? When did I ever provoke the woman?"

"Only every time you encounter her. Like remarking this afternoon that her reading would spur anyone to a rapid recovery."

"You cannot count that, my dear. Your cousin wasn't in the least offended, and it could even be inferred that I meant her soothing voice and admirable choice of reading material would prove beneficial."

"Not by anyone who knows you," she retorted, but couldn't help smiling a little.

"Well, perhaps not, but I am most contrite if I unwittingly created a tempest for you. I only thought the pup might be just what the old man needed to give him an interest in life."

"I thought so, too," Regina said, stopping at Penrod's box to stroke the black, silky head of her stallion. "It was a wonderful idea and something I had intended to try myself. Dr. Lyons told me poor Ramsey has lost the will to live, and needed something to care about if he is to regain his health."

"Unfortunately, Ramsey does not seem to agree with us, and I have saddled you with a pup," Balfour said, glancing back to where David dawdled, the pup frisking at his heels.

"Not I, Your Grace, but my brother. If Ramsey can't be brought to accept the dog, then I will tell Andy the creature is a gift to David from you."

"You are extraordinarily kind, my dear Regina. I can only imagine Sir Andrew's effusive gratitude."

"Well, do not let it trouble you. I still entertain hopes for Ramsey. He has always loved animals—horses, dogs, cats, whatever. Something may yet be contrived."

"I have one or two notions that might help. I have given the matter some thought, and if we can manage to leave the old man alone with the pup—"

"Careful, Your Grace," Regina warned, looking up at him with a teasing smile. "You are showing a great deal of consideration for a penniless old man. Your image as a heartless rake is slipping."

"There are ways to rectify that," he said, his arm coming

up to rest against the wall, trapping Regina between the box and the aisle. He was close enough to hear her quick intake of breath, and to see the way her lips suddenly parted. All he had to do was bend his head to taste her sweet mouth.

She gazed into his blue eyes, now filled with desire. For an instant, she longed to throw convention to the winds, longed to throw her arms about his broad shoulders and lose herself in what she was certain would be a most passionate kiss. But David was somewhere just behind them, and Jeremy's voice sounded from the other side of the stable. She wavered, but convention won out. A second later, she ducked beneath his arm, and glanced back at him from over her shoulder.

He smiled at her maneuver and Regina had the uncomfortable notion that he knew precisely what she'd been thinking. A blush tinged her cheeks as she hurried round the corner to the alcove where the parrot was caged.

"Here comes the duke, here comes the duke," Jake squawked from high on his perch.

"What is this?" Balfour asked as he came up behind her. "I gather someone has been teaching the bird a few new words."

Jeremy emerged from the mare's side of the stables, grinning broadly. "He learns quick, Your Grace. The problem is you never know what he'll choose to come out with. I've been coaching him for three days, and this is the first time he's said that."

"Is it?" the duke asked, drawing a cracker from his pocket and offering it to the bird. "Well, he's an intelligent fellow. No doubt he merely waited for the appropriate moment."

"Are you actually carrying crackers about in your clothes, Your Grace? Horrors! What is the world coming to?" Regina asked, shaking her head at this new evidence of depravity.

"One cracker only, my dear, and that as a measure of self-defense. I thought if I bribed the blasted bird, he might show a bit more respect for my attire. I take leave to tell you that

Desmond objects strongly to cleaning parrot residue from my shirts."

Regina laughed but left off teasing him. The conversation turned to horses and Jeremy told the duke that two colts, bred and trained at Whitechapel, would be running in the races at Newmarket. "I thought I'd attend opening day tomorrow and see how they do. If they win, which I expect they might, I can spread the word they came from here."

Balfour looked startled. "The meet opens tomorrow? Are you quite certain?"

"Why, yes, Your Grace. It always opens in—"

"I know, I know," the duke interrupted. "It just does not seem possible 'tis upon us already. Time gets away from one in this remote village. I had intended to be at Newmarket for the opening myself."

"Have you any horses running?" Regina asked, surprised. She knew Balfour did not normally race his stable at Newmarket.

"No, but as a member of the Jockey Club, I try to be on hand for the first day of each meeting. Most of us do—Bedford, Devonshire, York," he said, naming a few of the illustrious dukes who governed the racing fraternity.

"The company may not be as prestigious, but why not go along with Jeremy tomorrow?" Regina suggested. "It is only a short drive from here."

"I confess I would like to, but I dislike the idea of leaving you and David alone."

"Now you are being foolish. You said yourself that there has been no sign of those men about. Ben will be here and all the stable lads, and David and I will stay near the house."

"Have your forgotten that they came right in the house last time? No, it is out of the question. Forget I ever mentioned it, unless . . . Regina, why can we not make a day of it? You and David come, too," he suggested, his face lighting up with boyish enthusiasm.

"Oh, no! I could not possibly, but thank you for asking. That was kind of you."

"Why not, Regina," he pressed. "You can watch the races from the safety of our carriage. We will take Trudy with us, too, for propriety's sake. 'Tis high time you saw your horses run."

It was tempting. Very tempting. To see the horses that she had bred and trained actually competing in a race . . . she had dreamed of such a day. But she also knew how much Andrew and Cornelia would disapprove.

Balfour saw her hesitation. "What harm can there be? We can take a basket and dine alfresco. You need never leave the vicinity of our carriage. Come, Regina—a day away from here will do you good."

"I would truly love to go," she said, wistful longing in her voice. "It sounds delightful, but you must know it would be improper of me. Andrew would be furious."

"What? Is he such a pompous fool that he would object to his sister enjoying a harmless outing with her nephew, her maid and her groom in attendance? Or is it just my presence to which he would object? Will it help if I promise not to speak to you?"

"No, not at all," she replied, smiling at his nonsense. "I cannot imagine anything more uncomfortable than spending a day with someone who will not speak to one."

"Then I shall promise instead to keep you amused with all manner of aimless chatter," he said, determined now to win her over. He had proposed the jaunt because he enjoyed the race meets, but that no longer mattered. He was determined now to persuade Regina to go because he'd heard the longing in her voice and seen the desire in her eyes. "Come with us, my dear. There can be no serious objection. Other ladies will be in attendance, and David would enjoy it."

He could see she was strongly tempted. Hoping to persuade her, he called to her nephew as he approached. "What do you say, lad? Would you like a day at the races tomorrow?"

David had never been to the races. He had not the slightest notion of what it might be like, but if the duke proposed it, then it must be splendid. He replied with enthusiasm, "Could we, Uncle Cedric? And can I sit on the box beside you?"

Balfour laughed. "You may, that is, if we can convince your aunt to join us."

David looked up at her with round, hopeful, pleading eyes.

Jeremy added his approval. "It always helps to see what the competition has to offer, Miss Regina. I can give you reports, but there's nothing like seeing the horses firsthand. As a breeder, you know you ought to attend a few of the meets."

"There, the weight of opinion is against you, my dear. Give in gracefully and say you will come."

"Arguing with you is like tilting at windmills," Regina said, laughing. "You win, Your Grace. I will tell Mrs. Milligan to prepare us a basket." The decision made, she felt a heady sense of elation. "Newmarket! I can scarce believe I am going."

"Believe it, my dear. I will not allow you to back out now," Balfour said, smiling down at her. How absurdly little it took to please her, he thought, remembering the countless diamonds and emeralds he'd bestowed on other ladies—ladies who had received his gifts with much less pleasure than Regina showed over a simple outing.

They strolled back to the house, discussing their plans for the morning. Mrs. Milligan, when consulted, agreed to provide a nuncheon and positively beamed at Regina before hurrying back to her kitchen.

Cornelia was given no opportunity to voice her disapproval, as she was certain to do. She was still tending to Ramsey, and Regina said, quite casually, that perhaps there would be time enough in the morning to inform her cousin of their plans.

"Or you could just leave her a note," Balfour suggested with a devilish grin.

"I suppose you think I am cowardly for not facing her at once."

"I think you are many things, my dear, but never cowardly. Not after seeing you confront me with a pistol! Egad, I still shudder at the memory. No, 'tis merely that you are too kind to put your cousin in her proper place, whereas I have no such scruples."

Regina looked as though she might say something more, but David came in, demanding his game of chess, and she withdrew to a chair near the fire. Balfour watched her as he played, more entranced with the way her hair glinted in the firelight than with the precarious position of his king on the board.

"Check and checkmate!" David crowed.

Balfour glanced down at the boy, bemused. His king was indeed captured by a ten-year-old waif of a boy, and there was no room for him to maneuver. He looked across at Regina and suddenly realized the game was not the only thing lost to him. This tall, elegant and regal lady with the innate goodness and innocence of a child, had somehow captured his heart—captured it as easily and as surely as her nephew had caught his king.

Eight

The following morning, Cornelia stepped into the kitchen to have a word with Cook, and quite by accident discovered Regina's plans to attend the races at Newmarket. Cornelia's keen eyes had immediately spotted an oversized hamper sitting on the floor, although it was partially concealed by the table. Half expecting to find that Cook was stealing food, she instantly demanded an explanation, and her accusing manner made her suspicions abundantly clear.

Cook, who'd had several disagreements with Miss Davenport prior to that morning, naturally resented the slur on her character, and took a great deal of pleasure in retorting that she'd prepared the hamper on Miss Regina's orders to take with her to the races. She added that, in her opinion, it was high time Miss Regina got out a bit and enjoyed herself.

Cornelia retreated, wondering again at Regina's propensity for engaging servants who did not seem to know their proper place. When she had first arrived at Whitechapel, Cornelia had endeavored to show Cook a more efficient way to run the kitchens. The woman had not only been unappreciative, but she had spoken to Cornelia in a most disrespectful manner. Shocking, really, but when she'd told her cousin, Regina had merely said that Cook must order the kitchens as she saw fit.

It was all of a piece, Cornelia thought, as she took her morning constitutional in the gardens. Whitechapel, for all it was a pleasant enough place, was not run near so well as

Andrew's lovely home. Even though his estate was considerably larger, the house was orderly, meals were served at regular hours, and the servants kept to the line.

A rackety carriage pulling into the yard by the kitchen door drew her attention. She could not imagine anyone who had business with the kitchen staff arriving at this hour, and hurried over to intercept the young man climbing down from the box.

"Morning, ma'am," he said pleasantly, and doffed his cap politely. "Squire Poole sent me over. His hot houses are doing well and he thought Miss Westfield might enjoy some fresh strawberries."

"How thoughtful of the squire. Thank you, young man," she said, accepting the large dish of fruit he handed her. "You will please convey our gratitude to the Squire."

"Yes, ma'am."

Now here was a proper servant, Cornelia thought, and smiled warmly at him. "I do not believe I have seen you before."

"I guess not, ma'am. The Squire took me on just a few days ago," he said. His blue eyes held a hint of laughter and he confided, "I just hope he will bear with me until I learn my way about. I got lost on my way over here so it's taken me longer than it should have done."

"Well, the neighborhood is quite simple and I am sure you will become accustomed to it quickly."

"I hope so, ma'am. It's a nice place to work and I wouldn't want to lose my position, but learning the people and the estates is difficult for me." He turned as he spoke and stared at the house for a long moment as though to impress it on his memory. "I'll remember Whitechapel now. Thank you, Miss Westfield."

Cornelia blushed. To be mistaken for Regina could only be thought a compliment. She smiled coyly. "You are quite welcome, but I am her cousin, Miss Davenport. Miss Westfield is a much younger and taller person."

He nodded, repeating her name, then glanced at the house again. "Will Miss Westfield be about later? I kinda like to put faces to names to help me remember 'em, if you know what I mean."

"Yes, indeed I do. But my cousin will be away for the day. She and our guest, the Duke of Balfour, plan to attend the races at Newmarket."

He appeared suitably impressed by the mention of the duke, and a few moments later took his leave. Now that, Cornelia thought, is the sort of person her cousin should engage. A most well-mannered young man, and she would mention it to the Squire when next she saw him.

Her temper cooled, Cornelia took the dish of strawberries to the kitchen and directed Cook to prepare them for breakfast. The woman seemed about to argue, and Cornelia added, "They are best eaten fresh and I am certain Regina would like to have them this morning. I should not like to tell her you refused so simple a request."

Cook only nodded, but Cornelia left the kitchen somewhat mollified. She entered the breakfast parlor to find Regina not yet down, and seated herself to compose her mind. She must consider what she would say to her cousin over this Newmarket business. She would have to be very tactful. Regina had been a bit irritable of late, and while Whitechapel might be lacking in certain amenities, it was still a pleasant situation and one which Cornelia did not wish to lose. The thought that she had nowhere else to go was quickly suppressed.

"Good morning, Cornelia. I trust you slept well?" Regina asked as she entered the room and took her usual seat by the window. "It is a beautiful morning, is it not?"

"It is, my dear, but I have been out in the gardens and I fear it bodes to be unnaturally warm. I do hope you will limit your activities outside today for I should hate to see you overcome by the heat."

Regina glanced at her sharply, but Cornelia was sorting

the mail and looked entirely innocent. Taking a deep breath, she said quietly, "I do hope you are wrong. His Grace has very kindly offered to take David and me to Newmarket for the races. No doubt we shall be gone for the better part of the day."

"To Newmarket? Oh, my dear, pray tell me this is only one of your jests, for I cannot credit you are serious!"

"Quite serious, Cousin, but you need not be in the least concerned. Trudy will ride with me in the barouche. The duke intends to drive himself and has promised David he may sit next to him on the box—a treat which has my nephew in high alt, I assure you. And both Tenby and Jeremy will accompany us, though they will ride alongside the carriage."

"I see your mind is quite made up and there is no point in discussing the matter, although I think I might be excused for wishing that you had sought my advice before planning such an expedition," Cornelia replied with an injured air. "I will only say that I know Andrew would be most displeased with such a scheme, and if he were here, I am very certain he would forbid you to go."

"Very probably," Regina agreed with good humor. "But Andrew is not here, and for once I am going to do what pleases me."

"Pleases you or pleases the duke?" Cornelia could not resist asking.

"If you are referring to our trip to Newmarket, it pleases me immensely," Balfour said from the doorway.

Cornelia, misliking the intimate way he smiled at Regina, glared at him, but he did not even notice.

"Good morning, ladies," he said, sauntering into the room. "Regina, my dear, have you seen the size of the basket your cook has prepared? We shall have enough provisions to feed half of Newmarket."

"The waste in this household is positively disgraceful," Cornelia said, but when her cousin paid no heed, she rose from the table abruptly. "I pray you will excuse me, Regina.

As you are going to be absent all day, it appears I will be obligated to nurse Mr. Ramsey without any assistance, and there are several matters I must attend to first."

"Maisie will help you," Regina replied, feeling a small twinge of guilt, but her cousin had already sailed through the door.

"The classic martyr," Balfour said. "Do not allow her to depress you, my dear. You know she enjoys nursing the old man."

"I do know it, but I can still sympathize with her. My poor cousin is having a difficult time of late, and I am responsible. I rather got in the habit of allowing her to dictate to me, so she is not accustomed to my disregarding her advice." She smiled ruefully. "It is so much easier to simply agree with her."

"Promise me that you will not think of her today."

"I promise. In truth, I doubt I shall be able to think of anything but the horses."

"Well that certainly puts me in my place," he said, and grinned at her sudden look of comprehension. "No, my dear, do not apologize. Tell me instead, have you seen David? I thought he would be at the door, ready and waiting for us."

"I saw him in the hall when I came down. He has the puppy with him and is planning to fix a space in the garden for the dog so he won't be cooped up all day."

"Finish your breakfast then, and I will see if I can roust the boy out. We should be leaving at half-past nine if you can be ready."

Balfour rose and started for the door, nearly colliding with David as he came running into the room. The duke picked him up with one hand and swung him around. "Whoa, young man. What is this unseemly rush?"

David grinned, not in the least daunted. "I couldn't wait to tell you about the pup. I asked Mr. Ramsey to keep an eye on him, and he said he would!"

"Did he now? Well done, David."

"He said he couldn't chase after the pup, but if I fixed the dog near his chair in the garden, he would watch him. He's out there with the pup now, Uncle Cedric, and I heard him talking to it when I left."

Regina rose and swept round the table. "David, that is wonderful news!" She knelt before her nephew so that they were on eye level. "I think you are perfectly splendid," she said and planted a kiss on his brow before hugging him.

David squirmed and grinned up at Balfour over Regina's shoulder.

The duke smiled at the boy's discomfort. In a few more years the lad would know how to behave when a pretty lady hugged him. He would likely be seeking out their caresses rather than avoiding them.

Now if Regina hugged me like that, he thought . . . and was deeply thankful they were not related.

Jeremy had folded back the top of the carriage and Regina sat in the back with Trudy, enjoying the drive in the early morning sun. The day was warm, but not unbearably so. A soft breeze helped to alleviate the heat. Regina relaxed against the cushioned seat, admiring the scenery as they passed through Bury St. Edmunds and headed west on Bury Road to Newmarket. It had been years since she'd travelled this route, but she thought it little changed.

The duke appeared to have no trouble handling the team of chestnuts, despite his arm. Regina suspected her nephew posed a greater problem than the horses, with his unending questions. She could hear scraps of conversation as the duke tried to answer the boy. She thought she heard Escape mentioned and guessed Balfour was telling her nephew about the Prince Regent's withdrawal from racing. His Highness had once been a frequent visitor to Newmarket, and his patronage had done much to support the racing fraternity.

Regina had been only a child of six or seven when the

scandal had broke, but she could still remember the furor it had caused. The Regent's horse, Escape, a high favorite with the sporting crowd, ran a dismal race at Newmarket. Then, the following day, when the odds were long against the horse, Escape had won easily. Rumors that the Newmarket race had been fixed circulated swiftly and swarms of angry bettors had protested bitterly. In response, the Jockey Club had demanded the Prince Regent dismiss his jockey. He did so, but he'd bitterly resented the entire affair and had refused to race his stable.

For once, it appeared the Regent was blameless, and the Jockey Club belatedly presented him with a handsome apology. He had accepted it, but though he could once again be seen at all the major race meets, he refused to run any of his own horses. She had heard that the Regent had attended one of the meets at Newmarket last year and now she wondered if he would be present today. That would be something to see!

Regina knew they were drawing close to the town when she saw Bury Hill on her left, and a string of horses out for the morning gallops. She drew Trudy's attention to them as the horses raced down the hill. The beauty and the power of the high-strung thoroughbreds moved her, as always.

They passed several racing stables lining the road near Long Hill, then into town. High Street, the main road through Newmarket, crawled with traffic. Balfour reined in his team to a pace barely above a walk. Tenby and Jeremy fell into line behind them. Regina looked about her in amusement. Carriages of every size and description filled the road, along with dozens of riders on horseback. On this first day of the Second Spring Meet, Newmarket looked more like a carnival than a racing town.

The lusty, sometimes funny, cries of street vendors assaulted her ears as the men plied their wares. Every manner and type of food was offered up, from fresh strawberries to live chickens, along with the sound of ringing trumpets and bells to draw the crowd's attention. Regina noticed an oddly dressed little man, grinning widely as he shouted, "Stinkin' shrimps, buy my stinkin' shrimps." He spotted Regina's fascinated gaze and added loudly, "Lor' 'ow they do stink today!"

She smiled, shaking her head no at him, and at the enterprising young lad running alongside the carriage offering his fruit. "Fair lemons and oranges, twelve pence a peck," the boy cried, tossing a bright orange into the air.

Regina watched as he threw several lemons in the air at once, juggling them expertly—and caught them all safely. He was no sooner left behind, then an old woman lifted up her tray as the carriage halted briefly.

"Oysters, Miss? Only sixpence a pound and Fair Cherryes, too."

The duke drove on, the woman's shrill voice screeching after them until a new crier offered, "Hot Baked Wardens, Hot Baked Wardens." His voice rang in Regina's ears amid the cacophony of other vendors offering their goods. Onions, cucumbers, and eels were proffered as well as the opportunity to purchase "a fine singing bird," old cloaks, rare shoes, and thread laces—long and strong. So much to take in, Regina thought, hardly knowing where to look.

"La, Miss, did you ever see such a sight? And baked wardens, too! My ma used to stew pears like that, but I ain't had none in years," Trudy said when they finally left all the street vendors behind.

"It is certainly different than the peaceful quiet of Whitechapel," Regina said, but her green eyes glowed with excitement and she was enjoying every moment.

The duke deftly pulled the barouche into a line of fine carriages facing the five-mile course on Newmarket Heath. From there they would have an excellent view of the races. Their grooms reined in beside them a few moments later.

"I thought I'd lost you back there," Jeremy said. "Lord,

the street criers grow worse every year. Thank heavens there are not many of them on the race grounds."

"Did you see the man with the jack-in-the-box, Aunt Regina?" David asked, turning around in his seat. "He said it talked!"

"A ventriloquist, my lad, looking for unsuspecting buyers like you," the duke said as he descended from the carriage, then laughed at the boy's wide-eyed wonder. He helped David down, looking suspiciously at the lad's bulging coat pocket. "And what is that unsightly lump marring the line of your coat?"

"A bag of oats," David replied, grinning unabashedly. "For the horses, you know."

"You stay away from the horses, David," Balfour warned, struggling to hide a smile.

Regina did not hear their chatter. She was preoccupied with watching the crowds, but thankful that she was under the duke's protection. For the most part, the spectators seemed to be of the upper class. Expensive carriages, gigs and high-perch phaetons lined the course, and dozens of well-dressed gentlemen strolled the lawns. She inadvertently caught the eye of one man, and received a knowing wink and flirtatious smile before she hastily glanced away.

She noticed that not many women were present, but a few stylishly dressed ladies were walking about, brandishing lacy parasols to protect their faces from the sun, and accompanied by maids and aristocratic-looking gentlemen. Regina felt immeasurably better. Knowing she was in good company, she turned her attention to David and the duke.

Balfour was pointing out various sights to her nephew. She heard him describe one particular gentleman as a *black-legs,* and she glanced in the direction he pointed, clearly puzzled.

"I mean that man in the outlandish hat," Balfour said. "His name is Dandy Scrope Davies, but he is commonly referred to as 'blacklegs' or just 'legs.' As David opened his mouth, the duke added hastily, "No, lad, I do not know why. It is simply what bookmakers are called. He gives odds on the races and we shall place a few wagers with him later."

"Do you know which horses you mean to back?" Regina asked curiously.

"No, not yet. Normally, I walk about a bit and listen to the gossip, or else decide by instinct after they bring the entries out."

"Uncle Cedric!" David cried urgently, tugging on his sleeve. "Oh, do look at the clown!"

Balfour glanced around at a slender young man clad in particolored silk tights and a blouse of purple and white in a harlequin design. "Not a clown, you young jackanapes. That is one of the premier jockeys, and judging by his colors, I would guess he is riding for Lord Bedford. I wonder if Harry is here. That rather looks like his carriage down there."

"There are undoubtedly a great many people present that you know," Regina said. "Jeremy can stay with us for a bit if you would like to stroll about."

"I would, but I'd rather you come with me," he replied, offering a hand to help her down. "I want you to meet Harry Warwick, the Earl of Bedford. He's an old friend and the two of you have much in common. Harry is more fond of his horses than he is of most people."

"What of David?" she asked, hesitating.

"Tenby is watching him. He looks content enough for the moment and appears to have made a friend." David had approached a redheaded, freckled-face boy, playing with a large black dog behind the carriage next to them. "I think we may trust Tenby to keep an eye on him for a few moments. Come along, my dear. I am sure that after the long drive, you and Trudy will enjoy a walk."

When the groom had assured her he'd watch David, Regina accepted the arm the duke offered. With Trudy on her other side, she strolled slowly, admiring the carriages and the fine teams harnessed to them. She could not help being conscious of many curious looks in her direction, and guessed Balfour was a well-known figure at the race meetings.

The duke, aware of the speculation he stirred, knew the true reason. He was, of course, well known at Newmarket, but the young women who usually accompanied him on such occasions wore bits of muslin, nothing at all like the elegant young lady at his side, who looked particularly fetching in a well-cut blue and white walking dress. He ignored the stares of the curious and halted by a gold and white high-perch phaeton, coming up to the young man on the box, "Harry, old fellow, come down. I thought I recognized your rig."

The Earl of Bedford had his glasses trained on the race course, but he lowered them at once and looked around with considerable surprise. "Cedric! Where the devil have you been? No one has seen or heard from you for a month. The rumors have been flying. You should hear what they are saying in Town about you."

"I can only imagine. No, pray do not enlighten me. Are you coming down or am I to stand here getting a crick in my neck yelling up to you?"

"One second," his friend said, and obligingly climbed down. He had not missed Regina's presence, but though he darted a quick look in her direction, he was too well mannered to stare.

Balfour saw his furtive glance and smiled. "May I make you known to Miss Westfield? My dear, this hapless fop is the Earl of Bedford. I warn you—believe nothing he might say of me."

"I am honored, Miss Westfield," Harry said, bowing gracefully over her hand. "Are you perchance related to Sir Andrew Westfield?"

"My brother, sir."

"You don't say? A fine man, though I am not much acquainted with him. Still, I have heard of some of his deeds. Most commendable," he said, then glanced at Balfour, wondering how he came to be with pompous old Sir Andrew's sister. Not that the girl wasn't a looker, he thought. She was, but just not in the style Cedric favored. This one had respectability written all over her.

"I should tell you, Harry, that Miss Westfield breeds and trains some of the finest bloodstock you are likely to see. One of the horses she bred is running in the big race this afternoon, and another in the sweepstakes for three-year-old fillies."

"Really?" he asked, studying Regina with more interest. "Should I lay my blunt on then?"

"I have not seen the horses in over a year, my lord, and know nothing of their training since then, but both have excellent breeding and have performed well in the past."

"Let me have their names," Harry said. His brows lifted when she told him of Cavalier and Daylight. He knew both horses and was quite impressed to learn she'd bred them. The conversation turned naturally to other horses, and Balfour stood by, quietly amused as Harry questioned her. Then the trumpet sounded and a roar went up from the crowd.

"I think we had best return to our carriage, my dear. It looks as though they are bringing the first horses out. Harry, it was good to see you," the duke said, extending his hand. "Pray tell them in London that you saw me alive and well."

"You *are* looking extremely well, now I think of it," Harry said, and noted with surprise Cedric's clear eyes and tanned face.

"It must be the country air," Balfour replied, laughing. "Perhaps we shall see you later."

He drew Regina away, well aware that Harry was still standing beside his carriage watching their departure. Perhaps, Balfour thought, he'd made a mistake introducing her to Bedford, but he'd done so from the best of motives. If Harry chose to patronize her stud, Regina would have more business than she could handle, which would certainly please her.

The problem was that he did not want Regina's name linked with his own. Lord, how much he had changed—to be thinking of protecting a lady instead of seducing her. But Regina had come to mean too much to him. For the first time in his life, he understood what it meant to care for someone else more than himself. There was nothing he would not do for Regina. During the last week he had come to a decision. He intended to try to retrieve the tattered shreds of his reputation—a feat which might prove beyond even his capabilities. Aunt Sophia would help, once he convinced her that he'd turned over a new leaf. But that would have to wait until he returned to Town. In the meantime, he could say nothing to Regina.

He glanced at her, walking serenely beside him, secure in the belief that she was safe with him. In her own way Regina was as bad as David, investing him with qualities of some mythical hero. She thought him trustworthy! Lord, how the ton would laugh if they knew. But if it was within his power, he would see her faith in him was not misplaced. Even if it meant giving her up.

It was a depressing thought and he put it aside as they strolled to the rear of his carriage. David still played with the red-headed urchin, the pair of them taking turns throwing sticks for the mongrel to chase. Tenby leaned against the rear of the carriage, watching the boys. The duke stepped over for a quiet word with him.

"Any signs of trouble?"

"No, Your Grace. The boy seems okay. I had a word with his pa a few minutes ago. They hail from over Huntingdon way."

"Good man," the duke approved. Then, aware of the way his groom's eyes followed the horses, Balfour suggested, "Take a walk if you like. So long as one of us remains by the carriage, the boy should be all right."

Tenby was off at once, and Balfour smiled to himself.

Regina would be proud of him for considering his servant's feelings. Surprisingly, it felt rather good.

Regina, unaware of the duke's regard, tried to attract her nephew's attention. She called to him several times, but her voice never reached him amid the tumult of the crowds. Balfour stepped behind her and whistled piercingly.

David glanced up at once, then threw a stick as hard as he could before running up to them, his new friend trailing along behind him.

Regina put a hand on his shoulder. "David, the first race is about to begin. Do you and your friend want to come sit in the carriage with us? You won't be able to see anything from here."

"Can I not stay here with Freddy, Aunt Regina? We found the best dog!"

"But do you not wish to see the race?" she asked, truly astonished that anyone could pass up such an opportunity.

Her nephew shook his head. "Freddy and me are teaching the dog tricks. Please, Aunt Regina, may I stay here?"

She sighed. "Very well, but promise me you will not go out of sight of the carriage."

"I won't," he promised. "Come on, Freddy, let's see if we can teach the dog to roll over and play dead."

Regina watched the two young boys run the half-dozen yards back to where the dog sat patiently waiting. Their energy seemed boundless. She looked up at Balfour. "Were you like that at their age?"

"Worse," he said, grinning. He'd escaped his tutor at every possible opportunity and could easily understand David's desire to romp with a dog and a newfound friend. "He should be all right here," he assured her as he helped her into the carriage.

The bugle sounded and the jockeys in their colorful silks edged their mounts into position. The first race for three-year-olds would be run over the Rowley Mile. Balfour watched Regina as she studied the horses intently through the binoculars he had provided her. "Which do you prefer, my dear?"

"That black with the white blaze and rather long ears looks promising," she said, her gaze still on the horses.

Balfour stepped a little away from the carriage and nodded to one of the "legs" who came running. He placed a wager for Regina on the black stallion, impressed with her choice. Called Diamond Cut, the black belonged to Lord Stoddard and had won an impressive number of races.

He returned to the carriage just as the race started and called up to Regina. "I placed a wager on the black for us. He's called Diamond Cut—cheer him home."

The horses erupted in a swirl of dust, but Regina kept her eyes on the blue and yellow silks of the jockey riding the black. Seventeen horses were entered in the race, and she feared Diamond Cut had gotten boxed in. His jockey took him to the outside, and as they passed the carriage, he lay fifth, running behind a large chestnut.

A gasp went up from the crowd as one of the jockeys took a spill. Regina knew it was the lad they'd seen earlier in the distinctive purple and white silks. He'd been riding third when he fell and more than a dozen horses thundered over him. By some miracle, the jockey had curled into a ball and rolled to the side of the course, narrowly escaping a trampling by several tons of horseflesh.

She saw him climb groggily to his feet, then turned the binoculars back to the leaders. The black had moved up to third, racing on the outside. He passed the riderless horse, gaining steadily on the gray in second place. Regina cheered loudly as he inched closer to the lead. "Come on, boy, you can do it!"

Her voice mingled with the yells of the other spectators. The black was a favorite, but so was the showy chestnut in the lead. The cries seemed evenly divided between the two, and the pair raced neck and neck. Regina saw Diamond Cut's jockey lift his riding crop and bring it smartly down, urging the black to the lead. The chestnut was tiring—she could tell by the way he moved—and the black drew out in front by a neck, his long legs easily eating up the turf. A wild cheer went up as he crossed the finish line half a length in front of the chestnut.

Regina sat down, hoping she had not made a spectacle of herself. She had yelled encouragement to Diamond Cut until her throat was near raw. But how exhilarating it felt, and what a magnificent stallion! She looked about for the duke, but he'd disappeared. Jeremy grinned up at her.

"Looks like you picked right, Miss Regina. I think His Grace and Tenby went to collect your winnings."

"Did you wager on him, too, Jeremy?"

"No, Miss, worst luck. I backed the chestnut."

"Oh, how unfortunate. A shorter race and your horse would have won easily. The black needed the distance. Did you see? He got stronger towards the finish."

The duke returned clutching a fistful of notes which he deposited in Regina's lap. "Your winnings, my dear."

She stared down at the money in her lap. "Why, there must be above fifty pounds here. I cannot accept this."

"Nonsense. We got excellent odds as the chestnut beat Diamond Cut just a few days ago. Of course it was only a six-furlong race, but had I not taken your advice, I would have backed the wrong horse. I retrieved my stake, plus ten percent. The rest is yours."

"Then Whitechapel shall declare a bonus this year," she said, counting out the notes. "Trudy, here is five pounds for you, and five each for Maisie, Mrs. Milligan and Cook." She handed a sheath of notes down to Jeremy. "Divide this between you and Ben, and the stable lads."

The duke watched, bemused. He could not help comparing her to the scores of young women who had accompanied him to the races in the past. Any one of them would have flung her arms about him, kissed him soundly, and promptly stuffed the notes in her bodice. Regina, however, was having a grand time giving away her windfall. He could see she derived just as much pleasure from Trudy's open-mouth astonishment and Jeremy's wide grin as the other women did in acquiring a small fortune.

When the money was dispersed to her satisfaction, Regina asked Balfour to help her down. "I just want to see how David is doing," she explained, and sighed. "He probably did not see any of the race."

"But he is enjoying himself nonetheless," the duke assured her as they walked behind the carriage. "Give him a few more years and he will be badgering you for a pound note to put on the nose of the favorite."

"Then perhaps it is just as well he shows no interest," Regina said. "I can imagine Andy's horror were David to— oh, good heavens!"

Her nephew lay on the ground, wrestling playfully with the mongrel dog, allowing it to lick his face. His high-pitched laughter came clearly to her ears, so she knew he was in no danger, but his clothes! He had been immaculately turned out when they'd left the house, but now his coat and nether garments were stained with grass and dirt, and sadly wrinkled. He looked like a street urchin.

Balfour laughed. "We shall have to smuggle him into the house when we return. I can imagine what the she-dragon would say were she to see him now."

The freckled-faced boy from the next carriage came running back. Regina watched for a moment as they engaged the dog in a game of tug-of-war. The dog won and the boys went down in a heap, oblivious to the dirt and mud ruining their clothes. They giggled and shouted, crying on in the way of boys.

"I suppose there is no point in calling him back now," she said. "The damage is done, and he might as well enjoy himself."

"My thoughts precisely," Balfour said, smiling at her. Regina's hair was tousled, her eyes sparkled, and her cheeks were flushed. He thought he had never seen a woman look so desirable, and it took considerable self-control to focus his mind on the horses. He made the effort, saying, "Come, my dear. Let us look at the entries for the next race. It's a sweepstakes for two-year-olds. I sent Tenby off to learn what he could."

Regina walked back with him and was once again caught up in the excitement of the race. She picked a handsome gray who unfortunately ran a poor third, and she owned herself horribly deceived by the animal's good looks. "All show and no substance," she told Balfour when the horse faltered in the stretch.

"The best of us are sometimes deceived by appearances, my dear. Never mind. The mile race for fillies is next, and you will have the chance to redeem your judgment. I assume you want to back Daylight?"

"Of course, but I am prejudiced in her favor, you know."

"With good reason, I think," he said, and went off to place their wager. He returned with Harry in tow.

The earl had his doubts about Daylight, but he had backed her and wanted to watch the race with Balfour and Miss Westfield. He observed the horses as they paraded before the spectators. Lowering his glasses, he looked worriedly up at her. "She seems a trifle small, Miss Westfield, and the race is a full mile. Are you certain she has the stamina to last?"

"I am, my lord, if the jockey paces her. Daylight is what I believe you gentlemen refer to as a 'closer.' She runs her strongest race at the finish, when some of the other horses are tiring."

"I pray you are right," he murmured and trained his glasses on the field. Fourteen fillies were running and Daylight had drawn the fifth post. It was a good position, but the legs were offering ten to one against her—not a good omen.

Two fillies went down in a tangle as the race got underway.

Daylight was not involved, but she was running well behind the leaders. Harry had lost a bundle earlier when his jockey took a spill. The hundred pounds he'd staked on this smallish chestnut was all he had left. Sweat beaded his upper lip. The roar of the crowd was for Wimblederry, the odds-on favorite, now running well out in front.

The horses passed the half-mile marker and Daylight moved up slightly to fourth. She ran easily, her jockey laying off the whip. At the three-quarter mark, she moved into third place and looked to be closing on the front runners. A groan went up from the crowd as Daylight swept between the other two horses, and the trio raced for the finish. All three jockeys, hunched over the necks of their mounts, plied their whips freely, but Daylight pulled out in front at the finish line.

Disappointed cries sounded around them, but none so loud as Harry's whoop of glee. He tossed his hat into the air. "I am indebted to you, Miss Westfield. By jove, that little filly ran a splendid race!"

"Which, of course, you never doubted," Balfour said, catching and returning his friend's hat.

"I staked my blunt on her, didn't I? And now, if you will excuse me, I see Dandy Davies over there and mean to collect my winnings at once."

Balfour smiled as Bedford left. "You have made an influential friend, my dear. Poor Harry, for all his knowledge of horses he seldom backs a winner. He will likely be at your heels for the rest of the day."

"As he seems a most delightful young man, I shall not object," Regina said, laughing. "I rather liked his light-hearted air and enthusiasm. Is he always so easily pleased?"

"Only when he has backed a winner," Balfour said sharply, feeling an unaccustomed twinge of jealousy. He wondered if Regina was attracted to Harry, then cursed himself for behaving so churlishly. He'd wanted her to like the few men he considered friends. Forcing himself to smile, he added, "Harry is devoted to his horses, and his mood is often dependent on his luck, but he is the best of good fellows. I'd trust him with my life."

Regina, more attuned to the duke's moods than he knew, had sensed his displeasure at once. *He was jealous.* She knew it was unworthy of her, but the notion thrilled her nevertheless. She hid a smile and made an effort to speak lightly. "Tell me, Your Grace, are you not hungry? Shall we spread a blanket and enjoy some of this food Cook packed for us?"

"An excellent idea," Balfour agreed, and climbed up to lift the heavy hamper down. "I'll warrant David is starving after chasing that mongrel all day."

Regina and Trudy descended, and the maid took the heavy blanket. "Let me attend to that, Miss Regina. You go watch the horses with His Grace. Won't take me but a few moments to set everything out."

Regina, glad to stretch her legs, walked a little way with Balfour. She noticed that some of the spectators were already leaving, although the big race of the day was yet to be run.

"Losers," the duke said dryly, following her gaze at the departing carriages. "They staked all their money on the wrong horses, and having lost see no reason to remain for the rest of the races."

"What a pity, but even had I lost, I would still wish to stay and see the 2000 Guineas," she said.

"Ah, but you have a special interest in the race. Most of those leaving care little about the horses. It is the gambling that interests them."

"Miss Regina!" Trudy called urgently, hurrying towards them, her face white and her eyes wide with fear. "Miss Regina, I can't find David nowhere! He's completely disappeared. All that's left of him is his cap lying on the ground."

Nine

Icy fingers of fear clutched at Regina's throat so she could not speak. She hardly noticed the duke's strong arm supporting her, and seemed incapable of doing anything but clinging helplessly to his sleeve. Her green eyes pleaded with him to find David.

"Don't panic, Regina. We shall find him. David has likely wandered off after that dog."

The duke summoned Tenby and Jeremy and set them both to searching at once. The redheaded boy had disappeared and Balfour realized the carriage next to theirs was one of those which had left earlier. Confusion reigned as race-goers left and others arrived, but they questioned everyone in sight. No one had seen a small, dark-haired boy, or a large black dog.

Regina wanted to search for David herself, but Balfour persuaded her to remain in the barouche on the off chance that her nephew might return on his own. Trudy sat beside her, offering what comfort she could.

Regina prayed she was wrong, but she was convinced David had not merely wandered off. He was an obedient child and he'd been told to remain near the carriage. She knew he would not have willingly left the area. And if David had been abducted, she was entirely to blame. She had been too immersed in her own pleasure to keep a watchful eye on him. Now he was probably in the hands of those brutish men. The thought made her ill.

A deafening roar went up from the crowd, but Regina could not bear to look at the horses. She'd been wrong to come—now she was being punished for it. It was frightfully warm now and the noise of the crowd beat at her head like hammers. She could not endure just sitting there. Climbing down, Regina ignored Trudy's protests and walked towards the rear of the carriage. She saw Jeremy approaching, his shoulders hunched dejectedly.

"I am sorry, Miss Regina. I found the dog the boys were playing with—sleeping over there in the scrub—but there's no sign of David."

She nodded. It was no more than she'd expected. She scanned the grounds for Balfour and spotted him talking to an older man a short distance away. From his gestures, she guessed he was describing David. The duke seemed to listen intently for a moment, asked something, then looked in her direction.

Regina's fingers tightened on her handkerchief, praying silently that they had news of David. She took an unconscious step towards the men, but stopped when she felt Jeremy's hand on her arm.

"Best wait here, Miss Regina. Some of the toffs won't talk as freely in front of a lady. The duke will handle it."

Tenby came up on the other side. "Seems impossible, but ain't no one I talked to who recollects the boy," he said. Seeing Regina's white face, he added quickly, "Of course, that's to be expected, Miss. They was all watching the races and wouldn't be paying no mind to a child running about."

Balfour came striding across the grass and Regina hurried to meet him. He took both her hands in his, wishing with all his heart that he had better news. "My dear, for David's sake, you are going to have to be strong. That man I was speaking with remembers seeing a boy playing with the dog out here. He did not see anyone approach him, but he does recall a gig that pulled up back here not long ago. He remarked on it because it looked like a farmer's rig, and it is unusual to see such a turn-out at Newmarket. He said it appeared just as the last race started, and when he looked again, the boy was gone . . . and so was the gig."

"I . . . I see," Regina said, struggling not to let the hysteria she felt overtake her. "What should we do now?"

Balfour put his arm about her shoulders, gently directing her steps towards the carriage. "We drive back to Whitechapel at once. If it is the same pair who tried to abduct David before, there's a slim chance we might spot them on the road. They must have been watching us, just waiting for the right opportunity. But that means they are likely putting up some place near Bury St. Edmunds. I'll start searching there."

Regina went with him, but she paused before entering the barouche, looking around at the crowds and the carriages still lining the course. There must have been above two hundred people still on the grounds. "But if . . . if he is still here? Hurt, perhaps?"

"Jeremy will stay and continue searching until the crowd leaves. If David is anywhere about, he'll find him. But I don't believe he's here, Regina, and there may be a message for us at the house."

Balfour was certain the same men who'd tried to kidnap David before were responsible for his disappearance now. What puzzled him was how the pair knew the boy would be at Newmarket. The duke could swear no one had followed them—it would have been almost impossible to miss seeing another carriage on the long stretch of road between Bury St. Edmunds and Newmarket. Since Regina had agreed to attend the races only the evening before, no one other than the immediate household and stable staff could know of her plans.

The notion that one of the servants had betrayed Regina seemed ludicrous to the duke. They were all devoted to her.

He could not imagine any of them doing anything that might harm either her or David. But he thought it possible that one of the staff had dropped a word to someone outside Whitechapel. Innocently, of course, and without realizing the danger.

He'd questioned every one of the stable lads on his return from Newmarket. The lads had all sworn they had not talked to a soul, or even seen anyone, from any of the neighboring farms. At the time, Balfour had believed them. Now, he wondered if they were perhaps afraid to admit to a slip of the tongue. They all knew David had been kidnapped. Would they be willing to own up to it, knowing they might be blamed?

Balfour visited the stables again, speaking to each of the lads. He stressed that it was understandable if someone had innocently spoken of Regina's plans. No one would be blamed for that, he promised. But the boys still swore they had not spoken to anyone. Frustrated, Balfour left the stables after promising a reward to anyone who might remember seeing a stranger on the grounds.

He entered the house from the kitchen door. Cook was there with Mrs. Milligan, the two of them sitting at the round table, worrying over their mistress and the boy. They rose at once, the housekeeper daring to ask if there was any news of David.

Balfour shook his head, thinking these two should be questioned as well. "No, I am sorry. Nothing yet. Is there any tea left in that pot?"

"Why, yes, Your Grace, of course, but it's probably cold. I could bring you a fresh cup in the drawing room. Miss Regina is sitting in there with her cousin."

"Brand me for a coward, but I prefer the kitchen. I am in no mood to deal with Miss Davenport," he replied, a wry grin easing the harshness of his mouth. "Will you ladies allow me to join you?"

Mrs. Milligan and Cook glanced at each other. One did

not sit down at the kitchen table with a duke. It simply was not done.

Balfour smiled sadly. "Unless, of course, I am in disgrace with you as well?"

"As if you could be, Your Grace!" Mrs. Milligan said, making up her mind and drawing out the chair opposite. "Don't you be paying no heed to Miss Davenport. That one just talks for the pleasure of hearing her own voice."

Cook studied the duke for a moment, then busied herself about the kitchen. She sat a dish in front of him. "What you need is something to eat, Your Grace."

"What's this?" he asked.

"You'd best be having somethin'," Cook muttered. "I saw you no more than pecked at your dinner, and it won't be doing Miss Regina no good if you was to take sick."

"Thank you. It looks delicious but I fear I don't have much of an appetite. Just a cup of tea will be fine."

"The kettle's on the boil, Your Grace, and you shall have a nice hot cuppa, but whilst you're waiting, you just try a bite of that. It's my own recipe for shortcake and the strawberries is fresh. Squire sent them over special this morning."

Balfour stared at the appetizing dish of cake before him, but he made no move to taste it. Very slowly, he turned to look up at Cook. Her good-natured face watched him from above a pair of beefy arms folded over her ample chest. "The Squire, you say? Where does he live?"

Mrs. Milligan answered him. "Squire Poole? Why, just a few miles west of here. He's a kindly man, Your Grace. Well, you can see for yourself how thoughtful he is, seeing to it that Miss Regina has fresh strawberries for breakfast. Not many gentlemen as would give it a second thought."

"No, indeed not. Did he bring them himself?" Balfour asked casually. He forced himself to take a bite, careful not to alarm the women.

"Not likely," Cook said, chortling. "Nine days out of ten, Squire is laid up. Suffers terrible bad with the gout, he does."

"I see. Who brought the berries then?"

Cook shrugged her massive shoulders. "You'll have to be asking Miss Davenport. She brung 'em in. All full of herself, she was, ordering me to fix 'em for Miss Regina, as if I needed to be told what to do with fresh berries."

"Will you please excuse me, ladies," the duke said, rising.

"But your cake—" Cook protested.

"What about your tea?" Mrs. Milligan echoed, but Balfour's broad shoulders were already disappearing through the door.

He found Regina and Cornelia still in the drawing room, and paused at the door to calm his temper. Regina sat, pale but composed, near the fireplace. Her cousin paced back and forth, her strident voice full of censure.

"Of course, if you had listened to me, none of this need have happened. I *knew* it was a poor idea to drag little David off to Newmarket. I had a premonition something dreadful would occur!"

"Cornelia, please," Regina said, brushing a hand across her aching brow. "We have been over this a dozen times. I accept full responsibility for David's disappearance."

"That's all very well for you to say, Regina, but you know I am the one Andrew will hold accountable. He trusted me to see to it that you behaved sensibly, and I have failed him. I do not know how I shall ever face him."

Regina closed her eyes, leaning her head back against the chair. Balfour judged it was time he interfered. He tapped on the door, then strode in without waiting for leave.

Regina sat up at once, hope brightening her eyes. "Have you learned something? Is there any news?"

"Perhaps," he said quietly, then turned to Cornelia. "Tell me, Miss Davenport, did you receive the strawberries Squire Poole sent over this morning?"

"Strawberries? Why on earth are you worried about berries at a time like this? Really, Your Grace, one would think—"

"Answer me, please."

For all that his voice was silky smooth, Cornelia heard the menace underlying the words. She shrugged. "I do not see the point, Your Grace, but yes, I received the strawberries." She looked at her cousin and gave a small, tinkling laugh. "I had no chance to mention it earlier, my dear, but the fresh berries you enjoyed at breakfast came from the Squire's greenhouse. *He* is such a thoughtful gentleman."

"Who delivered them?" the duke asked, spacing out each word deliberately.

"Why, some young man the Squire engaged. I am deeply sorry, Your Grace, but I did not think to exchange cards with him!"

"Did you exchange anything with him? The time of day, perhaps? Or did you perhaps mention that—"

Annoyed, Cornelia turned abruptly to her cousin, and protested, "Really, Regina, must I be subjected to an inquisition? If anyone is to blame for David's—"

"Answer him, Cornelia. It may be important," Regina interrupted. She sat up in her chair, her hands tightly pressed together.

Cornelia glanced from her to the duke. Their unrelenting stares made her uneasy. She nervously plucked at the fringe on her shawl. "Well, I fail to see what all the fuss is about. He was a very courteous young man, and yes, I suppose I spoke a few words with him. He mistook me for Regina," she said, and tittered.

"Think very carefully, Miss Davenport. Did you tell him that I was taking Regina and David to the races?"

"I may have, but what of it? Surely, there is nothing in that to alarm anyone." She appealed to Regina. "He was merely trying to put faces to names. You know how difficult it is when one removes to a new neighborhood."

Her cousin ignored her, looking hopefully at the duke. "Do you think there is some connection?"

"Very possibly. I've been wondering how they could have known David would be at Newmarket."

"How ridiculous," Cornelia scoffed. "Why, any one of the stable lads could have ridden into the village and mentioned it, which is far more likely—"

"Except none of them left the estate today," Balfour said, cutting her off. "I questioned them all. Now, what did this pleasant young man look like?"

"You may have questioned them, but I doubt they would admit the truth. Those stable lads are a worthless lot. They would as soon lie as look at you."

"Cornelia, please!" Regina said, losing all patience. "Do you not realize that David's life could depend on our finding him? If you do not tell His Grace what he wishes to know at once, I will . . . I will ask you to leave this house."

"Well! I was merely trying to save you a fruitless search. I know that young man could have nothing to do with this, but if you insist on wasting time with him rather than grilling the stable lads, I will not object further."

"Thank you, Miss Davenport. What did this man look like?"

"He was a little taller than I am, and had sandy hair and very nice blue eyes. I suppose one would describe him as slender. He was dressed neatly and cleanly, though not above his station. There was nothing the least suspicious about him, I do assure you."

"I do not doubt it," the duke said dryly and turned away from her. His eyes softened as he faced Regina. "Try not to worry. I will take Jeremy with me to lead the way to the Squire's. Will you try to rest while I am gone?"

She nodded and he had to be content with that, though he would have liked to have taken her in his arms to comfort her. He knew she blamed herself for the boy's abduction, and that spurred his determination to find David. That and his very real affection for the boy. "I will be back as quickly as I can," he promised.

Regina watched him leave. For the first time since they'd discovered David missing, she felt a surge of hope. But she could not rest as she'd promised Balfour. She walked aimlessly about the room, straightening a table scarf, then picked up one of David's discarded books. She held it in her hands as though that could bring him closer.

"Well, I am glad he has gone. So much commotion over nothing. That young man cannot have had a thing to do with David's disappearance. Had you spoken with him as I did, you would realize that. But I shall say no more on that head for I can see you are quite distressed. I shall ring for Mrs. Milligan to bring us fresh tea," Cornelia said as she pulled the bell rope. "And this time I hope she will see that it steeps properly. It is outside of enough that with all this worry over David, we cannot even have a decent cup of tea."

"Mrs. Milligan is concerned, too. Please do not say anything to her," Regina said quietly.

"Really, my dear, you must be firm with your servants or they will take shameless advantage of you. I have had more experience than you, Regina, and you must trust me to deal with her."

"No."

Cornelia looked around, surprise in her eyes. "I beg your pardon?"

"I said no. I will not have Mrs. Milligan or Cook or the maids upset any further. I know you mean well, Cousin, but I grow weary of having my household disrupted."

"Is this the gratitude I am given for working my fingers to the bone for you? All day, I have run myself ragged, tending to a hundred small matters so that you, my dear, need not be bothered. And if I said something to that young man this morning, in all innocence, I am sure I cannot be blamed, what with so much on my shoulders."

"No one is blaming you, Cornelia."

"I should hope not! Why, just look how His Grace foisted that pup on us and then went blithely off to the races. And who was left to care for it, I ask you? And I will tell you," she said, her voice rising. "I am the one who had to tend to it. Mr. Ramsey refused to leave it alone in the garden this morning, so we had to carry luncheon out to him. And then, when he heard about David, he insisted on bringing that animal to his room, where, of course, it immediately soiled the floor. But do I get so much as a thank you for my labour?"

Regina stared at her. If luncheon had been carried out to Mr. Ramsey, she was very certain it was not Cornelia who had done so. And if the puppy had soiled the floor, she felt equally certain that it was not her cousin who had cleaned up the mess.

Cornelia realized abruptly that her voice had risen unbecomingly, and she had all but screamed at her cousin. She used her handkerchief to dab at her eyes and attempted to make amends. "I am sorry, Regina, if I allowed my emotions to overcome me. This is a difficult time for all of us—"

"There is no need to apologize, Cornelia, but I think it would be best if you retired to your room for now, and when this is all over, perhaps you should consider leaving Whitechapel. I believe you would be much happier in a . . . in a different sort of house."

Her face drained of color, her bosom heaving, Cornelia snapped, "This is all Balfour's doing. He has persuaded you to get rid of me because I don't fawn all over him. I am warning you, Regina, you will regret this day. Your infatuation with that man has blinded you—"

"I think rather it has opened my eyes," Regina interrupted. "Please leave me, Cornelia, before we both say something we shall regret."

Regina sat still, her head resting against the back of the chair, and her eyes closed. She allowed the angry words of her cousin to wash over her. Not until silence permeated the room and she was certain she was alone, did she open her eyes again. Her cousin was wrong, quite wrong, she mused. She was not infatuated with the duke. It was far more serious than mere infatuation. She had fallen hopelessly, irretrievably, in love with that disreputable rake, the Duke of Balfour.

Regina was still sitting in the tall wing chair, unaware of the dusk and the chill that had crept into the room, when the duke returned. He immediately rang for Mrs. Milligan, built up the fire, and lit several candles. Then, kneeling before Regina's chair, he took her cold hands in his own.

"Courage, my little one," he said softly.

"I am not little," she managed to say, knowing he expected it of her. She summoned a tremulous smile.

"Ah, that's better," he approved as he stood. "Here's Mrs. Milligan with some tea. You shall drink some of this, Regina, and then I will tell you my news."

She looked up hopefully, and the housekeeper tarried after setting down her tray.

"The Squire employs no one answering to the description your cousin gave us. And further, the Squire did not think to send you strawberries this morning. But it seems a man did stop there, rather early, and asked to buy some for an ailing aunt who craved fresh fruit."

"Then it was all a ruse?"

He nodded. "I suppose they were growing impatient and merely hoped to learn something useful. It was just unfortunate that the fellow stumbled upon your cousin. I am certain now that she told him of our plans for the day."

"Well, at least we have a description of the man. Perhaps someone in the village will know more," Regina said, striving to maintain some small hope.

"Better than that," Balfour assured her. "The Squire's groom recognized the gig the fellow was driving, and from what he said, it matches the one mentioned at Newmarket. He is fairly certain it was hired from the Angel Hotel in Bury St. Edmunds. Do you know the place?"

"Yes, of course. It is right in the center of town and faces Angel Hill. You can hardly miss it. There are two massive white pillars in front and stone steps on either side leading up to the porch."

The duke nodded. "I believe I must have passed it when I took David into the village. All covered with ivy, is it?"

Regina nodded.

"Then drink your tea, my dear, and keep a candle burning. I think I shall pay the Angel Hotel a visit."

"You are not going now?" Regina asked, glancing at the clock on the mantel. It lacked but ten minutes to nine o'clock.

"I doubt they will still be there, but the sooner we pick up their trail, the better. I'll take Jeremy and Tenby with me."

She nodded absently before looking up at him again. The candlelight reflected the softness in her eyes. "Thank you, Your Grace, for all you are doing—"

"There's no need to thank me, Regina," he said. "But if you wish to please me, you will try to eat something while I am gone."

She shook her head. "I cannot. I have no heart for food. I need to do something . . . would you allow me to come with you?"

He hesitated but could not stand against the pleading look in her eyes. She might be better off waiting at home for news, but he knew how she felt. Waiting was the worst part. "If you wish," he said, smiling down at her. "I'll order Penrod saddled while you change."

The ride into Bury St. Edmunds had been swift, but Balfour no longer worried that Regina would be unable to keep up the pace. Her white stallion had shown his mettle, and despite the hard ride, was hardly lathered when they arrived at the Angel Hotel.

The duke dismounted, then helped Regina. He told the grooms, "Tenby, you and Jeremy take the horses round back and nose about the stables. Regina and I will go in the front and order something to eat."

"I really want nothing," Regina murmured as he escorted her up the steps.

"You will have to pretend to be hungry, my dear," Balfour whispered, opening the heavy door. "It is our best chance to learn something."

It had been a long day, and the duke had not rested at all. He was tired, disheveled, and badly in need of a shave. Nor was he accustomed to announcing himself. Tenby or Desmond normally went ahead and did that sort of thing, or else he was readily recognized at the inns he patronized. But he need not have worried. The portly innkeeper knew quality at a glance and bowed obsequiously low.

"Is it a room you be wishing, milord? I have a fine front chamber available that overlooks the street—"

"No, thank you. We merely wish for a bite to eat and a pint of ale."

The innkeeper hid his disappointment and led them to a private parlor. Thinking that perhaps if the gentleman partook of a heavy meal along with a couple of pints, he might decide to rest at the Angel, the man rattled off a long list of dishes, promising it could all be ready in a trice.

"Nothing so heavy," Balfour said, drawing out a chair for Regina. "A few sandwiches will suffice, a pint of ale for me, and a pot of tea for the lady."

The innkeeper withdrew. There was nothing much to be gained from the gentleman, and he sent his serving wench, Molly, back to wait on the table. A buxom lass with laughing dark eyes and long, black curls, and a figure that had enticed more men than she could count, Molly had induced more than one gentleman to remain at the Angel. She served the sandwiches, bending unnecessarily low before the duke, and asked in a seductive voice if there was anything else milord desired.

Balfour, hoping Regina would understand, drew out a gold sovereign and dropped it in the girl's low-cut bodice. "I am hoping to find some gentleman, sweetheart."

Molly darted a glance at Regina. Her hair was hidden beneath the dark hood cloak she wore, and she kept her head down, apparently immersed in stirring her tea. Molly decided the lady didn't look the sort to pleasure a gentleman and whispered boldly, "Are you sure 'tis a gentleman you want, milord, and not a comely lass what knows how to please a man?"

"Unfortunately, yes," he said, grinning at her. Another sovereign appeared magically between his fingers. "I seek a tall, sandy-haired fellow with blue eyes and a slender build. Have you seen such a one?"

With one hand, Molly pushed her long curls back, her eyes never leaving the coin. She knew the one he meant. The man had tumbled her the night before, and been more rough than she'd cared for. Miserly, too, she thought, recalling the few coins he'd left her. But this gentleman had plenty of the ready. She regarded him with teasing eyes, "And if I have, milord?"

"Tell me where I can find him," the duke replied softly, and allowed the coin to drop into her bodice.

"Now, what would a fine gentleman like you be wanting with the likes of Jack?"

Balfour grabbed her wrist, impatient with the game. "Where is he?"

"He's gone," she said quickly, suddenly scared of the icy anger she saw in milord's eyes. "He left this afternoon in a bit o' a hurry. Him and them two louts he travels with."

"Describe them, my dear," the duke suggested, still holding her wrist. "If your answer pleases me, you'll be amply rewarded."

Molly did her best, leaving no doubt that Jack's friends were the same pair that had attempted to kidnap David. The duke let her go and drew out several pound notes. "Thank you, my girl. You've been most helpful. Now, tell me, did you by any chance see a young boy with those men?"

Molly shook her head, stuffing the notes in the skirt pocket of her gown. "Not whilst they was here, but I never saw 'em leave. They was gone before I knew it today."

A head peered round the door, and Molly went to shoo the intruders away from the private parlor.

"Let those gentlemen in," the duke called, seeing Tenby's face. "Bring them each a pint, and then you may leave us."

No one said a word until Molly had left the room. Then Regina put her hood back and looked anxiously at Jeremy. "Did you find out anything? Has anyone seen David?"

"No, but I think the gig they used at Newmarket is here. The ostler said it had been hired for the day and was returned late this afternoon. That ties in well enough."

"And the man who hired it?" Balfour asked, then shook his head. "No, let me guess. He left with two others."

Jeremy nodded glumly and Tenby added, "No one took notice of which way they went, Your Grace, even though we spread a few coppers about."

"Drink up, then, and let us fetch the horses," Balfour said. He reached across the table to clasp Regina's hand. "Hold tight, my dear. They won't escape us for long."

She nodded, not trusting her voice, and sipped at the sweet tea.

"You want I should bring the horses round front, Your Grace?" Tenby asked when he'd drained his tankard.

"No—I want a look at the stables. My dear? Do you come with us? Jeremy can escort you outside if you prefer. I won't be long."

Regina rose, drawing the cloak about her and covering her fair curls again with the hood. "I would rather go with you, Your Grace."

He nodded and, after tossing a few coins on the table, motioned to Tenby to lead the way. They passed through the public room and Balfour was thankful it was nearly empty, but even so he moved so that he blocked a clear view of Regina. They emerged into a long hall, and went down a flight of steps to a door which led into the yard.

The night had grown cool, and Regina shivered in her thin cloak. She thought of David in his light coat. The moon passed behind a cloud and darkness descended over the yard. She breathed a silent prayer that David was somewhere safe and warm.

They crossed the yard and stepped into the stable. Regina recoiled at the odor and the droppings that littered the floor.

Balfour saw the way her shoulders trembled and the unconscious way she held a handkerchief to her nose. "Wait here, Regina. There's no need for you to step into this pigsty."

She nodded and stood just outside the door, her thoughts on David, wondering if he was horribly frightened. She bowed her head, intending to utter a prayer. At that moment, a breeze chased the cloud away from the moon, and in the pale light she saw a tiny mound of grain at her feet. Oblivious of the filth in the yard, she knelt, scooping up a few precious oats.

It could not be a coincidence, she thought, tears filling her eyes. David had left them a message.

"Regina!" The duke, leading their horses out, saw her kneeling in the yard and for one terrifying moment, thought something had happened to her. He dropped the reins of the horses and ran to her.

Regina looked up at him, tears streaking her cheeks, and proffered the scant handful of oats she'd found.

Ten

Regina, who only moments before had cast herself into the duke's arms with joyful abandon, withdrew from his embrace abruptly. A look of incredulous disbelief on her face, she stormed at him, "David is out there somewhere, alone with those brutal men, and you—you, Your Grace, want to go home and sleep? I cannot credit what I am hearing!"

"Not merely to sleep, Regina, but to wait until daylight. It would be foolish to try to—"

"You may go back to Whitechapel with Tenby, Your Grace. Jeremy and I will search for David without you," she interrupted, twisting away from his arms.

"Regina!" Balfour grabbed her shoulder and forced her around to face him. He held her firmly before him, looking down into green eyes that glistened with a mixture of tears and anger. Her hood had fallen back and her blond hair seemed edged with silver in the pale moonlight. It shimmered as she threw her head back and glared at him. "Little witch," he murmured, thinking how incredibly beautiful she looked.

He was unaware that some of the emotion he felt was reflected in his eyes, and in the tenderness of his voice. Regina turned away, but she stood still beneath his hands.

"Listen to me," he urged, then waited until she finally looked up at him. "Do you wish to destroy our only chance of finding David? If we go blundering about in the dark, the horses could trample and scatter any piles of grain David may have been able to leave. I know how anxious you are, and if you insist on continuing the search now, I will go with you—but for the boy's sake, I think we should wait until daylight."

Regina bowed her head. Balfour was right, of course. It was only that she was so worried.

"I agree with His Grace," Jeremy said quietly. "There are so many clouds, the chances are slim we would see the oats even were we to walk the horses."

"We shall wait then," Regina said, her voice laden with pain and the disappointment that was so much worse after the brief flare of hope.

"They will take good care no harm comes to David," the duke said softly, his hands moving slowly down her arms to gather her chilled hands in his. "They know Andrew would never deal if they could not prove his son was alive and well."

Regina nodded mutely and allowed him to help her mount Penrod. She knew waiting was the only sensible course, but even so she could not help straining her eyes for a glimpse of a tiny mound of grain as they left the yard. There was nothing. She held Penrod to a walk for nearly a mile, but the cloudy night finally defeated her, and she set her stallion to a canter.

The duke had allowed her to lead the way, knowing she needed to be certain that a search now was futile. When she increased the pace, he nudged his own horse and drew alongside of her. "It will be after midnight when we reach Whitechapel. A few hours' rest and we can set out again, and reach the Angel just at daybreak."

She knew he meant the words to be comforting, but fear gnawed at her heart. She spoke more sharply than she intended. "I only hope it does not rain before then. If the storm breaks—" she bit her lip, letting the words hang in the air.

"The gods will not allow it," he replied, praying that he was right in guessing the storm would hold off. It was cloudy, and the slight breeze held a hint of dampness, but a few stars were still visible.

Regina managed a smile. It did not quite reach her eyes and the corner of her mouth trembled, but it was a smile nevertheless.

Balfour saw it and felt immeasurably better. "See if that vaunted stallion of yours can move any faster than a snail. There might be some word at the house while we are tarrying here."

It was all the encouragement Regina needed. She gave Penrod his head and left the duke two lengths behind. The rush of wind in her hair and the smooth stride of the stallion soothed her. Her mind was numb, registering only the motion of the horse and the sound of hooves striking the road.

Balfour spurred his horse, but his mount was not of the black's caliber and he was still a length behind her when they reached the gates of Whitechapel. He saw the house the same instant as Regina, and they both reined in abruptly. Every window was brightly lit.

"Something has happened," Regina said, and felt the fear rising about her like the dust in the road. She swallowed hard. "Cornelia would never permit such a waste of candles . . ."

"Perhaps there is news," the duke said, but he misliked the look of the house. As the grooms halted beside them, he said, "I think the stables first, lads. Ben will know what is afoot."

Of one accord, they all dismounted and walked the horses quietly round to the stables. Here, too, lanterns were lit, illuminating the yard as though it were already daybreak. A travelling carriage stood in the yard, and they saw Ben talking to an ostler. He broke off and hurried towards them the instant he saw their approach.

"Oh, good heavens," Regina cried, recognizing the equipage. "It is my Aunt Sarah and Uncle John! Ben, how long have they been here?"

"They arrived just after you left, Miss Regina, and Lady Rochdale was in a rare taking to find you had ridden out."

"I had best go in at once. Will you cool Penrod down for me?" The groom nodded and she turned to Balfour. "My aunt is outspoken at the best of times, Your Grace, and she is undoubtedly near hysterics at the moment. I can only imagine what Cornelia has told her. If you would prefer to retire to your chambers—"

"And desert you? What a contemptible fellow you must think me." He handed his reins to Tenby and taking Regina's arm, turned their steps toward the house.

"My aunt is bound to create a scene. You cannot wish to subject yourself to that."

"Worse than the she-dragon, is she?"

"No . . . but I would rather a scold from Cornelia than my aunt. She—she says such cutting things."

He felt her fingers tremble on his arm and wondered just what sort of things Lady Rochdale had said in the past. He knew Regina to be courageous, and absolutely fearless astride a horse. But when it came to unpleasant confrontations, she faced them with an inward dread that seemed to drain the life from her. He knew her fear must be deep-rooted and suspected her aunt might be the cause of it. He answered her lightly, seeking to allay some of her worry, but the lines about his mouth hardened, and his eye took on an unpleasant glitter.

Mrs. Milligan had been on the lookout for them and she threw open the door. "Thank heavens you are returned, Miss Regina. Lady Rochdale and Sir John are here—"

"Regina?" A diminutive, perfectly turned-out lady stepped into the hall.

"Aunt Sarah! How . . . how delightful to see you, ma'am. I regret I was not here when you arrived. If I had known you were coming, I would not have—" she broke off, uncertain how to continue, and unnerved by her aunt's coldly appraising stare.

"Would not have indulged in a moonlight ride?" Sarah Rochdale finished for her niece. Her small dark eyes flashed upwards at Balfour.

"It was hardly an indulgence, Lady Rochdale," the duke said, stepping forward. "Miss Westfield and I were searching for her nephew. I assume Miss Davenport has told you of his disappearance?"

"Cornelia has told me any number of things, but I fail to see how an effective search can be conducted at this hour of night. And I will add, sir, that I find it reprehensible of you to use the boy's disappearance as an excuse to lure my niece into behavior unbecoming a lady. Sir John is waiting in the drawing room for an accounting of your conduct. From both of you," she added, her dark eyes swinging round to Regina. "You will oblige me by putting off your cloak and tidying your hair before presenting yourself to your uncle."

She was gone before either could protest, and Regina looked helplessly at Balfour. "I did warn you, Your Grace."

He smiled, and could not resist smoothing one of her curls back from her brow. "You do look rather disheveled, my dear. Come, let us both go make ourselves presentable, and then we shall face the ogress in her den."

Regina, anxious to placate her aunt as much as possible, hurriedly changed and arrived in the drawing room before the duke. She had tried to rehearse what she would say while changing her riding skirt for a suitable gown, and combing the tangles from her hair. But no sooner did she step over the threshold then her mind went blank.

Her uncle rose at once, holding out his arms in welcome. "Regina, child, come give your old uncle a kiss. It seems an age since I saw you last, but you are still just as pretty as ever."

"Thank you, Uncle John," she said and kissed his leathery cheek before allowing herself to be enfolded in his embrace.

He smelled a little of brandy, cigars, and the stable, an oddly comforting aroma, she thought, closing her eyes briefly. But she could not stay in the shelter of his arms forever, and reluctantly stepped back.

"You look much improved, Regina," her aunt conceded a moment later, dutifully accepting the kiss her niece dropped on her brow. There was something subtly different about Regina, she thought, and it was not merely that for once her niece carried her height well.

"I am sorry you arrived at such an inopportune time, Aunt Sarah, but I know Cornelia has taken good care of you."

Her cousin sniffed. "Insofar as I was able, although being obliged to inform our aunt that you had disappeared in the middle of the night with that man, and without a word to me—"

"You were resting, Cornelia," Regina interrupted, her low voice holding an unexpected note of firmness. "I did not wish to disturb you further, but Mrs. Milligan knew where I had gone."

"As though I would question the housekeeper over your whereabouts! You may not care about the scandal you bring to this family, but I do. I would never gossip with the servants regarding your behavior, but heaven knows they are probably speaking of little else."

"I fear Cornelia is correct," Sarah said before Regina could utter a retort. "Your conduct certainly leaves much to be desired. However laudable your concern for David may be, it hardly constitutes a reason for riding off in the middle of the night with the Duke of Balfour. Had he chosen to search for the boy while you remained here, I would have found his actions commendable—if somewhat difficult to believe. But to use David to entice you into a moonlight ride goes beyond the pale. Had it been any other gentleman, your uncle would no doubt speak to him and he would do the honorable thing, but that you chose to ride out in the com-

pany of a noted libertine, a rake, a . . . a womanizer like
Balfour—"

"Did someone mention my name?" the duke asked, strolling into the room as casually as though he were presenting
himself for afternoon tea, and the clock was not chiming one
o'clock in the morning.

Regina not only admired his aplomb, but was near dazzled
by the splendor of his attire. Nor was it lost on her family.
Even Cornelia seemed a little awed by the duke at his most
regal.

"Will you present me, my dear?" Balfour drawled.

Something of his air of utter confidence infected Regina
and she managed a credible smile. "Your Grace, may I present my aunt, Lady Rochdale, and my uncle, Sir John
Rochdale?"

"Charmed, my lady," he said, executing a small bow in
Sarah's direction. He then extended a hand to Sir John, who
had heaved his considerable bulk out of the chair. "A pleasure to meet you, sir. Your niece has mentioned you frequently, and told me how highly she thinks of your stable."

"Well, I do have quite a nice little—"

"John, need I remind you that this is hardly the time to
be discussing stables," Sarah interrupted.

"Yes, dear, of course, you are right," her husband muttered, looking extremely uncomfortable. He turned to the
duke with an air of apology. "Your Grace, I must ask you
for an accounting of your conduct. You must comprehend
that I stand in place of a father to Regina, and naturally we
are concerned that her good name not be tarnished."

"Quite," Balfour replied. "I had intended to—"

"What nonsense is this?" Regina broke in furiously. She
faced her uncle, eyes blazing. "His Grace's conduct has been
above reproach! He has done nothing to warrant an inquisition from you or anyone else, and if he does not resent it, I
very much do."

"There, you see," Cornelia said with a titter. She leaned

towards her aunt, but her words carried clearly. "She is so infatuated with the man that she has lost all sense of propriety."

"Who are you to speak of propriety?" Regina demanded, whirling around to face her cousin. "You are a malicious cat, Cornelia Davenport. You have sought to make trouble in this house from the first, and when my aunt and uncle leave I hope you have the good sense to go with them, because you are no longer welcome here."

"Regina!" her aunt cried, truly appalled by such an outburst.

Cornelia rose, her thin bosom heaving. "I will leave, and gladly, so you may be alone with your precious duke. But do not come crying to me when he has ruined you, and he will, mark my words." She gathered her skirts about her and made for the door.

Balfour opened it for her with a flourish. "Good evening, Miss Davenport. I do so hope we will never meet again." He shut the door quietly and turned to Sir John. "Now, sir, as I was saying, I had intended to call on you, but your visit is fortuitous. Might I speak with you in private?"

"Certainly not," Sarah said. She quickly rose and moved to stand between her husband and the duke. "I believe you have done sufficient damage to this family, Your Grace. It was shocking enough that you remained here without reason, taking advantage of my niece's innocence, but now you have succeeded in coming between two girls who were reared as closely as sisters, and who share the same blood ties. Never would I have thought to see them behave so to each other, and I hold you fully to blame. I will not allow anyone in this family to have any further association with you, and I will thank you to take your leave at once."

"Aunt Sarah, you do not understand—"

"I understand all too well, Regina. You were reared strictly, perhaps overly so, and this is your first encounter with a gentleman who has a certain measure of address. It must have been relatively easy for him to influence you to such a degree that you forgot all bounds of propriety and correct behavior. I should have come when Cornelia first wrote me, but I discounted half of what she said. However, this unseemly display this evening has convinced me that, for once, your cousin did not exaggerate. For you, there is some small excuse. For him, there is none. He has taken advantage of your innocence and your lack of protection here to—"

"No! That is not true," Regina cried, with a distraught look at Balfour.

He stood perfectly still. There was no expression in the pale blue eyes, and his lips made a mockery of his smile. With elaborate care, he produced a snuff box and deftly removed a pinch.

"Do not listen to her," Regina pleaded, sensing the disillusionment behind the arrogant facade. "She doesn't know, she doesn't understand! Your Grace, please . . ." She would have gone to him save her aunt held her firmly by the arm.

He lifted his brows slightly, but there was no other trace of emotion on his handsome face. No trace at all of the man she had come to know. In desperation, she cried, "You cannot have forgotten David!"

"Regina, please," her aunt scolded, shocked at such an unseemly display. "Try not to make more of a fool of yourself than you have already done. This interlude with the duke is over. Done with and best forgotten. Your uncle will do whatever needs to be done to find David."

Balfour spoke at last. He addressed them generally, but his eyes remained on Regina. "I shall remove at once to the Angel Hotel. Miss Westfield, I am ever your servant." He nodded curtly to Sir John, and then he was gone.

Regina stared at the door, tears streaking her cheeks. She barely felt her aunt drawing her down to the sofa, or the pair of comforting arms about her as her body shook with racking sobs.

Sarah soothed her, murmuring foolish, consoling words

and patting her niece on the back until her sobs lessened. When Regina sat up at last, feeling drained and exhausted, her aunt tenderly wiped her tears away from her cheeks, and held tightly to her hand.

"You must listen to me, my dear. You are my sister's child, and I love you as though you were my own. You think I have hurt you dreadfully tonight, but that is nothing compared to what you might have endured had I not interfered."

Regina tried to speak but Sarah would not allow her.

"Hush, child and pay heed. I have been about in this world, and I know whereof I speak. The Duke of Balfour is not a fit person for you to know. Were he any kind of gentleman, he would not have remained in this house. If word gets about, your reputation will be all but ruined."

"I don't care what people think—"

"I am, sadly, aware of that, but do try to consider the rest of us," her aunt interrupted sharply. "Would you see the career Andrew has worked so diligently for, ruined? Even living retired as you do, which I always felt to be a mistake, you must know of Balfour's reputation. He is not received in polite circles. His scandalous conduct has closed all but the most liberal doors to him. What do you suppose Andrew will do if he hears the duke has run tame in your home for over a month? Or that you visited Newmarket with him, and went for moonlight rides?"

"It was not a moonlight ride. We were searching for David."

"So you have said, my dear, but I am afraid others would fail to see the distinction. Andrew would have one of two choices. He could insist Balfour offer for you, or he could call him out. I doubt either choice would be acceptable."

Regina stared at her. "Andrew would not . . ."

"Do not doubt it. He will be forced to do so unless I can hush this affair up," Sarah said. "If it were any other man but Balfour! Even were Andrew able to persuade him to offer for you, he would make you miserable, child. Oh, I know you think not. From what Cornelia wrote, you have enjoyed a lovely idyll here this past month, but how long do you think a man like Balfour would be content with such a life? It is a novelty now, but he is used to a very different sort of life. He is accustomed to gambling until all hours, to heavy drinking and . . ." she paused, wondering how to put such a matter delicately. "It pains me to say this, but I must be frank. I have heard he . . . he consorts with all manner of ballerinas and actresses. They are under his protection, Regina, if you take my meaning."

"If you are referring to his keeping a mistress, I know precisely what you mean," Regina said, daring to look her aunt straight in the eyes. "What he has done in the past does not matter."

"No? Are you also aware of the number of duels he has fought? Did you know he fled London after his last duel? He wounded some poor man foolish enough to call him out. It is said the gentleman has lost the use of his arm, and public opinion is much against your fine duke."

Regina hung her head, knowing there was nothing more she could say. There were no words that would convince her aunt that the man Regina had come to know was vastly different than the rogue she described.

Sarah patted her hand and then urged her to go up to bed. "Come along, Regina. I will have your maid fix you a potion to help you sleep. In the morning, when we are both thinking clearly, we can discuss all this. I know you will behave sensibly."

Regina lay in her bed waiting. The house at last settled into the silence of the night. Aunt Sarah would think she was sleeping. The potion Trudy had brought her was strong enough to put even Uncle John out for the night, but Regina had tossed it out the window. She had no intention of sleeping. Balfour had said he was removing to the Angel, and she knew with a certainty which defied logic, that could only mean he intended to continue searching for David. He was not heartless, no matter what her aunt thought.

David. The poor little boy was out there in the night somewhere, undoubtedly frightened, while his family sat in a warm drawing room debating propriety! And while they slept comfortably in their beds, the man her aunt had castigated so blackly would be out searching for him. Well, he would not be alone, Regina thought, as her clock chimed three. She climbed out of bed and made her way stealthily to the wardrobe.

Lighting a candle, she rummaged in the wardrobe for her other riding habit. She dressed as quickly as she could, but her fingers were half-numb with nervousness and there was no way she could reach all the buttons that ran down the back of her dress. It would have to do, she thought, leaving several undone. Her riding coat would cover them. Regina twisted her long hair into a braid, pinned it securely to the top of her head, and then covered it with her hat, unaware that its jaunty feather tilted at a rakish angle.

She lifted up her boots, holding them securely in her arms as she glanced about the room. It had an odd, lonely look to it, as though she had already left. The rumpled bed and pillow still held the indentation where she had laid her head. She'd left her night clothes piled in an untidy heap on the floor, and her embroidered slippers seemed somehow out of place in front of the wardrobe. Regina knew a moment's hesitation. Once she left this room, her life would never be the same again. *But if you don't go, you will never see him again.*

The thought came unbidden, but Regina knew it to be true. She'd seen the look in Balfour's eyes while he was listening to her aunt. He had not said a word in his own defense, perhaps because he thought he was as black as everyone painted him. But she knew better, and somehow she must convince him, too. And she had to do it at once—before he took some stupid notion in his head that she would be better off without him. It was just the sort of thing a man like Balfour would think.

Without a whisper of regret, Regina blew out the candle and inched the door slowly open. She stood in the hall for a moment, letting her eyes adjust to the dark, and listening to the sounds of the night. The house seemed wrapped in an eerie silence as she stood in the pitch darkness. Regina wondered if she might risk a candle.

A sudden noise startled her and set her pulse racing. She clutched her boots close to her chest and backed against the wall. It was another moment or two before she realized the noise was only the clock in the drawing room chiming the quarter hour.

Feeling foolishly frightened, Regina took a deep breath and edged along the wall until she reached the top of the curving stairs that led down to the center hall. The stairs were easier. With the banister to guide her, she hurried down the steps without mishap. She still didn't dare to pull on her boots. She had to cross the hall and make her way through the kitchen, then out through the garden.

The kitchen door squeaked when Regina pushed it open. She paused, holding her breath, but no one cried out. Gathering her courage, she stepped boldly into the kitchen. The pale moonlight streaming in the large windows illuminated the empty room, now neatly tidied for the night. Regina crept softly across the cold, stone floor and fumbled with the latch on the garden door. She would have to leave it off the latch, but it was nearly morning. Mrs. Milligan would be about in another hour or so. She closed the door quietly behind her and stood breathing in the cool night air.

Easy now to slip into her boots and make her way down the graveled drive to the stables. As she drew near, she saw a dim light coming from the tiny windows set high above the stalls. Jeremy and Ben! Of course they would be up and getting ready to leave. They knew Balfour's plan and would not leave him to search alone. The huge door leading into the stables was partially open and Regina slipped inside.

"Jeremy?" she called softly.

His dark head appeared over the half-door to one of the stalls. "I'm just saddling up Penrod for you, Miss Regina."

She smiled for the first time in what seemed like days. "Were you so certain I would come, then?"

"Me and Ben laid a bet on," he replied, grinning. "After the way the duke stormed out of here—well, I was pretty sure you would be wanting to come with us. His Grace said he'll be wanting to leave at four, and we can meet him round back of the Angel."

Regina nodded and then asked pensively, "Did he . . . did he leave a message for me?"

"No," Jeremy said reluctantly, noting the way her smile faded and the light died from her eyes. "But he hardly had time, Miss. He just said he'd been booted out, and the sooner he was away from here, the better for everyone."

"I see," she said, turning away to hide the glimmer of tears she felt on her lashes.

"I knew it wasn't none of your doing, and that it must have been that aunt of yours, but when I said so, he just laughed, hard like. Said he'd been asked to leave better places and likely would be again." Jeremy shook his head. "I'll tell you this, Miss Regina, I ain't never heard a man sound so . . . so bitter."

"Oh, lord! Jeremy, I must talk to him."

"Then let's be on our way. I got Commander saddled in his stall. If you walk Penrod out, I'll go fetch him. Ben's going to stay here to keep an eye on things."

Regina nodded and moved deftly into the stall. Her mind was on a thousand other things, but she automatically soothed and talked to her horse, her sure hands moving over him reassuringly before leading him out. She used the mounting block in the yard to boost herself up, and was already turning toward the gate when Jeremy rode out.

"You ready, Miss Regina? I'd like to be well away from here before that aunt of yours wakes. She—what the devil is that?"

Regina had already turned at the sound of a carriage pulling into the yard. Her heart raced. Had Balfour come back to meet her? Her eyes strained against the darkness, but it was another moment before she could make out the large travelling carriage. Hope died within her. Andrew had come home.

Jeremy was close enough to hear her low moan and saw the stricken look on her face. "We could just ride on out, if you want—"

"I cannot," Regina said. "It is my brother and he would only follow. That would be far worse. Jeremy, go on without me. Tell Balfour . . . tell him I must speak with him. Hurry."

Jeremy nodded and urged his horse to a trot. He circled round the travelling chaise as the doors opened. He heard someone shout, but he didn't look back until he was on the rise above the house. He could just make out Miss Regina standing beside her stallion. He couldn't be sure, but he thought she was looking in his direction. He waved once, then turned Commander towards town.

Regina lifted her hand in answer to Jeremy's salute, and wished with all her heart that she was riding off with him. Oh, God, she prayed silently, please let them all return here safely, and with David well and happy in their midst. She turned then and called for Ben. When his startled face appeared in the stable door, she ordered him to take Penrod in and unsaddle him.

"Regina!" her brother cried incredulously as he stepped down from his carriage. "What is the meaning of this? Why are you dressed for riding at this hour? Is it David?"

"It is true, then," Beth said, standing on the steps of the carriage. "They have abducted my son."

Regina crossed the yard, her eyes on her sister-in-law. Even in the moonlight, Beth looked ill—as though she had covered her face with rice powder. Regina reached up a hand and urged her down the steps, then hugged her warmly. It was like embracing one of Madame Salmon's wax mannequins, cold and lifeless.

"How long . . . how long has he been missing?" Beth asked, drawing back.

The pain reflected in her dark eyes tore at Regina's heart. She glanced helplessly at her brother. He, too, was showing the strain, and she was thankful that there was at least a glimmer of hope to offer them. "They took him yesterday afternoon. I had hoped we could—"

"Yesterday?" Andrew interrupted. "They sent me word a fortnight ago! I didn't believe them at first, but they sent the cross I gave David. The one he always wears . . ."

"It was not the first attempt," Regina said, realizing at once what must have happened. "Come inside, both of you. There is so much to tell you, and you look near exhausted. Did you drive all night?"

Andy nodded. "We were in France when the message came. We left at once, but then we had to cool our heels in Calais until the weather cleared. There were fearsome storms for a week, and no ship willing to set sail."

"The waiting was terrible," Beth added. "Not knowing what was happening, or even if it was true. I kept praying it was all some sort of ghastly mistake. But it is true and—" her voice broke on the words, and she turned her face away as tears streamed down her cheeks.

Regina hugged her. "Courage, darling. David is such a clever boy. He left a trail of sorts for us. That is where I was going with Jeremy when you arrived. By the time we get you settled, he may be back with David safe and sound."

"Good lord, Regina, I wish you had told me! I would have ridden with your man," Andrew said, trailing the women into the house.

"You are exhausted, Andy," she said over her shoulder as she led the way to the drawing room. "Anyone could see that, and there was no time to lose. We were only waiting for first light."

"We? Surely, you were not intending to ride off in the middle of the night with your trainer?"

A tap on the door saved Regina from answering at once. Mrs. Milligan stepped in, caring a large silver tea tray. "Pardon me for intruding, Miss Regina, but I heard the commotion in the yard. I took the liberty of putting the kettle on, and Trudy is preparing the Green Room for Sir Andrew and Lady Westfield. I told his man to take their things up." She glanced at Beth. "It should be ready by the time you drink a cup of tea, my lady."

"Bless you," Beth murmured, sinking wearily into the large wing chair.

Regina watched the housekeeper fuss over her sister-in-law, while she tried to think of a diplomatic way to tell her brother about the Duke of Balfour. Andrew was standing behind his wife's chair, and Regina thought she had never seen him look so spent. New lines were etched about his fine eyes, and his shoulders sagged beneath the weight of his worries. He glanced up to meet her gaze as the housekeeper withdrew.

"You must be wishing me at the devil, Gina," he said, using his old childhood name for her. "I was insane to leave David here with you. A woman alone—but I swear I never thought there was any real danger. When we get David back," he said, his hand gripping his wife's shoulder, "I'll make it up to you somehow."

"Do not be foolish, Andy."

"No, it was stupid of me. I not only placed my son in danger, but you as well. And you *were* planning to ride off in search of him, weren't you? It is well I arrived when I did. This is no game, Regina. I appreciate that you were willing to put yourself at risk for David's sake, but to go chasing off after those men in the middle of the night—"

"More like, it was to meet the Duke of Balfour," Cornelia

said, stepping into the room. She looked at Regina with spiteful eyes, her thin lips pursed into a hateful grimace. "Go ahead, Cousin. Tell Andrew how you were out half the night with the duke, and were creeping out of the house to run to him again. Tell him how you were too busy amusing yourself at the races with Balfour to pay any attention to David. Tell him how the boy was abducted from beneath your nose!"

Eleven

Were it not all so deadly serious, Regina would have laughed at the ludicrous expression on her brother's face.

"Balfour! What the devil does he have to say to anything? Cornelia, have you been drinking?"

"Certainly not!" she said, drawing herself up to her full height. "I wrote you several letters about this, knowing full well you would not approve of having a man of Balfour's character residing in your sister's house. Of course I first tried to persuade Regina to behave sensibly, but she is so infatuated with the duke, one can no longer reason with her."

"I cannot believe what I am hearing," Andrew said, looking incredulously from his sister to his cousin. He so far forgot himself as to sink into the deep sofa cushions while the ladies were still standing.

Regina turned her back on Cornelia, and quickly sat down beside Andrew, taking his hand in her own. "You must listen to me, Andy. We owe the duke an extraordinary debt of gratitude. He—"

"Regina, are you telling me there is some truth in what Cornelia said? Was Balfour actually staying at Whitechapel?"

"Oh, you grossly understate the matter," Cornelia broke in with a brittle laugh. "Not only was he staying here, but he took it upon himself to practically run the house. I believe he has bribed the servants, the way they cater to him. A pity you did not arrive sooner, Andrew, you would have met him.

Naturally, Aunt Sarah threw him out as soon as she arrived, but dear, sweet Regina was all prepared to go chasing after him."

Beth stood up abruptly and before Cornelia realized what she was about, she had crossed the room and taken her cousin by the arm. "I believe we should allow Andrew a few moments in privacy with his sister. Come upstairs with me and tell me what has been happening," she said persuasively, and with soft pressure, urged the older woman towards the door.

Cornelia moved reluctantly and opened her mouth to protest. One look at Andrew's stony face, however, convinced her that she would be wise to withdraw. She turned to Beth, her thin lips forming a pout, and her voice a muted whine. "No one realizes the terrible burden it has been on me. I have been at a loss to know . . ."

Regina sat on the sofa, her head bowed. She barely heard Cornelia's voice as the door shut behind her. Her cousin had made Balfour's presence in the house sound scandalous. There was little hope now of convincing Andy that the duke was not the rogue he imagined.

Andrew released her hand and stood up. He drew in a deep breath and, struggling to contain his anger, paced the narrow aisle between the sofa and the fireplace. He turned after several minutes and faced Regina, lifting his hands out in a gesture of helplessness. "You know how I feel about the Duke of Balfour. He is the embodiment of all that ails England. Regina, how could you entertain such a man?"

"I had little choice," she said, lifting her head. "The gentleman you speak so disparagingly of was wounded while saving David from the kidnappers. Did Cornelia not write you about that?"

"Whatever letters she wrote are no doubt still in the dispatch bag," he said irritably. "I never received them. You know I told you there would be no way to reach me directly."

"Perhaps it is just as well. Cornelia disliked the duke on sight and I am certain her letters are horribly biased, but what would you have had me do, Andrew? Order him out of the house? Refuse to summon a doctor for him?"

Her words brought her brother up short, and he shook his head as if trying to clear his thoughts. "Lord, I feel as though I have stepped into a lunatic asylum. My son is abducted, my cousin is raving mad, and my sister has been entertaining a libertine! Is it too much to enquire what Balfour was doing here? I know you were never acquainted with him."

Regina looked down at her hands, remembering that spring morning when Balfour had ridden so cavalierly up the drive. It seemed so long ago. When she spoke, her voice held the soft, gentle tones of one recalling a nostalgic moment. "We met by pure chance. His carriage overturned not far from here and the duke recalled seeing the house. He rode back to seek assistance. I was just taking Penrod out for a ride and met him in the drive." Regina paused and her lips curved into a smile. "I fear I mistook him for a tutor and sent him up to the house to await my return."

"You thought Balfour a tutor? Good God, Regina, one has only to look at the man to see him for what he is!"

"Oh, I admit I did think him rather arrogant, but he had driven all night through a storm and then been overturned. He did not look precisely ducal at the time—"

"Ducal?" Her brother snorted and threw up his hands. "He has never looked anything but evil incarnate. I know you have been sheltered, Regina, but I would have thought even you would recognize the Spawn of Satan. No, don't frown at me. That is what they call him in London, and I can assure you the epitaph is well deserved."

Regina rose and started for the door.

"Where are you going?" Andrew demanded, coming after her. He grabbed her arm. "We have not finished this discussion!"

Regina whirled about to face him, her eyes flashing with anger. "What discussion? You do not wish to hear what happened. All you want is to cast aspersions on the man who saved David's life. The man who is even now out trying to rescue your son. Well, speak to Cornelia then! She is as closed-minded as you, and will agree with all your petty, narrow-minded judgments of a man you know nothing about."

It was as though she had slapped him. Andrew stared at her, anger coursing through him. The pulse beside his eye throbbed and his voice shook. "Cornelia was right. You are obviously infatuated with Balfour! Did he make love to you? Tell me the truth, Regina. If he had the unmitigated gall to touch you, I swear he will pay for it!"

Regina was stunned. This man was her older brother, and though they had been apart a great deal, he was the closest member of her family. Andrew was the one person she had loved through all the years. Now, with his face contorted by hate and rage, he seemed a stranger. She was tired, more tired than she could ever remember being and she turned away, too weary to argue further.

Andrew seized her arm. "Answer me, Regina."

Tears filled her eyes. "No, Andrew, he did not make love to me, though in truth I would not have resisted had he tried, but Balfour was too much the gentleman. Does that satisfy you?"

He checked the retort on his lips, cursing silently, as Regina covered her face with her hands and sobbed softly.

Neither had heard Beth quietly open the door. Regina was not aware of her presence until she felt her sister-in-law's arm about her waist and her gentle voice urging her to be seated.

Andrew opened his mouth to speak but his wife gave him a look of such anger that he subsided and went instead to the table to pour himself a much needed cup of tea.

Beth murmured soothingly to Regina, allowing her to cry for several minutes. Then she spoke to her husband. "I believe you owe your sister an apology, Andrew. You have been immersed with scandals of the court for so long, you forget to whom you speak."

"You do not understand, Beth—"

"I understand all too well," she interrupted, her voice icy for all its softness. "I did not protest when you worked so diligently to prove that poor little boy, William Austin, was Princess Caroline's illegitimate son, though my heart ached for both of them. Nor did I object when the Prince Regent insisted you follow the Princess abroad and obtain evidence of misconduct against her, though his own conduct is scarcely above reproach, and I found such actions reprehensible. Still, I did not utter one word of protest, not even when the Whigs threatened you and put our only son in danger. I understand these are affairs of state and such actions must be taken for the welfare of England, but I will not stand quietly aside if association with such people can turn you into the sort of man who could speak as you did to your sister."

"That's all very well, my dear, but did you not also hear what my sister answered?" he said, much on the defensive, for Beth rarely criticized him.

"I did, and so should I answer had you dared put such a question to me!"

Andrew, tasting the hot tea, very nearly choked on it, and the tea splashed over his hand burning his fingers. He grabbed up a napkin and wrapped it round his fingers while he glared at his wife.

Regina glanced up and gave her sister-in-law a watery smile. "Thank you," she said and dabbed at her eyes with the lace handkerchief Beth provided.

"You must forgive your brother, my dear. This business is driving us near mad and for all he does not show it at the moment, Andrew has been quite frantic with worry over David. Now, you must tell us what happened. I could not get any sense out of Cornelia, save that some men followed you to Newmarket and . . . abducted David during one of the races."

Beth's calm manner helped to restore Regina's composure, and keeping a tight hold of her sister-in-law's hand, she managed to relate what had occurred. Andrew interrupted only twice, once when Regina mentioned their visit to the Angel Hotel the evening before, and again when she told them of their plans to begin the search anew at daylight.

"So you were planning to ride out to meet Balfour when we arrived this morning?" he asked, but under his wife's warning glance, kept his voice reasonably calm.

"I was. I wished to help search for David, but I also intended to offer my apologies to Balfour. Am I the only one in this family who can see the debt of gratitude we owe him?"

"Do we?" Andrew asked as he rose and stretched his stiff limbs. "It seems to me deuced odd that Balfour should show up here at such a time. And why did he remain? Yes, I know you told me his carriage had to be repaired, but surely that was done long since?"

Regina's taletell blush betrayed her, but she answered steadily enough, "I believe he was concerned about David. The duke has become very fond of him."

"Ha! I wish I may live to see it. Balfour cares for no one but himself, and if he pretended to care about my son, you may be sure it was for reasons of his own."

"You were not here, Andrew. You did not see him with David. Even Cornelia will tell you that they were together almost every afternoon and evening. Balfour knows a good deal about mythology, and he was willing to answer all of David's questions. I will wager he spent more time with your son this past month than you have all year, and I must warn you—David worships him."

"It appears he is not the only one," Andrew replied, annoyed at her implied criticism. "But as I said, if the duke went out of his way to befriend David, I am sure he had his own reasons. It occurs to me that Balfour is well acquainted with Princess Caroline. He was a frequent visitor when she resided at Montagu House, and it could prove most beneficial to him to protect her. She will wield a great deal of power if she becomes Queen. It could even be that Balfour is behind David's abduction."

Beth heard Regina's gasp and intervened quickly. "Surely, Andrew, you are the one who told me that the duke has no political leanings. That he could not be bothered to take a stand on any of the issues."

"The very idea is absurd," Regina added. "If Balfour was behind the attempt, then why did he foil the kidnappers the first time they tried to take David? Instead, he took a bullet in his shoulder for his trouble—and do not forget he was with me at Newmarket when David was actually taken."

"I am hardly likely to forget that, my dear sister, but obviously he would have had accomplices."

The discussion would have deteriorated into another argument but the door opened again, and all three turned expectantly towards it. Regina was the first to see the puppy's head peering round the door, and she smiled with relief. She had feared Aunt Sarah had risen and would join forces with Andrew against her.

The pup, sure of its welcome, trotted happily in and made directly for Andrew's chair. After sniffing his boots for a moment, the small collie sat at his feet, wagging his tail, his bright eyes looking up hopefully.

"When did you acquire a dog, Regina?" Andrew asked, and unable to resist its appeal, knelt to scratch the animal's head.

The tension in the room eased perceptibly. The argument was far from over, but at least Andrew was willing to set it aside for the moment. Regina gave him a small smile. "In truth, he belongs to you—at least in a manner of speaking."

"What? Get down, you ill-mannered cur," he ordered with

mock ferociousness as the pup, in a fever of excited ecstasy, tried to lick his face.

"The duke bought him as a replacement for poor Mr. Ramsey's dog, but the old man doesn't seem to want him, and David has been caring for it. He's a good pup, Andy, but as you may have noticed, somewhat in need of training."

"David wants a dog?" he asked, surprised. His son had never shown any interest in anything beyond his books. Andrew caressed the pup's silky ears, a shadow of remorse flickering in his eyes. "Why did he never tell me?"

Neither Regina nor Beth would answer him. The obvious truth was that he had not given his son the opportunity, and the thought loomed in all their minds that David might never have the chance again.

Andrew kept his head down and when he spoke, his voice was suspiciously hoarse. "Where is Ramsey now?"

"He is staying here," Regina said. "But when I looked in on him earlier, he told me he wishes to return to his cottage tomorrow. Dr. Lyons said he is well enough, but he was beaten so brutally, I fear he should not be alone."

"Remind me then, and I shall have a word with him. I feel partially responsible, since it was David those thugs were after."

"Thank you. I am certain he will appreciate that. I don't know what else to do for him."

"Perhaps we should take Mr. Ramsey home with us," Beth suggested in her quiet way. "The memories here may be too painful for him. Andrew, we have that cottage vacant near the kennels, and you keep saying it should not be left untenanted."

"I'll speak to the old man," he agreed as he stood up and brushed off his hands. "Well, it appears I have acquired a dog and a new tenant. Have you any other surprises in store for me, Gina?"

"Only one. You owe me fifty pounds for a colt. David has named it Boreas and he wishes to break it himself."

Andrew's eyes grew round. "You are jesting. Why, David cannot even ride. He has always feared horses."

"He rides very well now and will improve considerably, given time," Regina said. She could not resist adding, "Balfour has been teaching him." She rose before her brother could reply and turned to Beth. "Would you like to rest for a while? I know you must be exhausted."

"No, thank you, dearest, but I cannot. Not if there might be news of David soon."

Regina felt a surge of admiration for her tiny sister-in-law. She knew Beth must be near frantic with worry over David, but she had set aside her own feelings to try to keep peace in the family. How maddening it must have been for Beth to listen to their petty bickering while her son was missing.

Full of remorse, Regina did not argue. She leaned over and hugged her sister-in-law. "Will you excuse me for a few moments then? I wish to change before Aunt Sarah and Uncle John come down. Ring for Mrs. Milligan if you need anything."

When Regina returned, properly clad in a becoming green and white daydress, she found the entire family gathered in the breakfast parlor. Aunt Sarah told her curtly that they had agreed to wait until eight o'clock for news of David, then an extensive search would be mounted.

The appetizing aroma of bacon, ham, and fresh-cooked sausage filled the small room, but no one was eating except Aunt Sarah and Cornelia. Regina sat down at her usual place and allowed Trudy to pour her a cup of coffee.

"I do not know how you can drink that vile concoction," Lady Rochdale said, watching her niece. "I do not allow it in the house. It is such an *American* drink."

"Not any longer, Aunt," Andrew said, holding out his own cup for a refill. "Coffee has become very popular, not only with the Prince Regent and his set, but in all the larger cities of Europe as well. Paris, Rome—"

"Thank you for sharing your opinion with us, Andrew. I hope you will be equally forthcoming when you explain your purpose in leaving David at Whitechapel, even though you apparently knew there was reason to believe him in danger. But we shall discuss that later, in private."

Andrew was silenced and Regina sent him a sympathetic look before her eyes were drawn irresistibly to the window. Odd, she thought, how little different it looked. Her world had been turned upside down, but the sun was still shining and the grass sparkled with morning dew. Superstitiously, she crossed her fingers tightly in her lap. She would give anything to see Balfour come striding up the garden path, with David tagging along at his heels.

Her aunt called her sharply to attention. "Regina, I realize you have not had a great deal of sleep, but sitting there and fantasying will not bring David home any sooner. Nor will it do the boy the least bit of good for you to forsake your breakfast."

"I am sorry, Aunt Sarah. Of course you are right—" she began, but broke off suddenly as she heard a carriage pulling into the yard. Regina pushed her chair back and was running from the room before her aunt could stop her.

"Andrew, John, go after her," Lady Rochdale ordered, but it was hardly necessary. Both gentlemen had risen and were across the room before she'd finished speaking.

They caught up with Regina easily at the end of the footpath. She had stopped abruptly, staring at the strange carriage. She'd recognized Jeremy at once, of course, but why was he driving a strange chaise? Where was his horse? Fearful of the answers, she froze and it was not until Andrew came up behind her that she found the courage to cross the yard.

Jeremy was climbing down as they neared the carriage and he hailed them at once. "Good news, Miss Regina. We found the lad right enough. He's fine—curled up inside, sound asleep."

"Thank God," she breathed and matched Andy stride for stride as they ran the remaining few feet. She was right behind him as Jeremy flung open the carriage door and tenderly lifted David down. The little boy's hair was tousled and his clothes rumpled, but he looked wonderful. She watched Jeremy hand him over to Andy, then peered over her brother's shoulder. David's dark lashes lay against his flushed cheeks, and his small mouth pursed open as he breathed slowly, but he didn't stir.

"I'm afraid they drugged him a bit, Miss Regina. He never batted an eye the whole time, not even when the shooting began."

Regina closed her eyes briefly, the ground beneath her seeming to tilt at an alarming angle.

"Are you all right?" Jeremy asked, reaching out a hand to steady her.

Regina nodded. She'd never fainted in her life, but she had a notion the dizzy sensation she was feeling must be near to it. She took a deep breath, holding tightly to Jeremy's arm. "Andy, take David on up to the house. Beth must be anxious to know what's happening. I'll send Ben for the doctor and join you in a few moments."

Andrew, so thrilled to have his son restored to him, scarcely noticed his sister, and he paid no heed to what Jeremy had said. All his attention was focused on the boy in his arms. It would have been difficult for him to see in any event, for he found his eyes were unaccountably blurry. He kissed David on the forehead, mumbled something Regina did not understand, then stumbled towards the path.

She waited until he was out of hearing before turning anxiously to her trainer. "Tell me quickly, Jeremy. What shooting? Was anyone . . . was anyone hurt?"

"Lord, Miss Regina, I didn't want to be the one to tell you, but I got to say, it was the bravest thing I ever saw. The boy's a knowing one and we followed his trail easily enough. Led us straight towards Ipswich and this deserted old barn set off the road a ways. The duke, well he figured we might catch 'em sleeping, and we crept up to the side of the place. Couldn't see a thing with the windows all boarded up. Well, His Grace goes to the front, and before I knew what he was about, he'd kicked in the door. They must have heard us coming. That big fellow, Jasper, he was standing there with a pistol pointed at us. He says, 'Take one more step and you're a dead man.' The duke, he never hesitated. Went right for him and couldn't have been more than a couple of feet away when that thug fired straight at him. I'm sorry, Miss Regina—"

She moaned and pitched forward into his arms.

"Oh, Lord!" Jeremy muttered as he caught her.

Beth stood on the landing outside Regina's room, her slender body shaking as she cried against her husband's shoulder. It was the first time she'd seen her sister-in-law since Jeremy had carried her into the house yesterday. Aunt Sarah had told her then that Regina was distraught, and Dr. Lyons had given her laudanum to help her rest. Beth had not been overly worried. She knew Regina had been without much food or sleep, so it was hardly surprising that she'd fainted. And, of course, Beth had been too much concerned with her son to give her sister-in-law much thought.

David had slept for several hours and Beth had sat by his bed, watching over him. Her own tiredness had disappeared once she had her son safe beside her, and the doctor's assurances that her boy was in no danger. David had awakened late that afternoon, sleepy-eyed, disoriented, and hungry. She had stayed with him while he ate, and until he fell asleep again. Then she had gone in search of Regina, but Aunt Sarah had refused to allow her in the room. She'd said Regina was sleeping and should not be disturbed.

Beth had thought it understandable. She was near exhaustion herself, and she finally gave into Andrew's pleas that she rest. She'd slept through the night, but the terrible cries she'd heard in the morning had awakened her. When she realized they were coming from Regina's room, she'd rushed in. She had held Regina, giving her what comfort she could—though it was little enough—until the doctor arrived. She was still sitting by Regina's side when Dr. Lyons gave her another dose of laudanum. Beth left the room badly shaken.

It had been horrible. Poor Regina. Her hair, tangled and damp, had hung limply about her shoulders, and her swollen, red-rimmed eyes had stared vacantly from the pallor of her face. But what had frightened Beth the most was the way Regina seemed not to care what was said or done to her.

Beth said in a choked voice, "You have to tell her the truth, Andy. She thinks he is dead, and she's making herself terribly ill."

He hated it when women cried. He patted her clumsily on the shoulder. "Leave it be, Beth. It's better this way. She will get over him soon enough."

"How can you say such a thing?" she asked, drawing away from him. "Did you see her? Did you hear the way she's crying? She loves him, Andy."

"I know," he said, and sighed. "But what use would it be to tell her the truth? Even if this was an alliance I could give my blessing to, Balfour would never marry her. He returned to Town without a word to her, didn't he?"

"Of course he did! You know he had to have his arm attended to at once."

"He should have let Dr. Lyons amputate it. I don't know what he thinks that army physician can do. Lyons said the bone was completely shattered."

"Sir John Pringle has a wonderful reputation. If anyone can save Balfour's arm, he can."

"And if he can't?" Andrew asked, looking down at her.

"What then, Beth? Even if Balfour was willing, would you have my sister wed an invalid? I tell you, it is far better this way. By the time she learns he is still alive, she will have recovered from this mad infatuation with him. You must trust that Aunt Sarah and I know what is best for Regina."

Do you, Beth wondered, but remained silent. She knew it was disloyal of her to question her husband's wisdom, and it was his sister they spoke of, but she doubted she would ever forget the haunted look in Regina's eyes.

Two days later, Regina came below stairs for the first time, and Beth's doubts increased. It was difficult to say what precisely was wrong, but for all that Regina looked and sounded fine, there was a subtle difference about her. Beth watched her covertly.

Her sister-in-law smiled pleasantly, begged her aunt's pardon for the inconvenience she'd caused, and even teased Andy over acquiring a collie and a horse. Beth listened to the banter between brother and sister. It sounded perfectly normal, but she could not shake the feeling that something was dreadfully wrong. Andrew would say she was imagining things, but it seemed to her that the fire which had once burned so vibrantly in Regina, had died.

No one else seemed to notice anything amiss. Regina took charge of her household again, dispensing orders and instructions with her customary competence. When she excused herself to walk down to the stables with Uncle John, Andrew nodded in satisfaction.

"There. I told you all Gina needed was a few days' rest. She will be fine now, and I think we should plan on driving to London in the morning. I have already delayed longer than I should have and the Regent will be anxious for my report."

"Will you tell him about David?" his aunt asked.

"Yes, of course. One of the kidnappers talked quite freely

once he realized the game was up." He shook his head regretfully. "I still find it hard to believe that Lord Kensington was behind all this. A man I have known and liked for years. I knew he was a staunch Whig, but even so, to go to such lengths . . ."

"I don't believe the Regent realizes how much opposition there is to his scheme of divorcing Princess Caroline," his aunt interrupted. "You would do well to advise him, Andrew. She has the support of the people, and if he continues with this folly, he will regret it."

"His advisors have told him so, Aunt. Over and over, but the Regent is obsessed with the notion of ridding himself of Caroline. He will not listen to reason and refuses to even read her letters."

"Then you would do well to withdraw from court for a period. Use David as an excuse if you must, but distance yourself from the scandal that is certain to erupt."

"Perhaps," Andrew said, and glanced at his wife. The hopeful way Beth looked at him touched him, and he smiled at her. "After I have made my report, we could drive up to the lodge, if you don't dislike the notion?"

"I should like it above all things," she said softly.

The intimate look in his wife's eyes held a promise Andrew had not seen there in several months. It drove all other thoughts from his mind. He was totally unaware of how foolish he appeared to his aunt as he sat grinning quite fatuously at his wife.

"Well," Lady Rochdale said, rising. "I believe it is time Sir John and I took our leave as well. We are taking Cornelia back with us. This unfortunate incident has caused a rift between her and your sister, and I think it will do Regina good to spend some time alone, and to meditate on her behavior. What time do you plan on leaving, Andrew? I believe we will drive down with you as far as Chelmsford."

It was settled they would depart at nine the next morning, and Andrew walked down to the stables in search of Regina.

He found her with David beside the paddock, watching the gray colt his son wanted for his own. He cast an eye over the animal, but his knowledge of horses was slight and it was sufficient that David wanted the creature.

"A fine-looking colt, lad," he said, putting an arm about his son's shoulders. "But I think we must ask your Aunt Regina if she will keep him for you for a while yet. We shall be leaving for London in the morning, and from there your mother wishes to go up to the Lake District for a few months."

"Can I not stay here?" David asked.

"No, son. Your mother wants you with her, and while I'm busy in Town, I will depend on you to look after her."

"Don't worry, David," Regina said, managing a smile for her nephew. "I shall take good care of Boreas."

He nodded, his head down, aware that it was useless to argue.

Regina hugged him, knowing just how he felt. It was terrible when other people ordered your life for you, and one was helpless to do anything about it.

"Aunt Sarah and Uncle John will be leaving, too," Andrew said. After an awkward pause, he added, "Will you be all right, Gina? I dislike the idea of leaving you here alone."

"I will be fine," she said and leaned across David's head to kiss her brother's cheek, hoping he had not seen the relief in her eyes. If there had been a polite way to ask her family to leave, she would have done so that morning. Above all, she wished only to be left alone.

"We could stop here on our way back if—"

"Do not be absurd, Andy. It would be a great deal out of your way and I know Beth must be eager to visit the Lodge. I appreciate your concern, but don't worry about me. I have written to Mrs. Arbuckle and asked her to come visit."

"Wonderful," Andrew said, recalling the dowdy little widow who had once been his sister's governess. "That's settled then. I'll go up and tell Beth. Come along, David. Your mother wants a word with you."

Regina watched them go, wondering idly why she didn't feel more guilty for lying to her brother. It didn't seem to matter. Nothing seemed to matter except that she be left in peace.

Twelve

Regina stood in her bedchamber by the window and watched the carriages departing. Her family was leaving and she felt nothing but impatience for them to be gone. Was it unnatural of her, she wondered? These were the people who had cared for her, protected her, and loved her all her life—but now she could not summon even the mildest regret at their leaving.

Regina let the draperies fall shut and turned away. She glanced at the bed and resisted a strong urge to crawl beneath the covers and pull the quilt over her head. Do not even think of it, she told herself, knowing that if she gave in to the desire, she might never get up again. It would be so easy to take a large dose of laudanum and let the opium carry her into dreams that had nothing to do with reality. And it was reality that she had to come to terms with. A reality that did not include Cedric Everild, the Duke of Balfour.

His image came to mind instantly, and Regina blinked back tears. She could not, and would not think of him, she told herself sternly. But the vision persisted. She could see all too clearly the way his left brow arched when he was surprised and the way his lips curled into a raffish grin when he was amused. If she closed her eyes, she could almost hear his voice tenderly calling her "little one" and feel the touch of his gentle hands on her shoulders.

Regina stood still for a moment, holding tightly to the bedpost and leaning her head against it. In spite of her efforts, a few tears escaped from her eyes. She thought of how bravely the duke had stepped in front of a pistol in order to save David. Had he died instantly, or had he endured a lot of pain?

The thought tortured her and she realized she needed to know the answer. No one had told her what occurred after the duke was shot. Andrew had refused to discuss it. She drew a linen handkerchief from her pocket and wiped at her eyes. Perhaps, once she knew the whole story, she would be able to stop thinking of Balfour so much.

Jeremy knew what had occurred, and Jeremy could be counted on to tell her the truth. With a new sense of purpose, Regina hurried downstairs. She heard the housekeeper in the breakfast parlor and slipped quietly into the drawing room and out the doors to the garden. She did not want to have to deal with Mrs. Milligan or Cook. At the moment, Jeremy was the only person she wanted to see.

She found him near the paddock, overseeing the lads working with the colts. He was discussing the progress of a promising two-year-old with one of the grooms, but for once Regina ignored her prized horses. So intent was she on her errand, she broke in on their conversation without apology. She barely heard the stable lad greet her deferentially or her trainer's surprised good morning.

"Jeremy, I need to speak with you. Will you tell me what happened when . . . when David was rescued?"

Her trainer stared at her, wondering if she was feverish. Regina's eyes looked luminous and overly large against the paleness of her face. He doubted she was even aware of the urgent way her fingers gripped his arm, or of the groom gawking at them. He gave the boy terse instructions and sent him hurrying back to the stables, before turning to Regina. "Are you feeling well, Miss Regina? Do you want to go sit down somewhere?"

She laughed shakily. "Don't worry, Jeremy. I am not going to faint again, but I must know what happened when you and the duke rescued David. Andrew would not tell me anything, as though not talking about it could make it less real. I keep having these visions—dreadful visions—of Balfour." She paused for a second, blocking out the image she'd seen so vividly of a pistol exploding. A shudder rippled through her body, and her hand tightened on his arm. "I *must* know, Jeremy. You do understand, don't you?"

She was pleading with him. It was in her voice and in her eyes. Jeremy looked away uncomfortably. He remembered all too clearly Sir Andrew's instructions to him. *Say nothing to her.* Jeremy had protested, but Sir Andrew had been insistent. He believed Regina would forget the duke in due time, and if she thought him dead, she would get over him all the sooner.

Jeremy had argued, but although Sir Andrew had thanked him profusely for his help in rescuing David, his manner made it clear that he would not accept the trainer's judgment when it came to his sister. Not even Jeremy's bitter comment that Regina would be furious with both of them when she learned the truth, had moved Sir Andrew. He had merely shrugged and said Regina would understand that they had acted for her own good.

"Jeremy? Was it so dreadful you cannot tell me? Surely, it cannot be worse than what I have been imagining."

The lanky groom sighed. Either way he decided, he was bound to end up in the basket. Sir Andrew was certain to hear of it if he told Miss Regina the truth. And she was certain to find out sooner or later that Balfour was alive, and she'd be furious that he had not told her. Still, when all was said and done, he would rather have Sir Andrew angry with him. Miss Regina was the one who paid his wages, and she was the one who deserved his loyalty. Making up his mind, he hoped she wouldn't faint again. Eyeing her warily, he suggested they move to the rose garden where she could have a seat on the stone bench.

The trainer's concern for her increased Regina's nervousness. She accepted the support of his arm as they walked along the path leading into the garden. She felt a little fearful now of what she might hear, but was still determined to know the worst. When she was seated, she twisted her hands together in her lap, swallowed past the lump in her throat, and looked up at Jeremy. "Well, sir?"

A bee buzzed about his head, and he swatted at it. His gaze followed its flight, and he watched it settle on a large pink blossom. He kept his eyes focused on the tiny creature as he began. "Well, Miss Regina, I told you how we crept up to the place, and the duke kicked in the door. This cutthroat was standing there waiting for us with a loaded pistol in his hand. He threatened the duke, but His Grace never hesitated." Jeremy paused, glancing at her.

"Go on," Regina said, sounding calm enough, but she looked as though someone was about to strike her. Her hands were so tightly clenched, the knuckles were turning white.

"The duke must have seen the pistol come up. He dived at the same instant, and the bullet went into his arm instead of his heart, but it was the same arm he'd been hit in before. I could see he was hurt bad, but there wasn't time to do nothing. Tenby threw himself on Jasper like a fury, and they went down in a tumble. I went after the other fellow. He was still holding a gun, but the fight had gone out of him. He threw his pistol down and held up his hands. The duke yelled for me to—"

"He was still alive then?"

"Yes, Miss Regina, though his arm was bleeding something fierce. I got hold of the other fellow and was turning to help Tenby. Jasper had him down on the floor and was sitting on top of him, choking the life out of him. Before I could move, the duke yelled to stand clear. I don't know how he managed it, but he put a shot right through that cutthroat's eyes. Then the duke, well, he just sort of collapsed on the floor."

"I see," Regina said, lowering her eyes.

"I doubt it, miss," Jeremy said. Taking a deep breath, he continued, "While Tenby was seeing to the duke, I trussed up the ruffian I was holding with a piece of rope we found, and then I went to look for David. I found him in the next room, curled up on a cot, sound asleep. I couldn't believe it. It was only later we realized he was drugged. Right then I carried him out to the carriage, and then came back. Tenby had managed to stop most of the bleeding, but the duke was out cold, and a dead weight. It took both of us to cart him out to the carriage, and then Tenby drove like the devil was after him.

"We hunted up the doc and by that time I guess all the jostling in the carriage had stirred up the duke. He was conscious when we stopped, but the boy was still sleeping. His Grace suspected David was drugged and he insisted they see to him first. Dr. Lyons looked the boy over and said to take him home and put him to bed. He would sleep off the effects of the drug. Then he set about tending the duke.

"That arm was sure a mess, Miss Regina. Pieces of bone completely shattered. I don't know how the duke stood the pain. Doc wanted to amputate it right then, but His Grace refused. Ordered him to bandage it up and said he would see a surgeon when he got back to London. He told Tenby to get the carriage ready to leave at once, and ordered me to bring David on home. Said you would be getting anxious, and he didn't want for you to worry none. That's all he said, before he went off again."

Regina sat motionless, trying to absorb what Jeremy had said. It took a moment before she dared to put her thoughts into words. "Jeremy, are you telling me—is it possible that Balfour is still alive?"

"He was the last time I saw him, though I can't say for certain what might have happened once he got to Town."

"But why didn't anyone tell me? I thought . . . I thought he was—" she broke off as tears rolled down her cheeks. But these were tears of relief, and she smiled up at Jeremy.

"Forgive me. You must think me terribly foolish, but I do not understand why no one told me about His Grace. We must find out at once how his arm is . . ." She allowed her words to trail off as she became conscious of the odd expression on her trainer's face. He looked uncomfortable, almost embarrassed. "Jeremy? Is there something else you are not telling me?"

"Not really, Miss Regina. It's only—well, your brother thought you would be better off believing the duke had died—seeing as how he went back to Town without a word for you and all. Sir Andrew thought it would be best, and, well, he ordered me not to say nothing."

She sat quietly for a moment, then nodded. "Yes, it would be just like Andrew to arbitrarily decide what is best for me. He never learns. Well, I shall have a few words to say to him on this head. The idea that he would keep such a thing from me is monstrous." She paused, noticing that Jeremy was keeping his head down and shuffling his feet. "You do not believe Sir Andrew is right, do you? Is it true that Balfour left no word for me?"

The trainer nodded, wishing he were anywhere else in the world. "I'm sorry, Miss Regina, but His Grace wasn't himself, you know. His arm all shattered and losing all that blood—I doubt he was thinking clearly."

"I see. Thank you, Jeremy, for telling me this. You may leave me now," she said, not looking at him.

"Miss Regina, are you—"

"I shall be fine, Jeremy. I just need a few moments alone, if you please."

"Yes, miss," he murmured, replacing his cap. He lifted a hand to her, but Regina never glanced up. As he turned the corner of the path, Jeremy glanced back. She was still sitting in the same position, just the way he'd left her. Like a statue, Jeremy thought, shaking his head.

* * *

At first, Regina was more than willing to grant Balfour the benefit of doubt. She reasoned he had not sent word to her because he knew her family was with her, and Aunt Sarah had made it clear what kind of reception he could expect from them. And there was his arm. She knew he must have been in terrible pain when he'd left Jeremy, too terrible to even think of sending her a message. She consoled herself with these thoughts, went about her business with a cheerful face, and haunted the gate in the mornings, waiting for the arrival of the penny post.

Her efforts were poorly rewarded. She received two letters from distant cousins, a long missive from her Aunt Sarah abjuring her to meditate on her past behavior, a brief letter from Beth thanking her for her care of David, and a short note from Lord Sayers enquiring about prospective colts. She put his note aside and toyed with the notion of writing to Andrew. He had been in Town and must surely know how Balfour was faring, but then she discarded the idea. Andrew would, no doubt, only tell her to put the duke from her mind. It was what he had replied when she'd written, taking him soundly to task for his deception.

Frustrated, Regina realized her reclusive way of life had limited her circle of friends to those who lived in the vicinity of Whitechapel. She knew no one in Town of whom she could apply to for news. In desperation, she took to poring over the issues of the *London Gazette* for mention of his name.

She found what she was seeking a few weeks later. It was a small item, and she nearly missed it. Regina scanned the few brief lines of print. Lady Maidstone had entertained a small, select party at Stoneleigh Towers, her home near Leeds. A catalogue of the guests followed, and there among the names of the most elite of London, appeared the Duke of Balfour, with a brief notation that he was Lady Maidstone's nephew.

She read the paragraph a half-dozen times before folding

it carefully and laying it inside her ledger, then closed the book decisively. The duke was well. At least she knew that much. That he was well and had not written her was something she could not bear to think about. She pushed the ledger across the desk and determinedly drew forward the Racing Calendar. She'd been neglecting her horses and it was past time she concentrated on her stable, but the fine type on the pages blurred before her eyes, and she felt the beginning of a throbbing headache.

Regina stood up abruptly. Her small office suddenly seemed stifling, and she thought if she remained inside another moment, she would surely scream. She hurried down the hall and found Trudy in the drawing room. She told the maid to inform Mrs. Milligan that she'd gone riding, and was not certain when she would return. She spoke curtly, not giving Trudy a chance to reply, and then went out to the stables. It was as though the years had been wiped from the calendar, and she was once more a shy, gawky girl seeking solace among the horses.

After that, Regina rode every afternoon, often disappearing for hours at a time. There were days when she pushed Penrod to the limits of his endurance, and brought him back to the stable near spent and heavily lathered. It did little good. No matter how far she rode, or how fast, she could not escape the memories of Balfour.

It was on such an afternoon that Jeremy came to fetch her.

Regina had just finished grooming Penrod, and while the stallion appeared much improved, she was near exhaustion and looked it. Her hair had long since escaped its customary neat bun, and cascaded wildly about her face and down her back. The coat and skirt of her riding habit were badly stained and traces of the fresh straw she'd just put down clung to the material. Her boots bore so much mud, they would have caused her aunt to succumb to an apoplexy had she been present, and her gloves were fit only for the dust heap. Regina knew how disreputable she looked, but was too tired to care—too tired to even consider dinner. All she wished was to wash the dirt from her body and collapse into bed.

She tossed the ruined gloves into a large container that held the refuse from the stables and picked up her hat.

"Miss Regina, there's someone here to see you," Jeremy told her as he entered the stable.

Hope flared briefly in her eyes and her spirits soared. For a few seconds, she forgot everything. Then Jeremy added that it was some gentleman down from London, asking about the horses.

"You deal with him, Jeremy. I am not fit to be seen." Weariness settled over her, deadening her voice and weighing down her arms so that she struggled with the latch of Penrod's stall.

"He asked to see you, Miss Regina," the trainer insisted, and extended a calling card. "The gentleman says his name is Lord Bedford and he met you at Newmarket Races."

Regina glanced at the engraved card, remembering the duke's lighthearted friend, Harry Warwick, the Earl of Bedford. It seemed a lifetime ago. She handed the card back. "You will have to talk to him, Jeremy. Give him my regrets, and explain I cannot possibly see anyone just now."

"I thought you'd feel that way, Miss Regina, and I did try to be of help, but the gentleman is determined to speak with you. Said he'd ridden all the way down from London, and that you had invited him to call. I'm sure he would be willing to wait if you was wishful of changing first."

"Jeremy, I—"

"I think you ought to see him," he interrupted doggedly. "I know I'm speaking out of turn and it's not my place to be telling you what to do, but I got to say what I think. To hear this lord talk, he wants to buy a number of our horses. We got a yard full of two-year-olds eating their heads off, and no buyers in sight except Lord Sayers. The truth is, Miss Regina, if you don't start thinking about business soon, there won't be a business."

She didn't answer for a moment, but watched her trainer twisting his cap in his hands, his face red with embarrassment. She knew it had cost him a great deal to speak so bluntly, and, of course, he was right. Whitechapel was all she had. "Very well, Jeremy. Show Lord Bedford the horses, and then bring him up to the house. I shall try to make myself presentable before you get there, but take your time, please."

He grinned, "Yes, miss."

Regina hurried.

Even with Trudy's help, it was nearly an hour before she felt fit to be seen. She had lost weight and all of her dresses seemed to hang loosely on her slim figure. She rejected gown after gown, until Trudy finally pulled an apple green daydress from the back of her wardrobe. It was a dress Regina had not worn in years, and though it was sadly out of style, it had the advantage of fitting her properly. She nodded her approval and then allowed her maid to lace a matching green ribbon through her curls.

Lord Bedford was waiting in the drawing room. He stood at once as she entered, and the admiration in his eyes was balm to Regina's battered ego and worth the effort she had taken. She gave him her hand and did not even protest when he held it longer than could be considered proper.

"Miss Westfield," he said, bowing gracefully. "How delightful to see you again, and may I say that you are even lovelier than I recalled. Now I can understand what kept Balfour from London for so long."

It required a great deal of effort to keep smiling, but she managed somehow to answer him pleasantly. She was aided by Mrs. Milligan's arrival with an elaborate tea tray and fussing with the cups and cakes gave her time to regain her composure. When they were comfortably seated and Lord Bedford's cup was full, she could not resist the temptation any longer. With a pretense of casualness, she asked, "Have you seen His Grace recently, my lord?"

"Cedric? Not for a month or so," he said, helping himself

to a large slice of bread and several pieces of cheese. He swallowed. "I saw him when he arrived in Town with his arm all torn to pieces. He told me what happened, and I do hope your nephew is recovered from his ordeal."

"Quite. My sister-in-law wrote me recently and judging from her letter, David regards his abduction as a huge adventure. Of course, he was sleeping when His Grace was shot, and knows nothing of that."

"A nasty piece of business. It's sheer luck Cedric didn't lose his arm. Still, it may prove the making of him. From all accounts, he's given up his wild ways and has turned nearly respectable. But tell me, how did he ever find you in this remote hamlet? Not that seeing you isn't worth the drive, but I had the devil of a time finding the place."

Talking of Balfour revived the ache of missing him sorely. Regina was thankful to turn the conversation, and replied, "I chose to buy Whitechapel because of its proximity to Newmarket. There are persons in the area who would dispute with you, sir, and find our situation most convenient. We are not too far from London, after all."

"No, not if one knows the way, and now that I do, I hope to be a frequent caller. Miss Westfield, your trainer showed me some of your horses, and if he has not exaggerated their time, I am ready to make you firm offers on four of them. Impressive colts—most impressive. I can't think when I've seen better except perhaps for Lord Derby's crop. Out of Eclipse, you know."

"I know," she said with a sigh. "I wish I could convince Lord Derby to sell me one of Eclipse's foals. It has been a dream of mine for years. If I could mate a descendant of his with one of my dams—" she broke off, growing embarrassed. This was *not* a proper drawing room conversation!

"Ha! Slim chance, my dear," the earl laughed, seemingly unaware of her lack of decorum. "No one has been able to convince Derby to sell any of Eclipse's offspring. Had a go at him myself, but he wouldn't hear of it. Still, you've nothing to hang your head over. Those colts I saw in the yard are exceptional. I looked for you at Newmarket, you know. I wanted to congratulate you on Cavalier winning the 2000 Guineas, but you'd gone."

"Yes," she said, her hands trembling slightly against the teacup. "That was when David disappeared."

"A pity you missed the race," Harry said, unaware of her distress. He was not insensitive, but horses were his passion. When he was involved in discussing them, watching them or wagering on them, little else penetrated his mind. "Cavalier did you proud, Miss Westfield. He took the lead at once, then widened it by a couple of lengths. I don't mind telling you, he made me a bit nervous. I was afraid he'd tire before the finish, but what power that horse has! Never faltered once, and the rest of the pack couldn't draw close."

"I am pleased to hear he performed so well," Regina said, and pushed another cake near the earl's hand. His appetite was nearly as voracious as his enthusiasm.

"An understatement, my dear, and if any of those colts I'm buying perform half as well, I shall be pleased beyond measure."

"Which ones are you interested in?" she asked politely.

"Well, to say the truth, I like them all, but your trainer recommended a bay colt. Clio's Pride, I think he called him."

"An excellent choice, my lord. He's out of the same dam as Cavalier. She's the mare I want to mate with an Eclipse foal."

"Gad, what a combination that would be. Pity old Derby won't allow it, but I'll speak to him again on your behalf if you like."

"I would, sir, above all things," Regina said, catching a bit of his zeal. The tea grew cold while they talked of past races and triumphs, and disasters.

Harry was at his most engaging. He was astonished by Regina's knowledge of horseflesh, and he spoke to her as naturally as he would to another gentleman, entertaining her with tales of race meets and the sales ring at Tattersalls.

It was not until the room grew dim and Mrs. Milligan came in to light the candles that Regina realized the lateness of the hour. The earl was putting up at the Angel in Bury St. Edmunds, but she invited him to remain for dinner, and he was quick to accept. Cook contrived to set an adequate meal before them, but it is doubtful either knew what they ate. They lingered at the table long after the covers had been removed, and it was with a great deal of reluctance that the earl finally took his leave.

Regina saw him out and accepted his effusive declarations of gratitude with a smile. "It is I who must thank you, my lord, for a most pleasant evening. I do hope you will call again and let me know how the colts are doing."

"Gladly, my dear," he said, and bowed over her hand. He straightened up and grinned, "I can't think when I've enjoyed myself more. I can see now why Cedric spent so much time here. If I was a marrying man, I daresay I'd give him a run for his money."

The earl never noticed that some of the sparkle disappeared from Regina's smile, or that the brightness of her eyes dimmed. He set his hat at a cocky angle, and whistled as he walked out to his carriage.

Thirteen

The Earl of Bedford's visit helped to bring Regina out of the doldrums. She reestablished her old routines and took to riding Penrod for an hour or so in the mornings. Late afternoons, she spent working closely with Jeremy, breaking the new colts and training the four that Lord Bedford had purchased. She forced herself to sit down to dinner at six every evening and tried to do justice to the dishes Cook prepared especially to tempt her appetite. After dinner, she retired to her office and worked for several hours on her books, solidifying her plans for the mares' coming season.

She sighed again over Lord Derby's refusal to allow Full Moon, a great-grandson of Eclipse, to stand to stud with her own mares. Harry had sent her a note that old Derby remained adamant and had turned a deaf ear to his entreaties on her behalf. Still, it hardly mattered. Harry had obligingly spread the word about her stock, and she now had more offers for horses than she could possibly fill. Jeremy was jubilant. The post brought new orders every day, and she'd even accepted two provisional offers for future colts or fillies. Whitechapel Stables was a tremendous success.

Regina hoped Balfour knew. With her new affluence, her pride had resurfaced. She was more determined than ever to make Whitechapel the premier breeding farm in England, and when she succeeded, she intended to flaunt her triumph in the duke's face. When she thought of Balfour now, it was to imagine him returning, hat in hand, to plead for one of her horses. Some days she indulged in a dream where she behaved magnanimously and graciously agreed to provide him with bloodstock. Other days, she envisioned herself informing His Grace that, much as she regretted it, she was unable to accommodate him. She would be charming and cool, and he would be utterly dejected.

Unfortunately, she could not quite picture Balfour either pleading or dejected. And from Harry, when he could be brought to discuss anything besides horses, she heard of His Grace's preoccupation with the social whirl of London's elite. Much to Harry's disgust, Balfour had not been seen on a race course since Newmarket.

There were now hours at a time when Regina did not think of the duke. Hours when she was either too busy or too tired. Summer was over and as the days shortened, her work increased. September arrived, bringing cooler weather and a new set of domestic problems. Maisie had given notice, blushingly telling Regina of her engagement to a young man from a farm in a neighboring village. The first banns had already been called.

Regina sincerely wished her joy, but regretted the necessity of interviewing prospective maids. She prayed she would find someone who would be able to adapt to the comfortable routine of the household, but knew it would not be easy. She also knew it was past time that she wrote to Mrs. Arbuckle. The post had brought a letter from Beth, and she and Andrew planned to visit at Thanksgiving. Her brother would be furious if he learned she had not written to her old governess before this, and Regina was reluctant to start another argument with him. But still she put it off.

Mrs. Milligan took matters into her own hands a few days later. She waited until Regina had finished breakfast and was opening the mail, and then asked if she might have a word with her.

"Of course," Regina murmured absently. She laid aside her letters and tried to give her attention to the housekeeper, but her mind was occupied with the vast number of things she needed to do before Andrew's visit.

"She is a nice little thing," Mrs. Milligan was saying. "And I think she'd do well here."

"I beg your pardon?"

"Annie Mowbray," the housekeeper repeated patiently. "She will do well as a replacement for Maisie, and though she don't think I know it, I heard she has been stepping out with our Jeremy."

"Jeremy is courting a girl?" Regina asked incredulously as she glanced out the window towards the stable. "I cannot believe it. Why, he never said a word to me."

"All you have to do is look at him, Miss Regina. He's been smelling of April and May for some time now. But what I was thinking is, if he does come up to scratch, well, it would be good for you to have his wife here, too."

"Definitely," Regina agreed. The idea of losing Jeremy did not bear thinking of.

"That's settled then. I've arranged to have Annie here to-morrow afternoon, if that's agreeable to you?"

"Fine, Mrs. Milligan—and thank you." Regina remained at the table thinking about her trainer. She was a little hurt that Jeremy had not confided in her, but she also realized that, had she been more observant, she might have guessed. Well, she would talk to him later, and if he were indeed going to set up housekeeping, she would give him a cottage as a wedding present. He deserved nothing less. Whitechapel's prosperity was due in large part to Jeremy's dedication.

Her trainer was not in the stables when she went out for her morning ride, but he was there when she returned. It appeared to Regina's bemused eyes that every member of her staff was out in the yard. What on earth had happened to cause such a flurry of excitement, she wondered, riding in amidst the clamor.

Several voices hailed her at once, but it was Jeremy who reached her side first and helped her down. Uncharacteristically excited, he told her, "Just wait until you see what arrived, Miss Regina. The most perfect-looking stallion I ever saw!"

"Pay no attention, Penrod," Regina said, giving her own stallion a pat as she handed over the reins to the groom. "Obviously, the man is delirious from too much sun."

"Wait until you see him," Jeremy repeated as he led her towards the small paddock where the new stallion had been turned out. "A groom brought him down in easy stages. Said it took a fortnight to get here, and he has orders to release the stallion to no one but you."

Regina was understandably confused. "A stallion? But we have not bought any new stock."

"Are you Miss Westfield?" a groom asked respectfully as he stepped away from the fence.

Regina nodded, noting the rich livery the man wore. She didn't recognize the yellow and deep blue colors as any of her clients.

"Then this is for you, Miss, with His Grace's compliments." He proffered an ivory envelope, heavily embossed.

His Grace. The words rang in her ears and her hand shook as she accepted the envelope. There was only one person she knew who was addressed in that manner. She was very nearly afraid to open the envelope and postponed the moment, watching the stallion. A beauty, she thought, admiring the rich deep black coat. The horse, as though sensing her regard, tossed his head and then trotted halfway round the ring. Jeremy was right, she silently acknowledged.

This stallion was something special. It showed in the way he moved, the way his powerful muscles rippled smoothly beneath the glossy coat. She watched him paw the ground, then rear up, showing off two white stockings on his forelegs. Only her fondness for her snow white Penrod kept her from owning aloud that the new stallion was the best-looking horse she had ever seen.

She glanced at the envelope in her hand, wishing she was

alone. Jeremy's eager eyes watched her, and the stable hands were crowded round the paddock. They all wanted to know where the handsome brute had come from. Hesitantly, she drew out a sheet of heavy vellum stationery. It contained only a few lines, the writing a dark scrawl. Her gaze flew to the signature at the bottom. Cedric. She drew in a deep breath and quickly read the few words.

My dear Regina,

    I would gladly place my wealth and all my world possessions at your feet, but I know you have little regard for such commodities. The things you value—integrity, honor, decency—have not been much in my line, but I am doing what I can to cultivate them.

    You once said what you desired most in the world was a stallion out of Eclipse. I am thankful that it lies within my power to fulfill at least one of your dreams. Introduce yourself to Half Moon. He belongs to you—a fate which I most sincerely envy.

It was simply signed "Cedric." She read the note through twice, then looked up through a mist of tears at Jeremy. "It's from—" she began, then had to break off to clear her throat. "Balfour sent him. Jeremy, he's out of Eclipse!"

"Well, no wonder he looks so grand. How in the world did the duke manage it? I thought old Derby would never part with one of his get."

Regina shook her head helplessly, torn between laughter and tears. Happiness bubbled inside her and she felt like hugging someone. She tried to appear calm, and replied, "I have no idea."

They both turned to the young groom who had delivered the horse. The lad appeared absurdly pleased, and Regina suspected he knew a bit more. She smiled at him and asked,

"Did the duke send no other message? Do you know where he is?"

"His Grace is putting up at the Angel, Miss Westfield. He said I should tell you that he would be visiting the old man this afternoon, if you was wishful of a word with him. His Grace said you would know who he meant." He paused, fingering the gold sovereign in his pocket. A bonus from the duke, the groom had the promise of another if the lady kept the rendezvous. But first he had to deliver the rest of the message. Superstitiously crossing his fingers, he told her, "His Grace said, Miss, that he would quite understand if you did not come and that the stallion was yours to keep either way."

"I see," Regina said softly. So Balfour was not entirely sure of his welcome. Good. He had audacity, sending such a gift and cryptic message after leaving her without so much as a word all summer. Let him wait. She turned to find a circle of curious faces watching her and blushed. She focused on her trainer. "Jeremy, take care of our new horse, please. I will be in my office if you need me."

He nodded and Regina started for the house.

The groom stepped forward, mindful of his promised reward. "Pardon me, Miss Westfield, but are you going to see His Grace?"

It was the boy who turned a bright red this time as Regina glanced at him, her brows raised in surprise at his impertinence. Jeremy cuffed the messenger soundly on the arm.

"I have not decided," she said before walking away with her head held high. She had to force herself to walk slowly, and barely conquered the urge to have Penrod saddled at once. She reminded herself that she had waited months for word from Balfour. Let him wait now.

Regina paced her office for precisely one hour and two minutes before sending Trudy with a message for Jeremy.

She wanted Penrod saddled and brought round to the drive. She could not face the grinning stable lads. Not yet. Jeremy offered to accompany her, but she shook her head and set off on the trail alone. Her thoughts were in a turmoil as she tried to imagine what Balfour would say, and she very nearly paid for her distraction when Penrod suddenly reared.

She brought the stallion under control, but he was skittish, seeming to sense her own nervousness in the uncanny way that horses have. He shied at every leaf that fell in the woods, and every small creature that scurried in the brush. Regina cantered into the clearing near Ramsey's cottage before she had decided on what she would say.

She saw the duke at once. He waited outside the cottage, and as soon as he saw her, he strode towards her.

Regina reined in and slid off Penrod's back before Balfour could assist her. She turned to face him. The afternoon sun was behind him, and his dearly beloved face was shadowed, but he looked wonderful. Elation, joy, whatever it was she felt, set her blood surging through her, and if he had opened his arms, she would have run to him. But Balfour halted a few steps away. For the first time since she had known him, he seemed uncertain, unsure of himself.

"You came," he said simply, his eyes roving over every inch of her slender body with a greediness that sent delightful shivers down her spine.

"Did you think I would not?" she asked, pleased that her voice sounded so steady when her insides were a bundle of quivering nerves. "How could I not come and thank you for such an extravagant gift?"

Her tone was saucy, teasing—but Balfour was not amused. "Is that the only reason you came, Regina?"

She glanced away, unable to bear the intensity of his gaze. She busied herself with tying Penrod's reins to a sapling, and replied over her shoulder. "No, I confess I was . . . curious. I had thought to hear from you after you returned to London. When I did not—"

She shrugged and walked the few feet to where a late-blooming rosebush displayed the last of its flowers.

"You look remarkably well," he said, following her. "I am glad to know you were not distraught. Of course, I heard you contrived to amuse yourself tolerably well. Bedford has been singing your praises all over London."

"Oh, Harry," she said, managing to give a convincing laugh as she broke off a rose and plucked the petals from it. "He is rather amusing, and of course we have a great deal in common. Did he tell you he bought four horses from me?"

Balfour grabbed her shoulder and swung her around to face him. His voice deathly cold, he demanded, "How often has he been down here, Regina?"

"Really, Your Grace, I fail to see in what way that concerns you," she replied, and lifted her chin defiantly, but she wished he would put an end to such nonsense and kiss her.

The duke dropped his hands from her shoulders. "My apologies, Miss Westfield. You are correct. I have not the right to question you, and if you tell me you prefer Bedford, I shall leave at once."

Regina lowered her lashes. He was jealous, she thought, and the knowledge thrilled her. "Prefer Harry to what, Your Grace?" she answered, her words so soft he had to lean close to hear.

"As a suitor," he snapped, dangerously close to losing his temper.

"Oh. 'Tis odd, but I never really considered him in that light," she murmured. "Though, I must admit, compared to certain gentlemen, he does possess one advantage. Harry writes to me from Town. Rather short letters, for he is not at all bookish, but at least I know that he is well, and that he occasionally thinks of me. You cannot imagine, Your Grace, how much such small attentions can mean—"

"Regina, I had reasons for keeping silent. Egad, if you only knew how desperately I missed you," he said, running a hand through his hair.

"Did you?" she asked softly, looking up at him. Her lips parted slightly and her eyes held a warm invitation.

It was too much for his self-control. He pulled her roughly into his arms. His mouth sought hers hungrily, bruising her lips as he possessed himself of the one thing he had so much desired and been so long denied. His arms held her tightly crushed against him, and they both gasped for breath when he finally lifted his head.

Regina raised a trembling hand to his face and with a delicate fingertip traced the line of his mouth. "Harry never did that," she said, making no effort to move from his arms.

"Fortunately for him," Balfour said, but the anger had gone and he even managed a droll smile. "I should hate to run him through."

Regina laughed. "You would have a difficult time, Your Grace, unless you dueled in the paddock. Harry haunts the stables. I have never seen a man so obsessed with horses."

"I did warn you, my darling girl," he said, then kissed the lobe of her ear. "Do you think we might lure him away sufficiently long to act as groomsman?"

Regina stilled in his arms. "Are you proposing, Your Grace?" she whispered at last.

"I am, dear heart, and if you are thinking of your brother, you may set your mind to rest. I have his assurances that if you are agreeable, Andrew will give us his blessing."

"I do not believe it," she said, her eyes opening wide. "When Andrew left here, he did not even wish me to know that you were still alive."

He kissed her again. A lingering caress that brought a soft moan from her throat. Balfour had to struggle to recall what he had been saying. "I own your brother has his faults, but he has come to see the error of his ways. Does it make any difference to you, Regina? Would you still have me if Andrew disapproved?"

"Do you need ask, Your Grace?" she murmured, hiding

her face against his neck and tightening her arms about his shoulders.

It was several moments before he released her, and another before he regained his breath. "I think it is time you started calling me Cedric. Now, come over and sit down like a good girl before I lose all control."

"What would happen then, Cedric?" she asked, her voice lingering over his name, her eyes full of mischief.

"You shall find out soon enough, little one. Your brother and sister-in-law will be here for Thanksgiving. Your aunt and uncle, too. If you agree, I thought we might be wed then."

"Little one," she repeated. "I never thought to hear you say that again. 'Tis foolish, but it sounds so . . . so wonderful. But how on earth—lord, I do not understand how any of this came about. You say Andrew is willing to give me his blessing, and even Aunt Sarah approves?"

"Perhaps approves is too strong a word, but she is agreeable. 'Tis what I have been trying to tell you, my dear. I kept away from you for two reasons. One, I was not certain this arm of mine would heal—"

"As if that would matter!"

He dropped a kiss on her brow. "There were sufficient cards stacked against me without facing your brother as an invalid. And secondly, I needed to polish my rather tarnished reputation. Aunt Sophia helped. She is as high in the instep as your brother, and it took considerable persuasion to convince her I had mended my ways—"

"No, have you?" she asked, unashamedly hoping for another kiss.

"I have," he replied firmly, but couldn't resist the temptation of her open lips. When he raised his head again, he frowned at her. "Really, Regina, I agonized for weeks over this explanation. You might at least pretend to care why I neglected you all summer."

"But I don't," she replied with incurable honesty. "I am

too grateful merely to have you back. You have no idea how much, how very much I longed to see you."

He groaned aloud and rose abruptly. "Lord, Regina. No man on earth deserves such devotion, and certainly not me, but I swear to you that you will never have cause to regret it. I finally convinced my aunt of that, though I suspect the thought of seeing me respectably wed at last and setting up a nursery had a great deal to do with her capitulation. She is most anxious to see us wed."

"I believe I shall like your Aunt Sophia."

"I hope so, my dear. She certainly exerted herself to persuade your brother that the connection would be a desirable one. No doubt she will expect our first one to be named after her in suitable gratitude," he said with a comical grimace.

Regina gravely shook her head. "I fear we cannot do that." At his questioning glance, she blushed, but met his gaze steadily. "Our firstborn will be named Cedric after his father."

"Sure of that, are you?"

"I am an expert breeder, Your Grace. Need I remind you that bloodlines are my specialty?"

"Lord, but I have missed you!"

"And I, you. Will you stay in Bury St. Edmunds until the wedding? I do not think I could bear to have you go away again."

"Never again," he swore, then held out his hand and pulled her to her feet. "Come, my sweet, and let us say hello to old Ramsey before I ravish you on the spot."

Regina laughed and stepped into his embrace. She brought her arms up and locked her hands about his neck. Her eyes were dark with passion and her voice husky. "I fear you will be disappointed, Cedric, but you cannot see Ramsey. He now lives on my brother's estate. The cottage is empty."

"Really?" he drawled, and with only the ancient trees for witness, he kissed her sweetly. Time stood still in the small glade, as he told her of his love in ways as old as the hills, and as new as the dawn.

ZEBRA REGENCIES
ARE
THE TALK OF THE TON!

A REFORMED RAKE   (4499, $3.99)
by Jeanne Savery

After governess Harriet Cole helped her young charge flee to France — and the designs of a despicable suitor, more trouble soon arrived in the person of a London rake. Sir Frederick Carrington insisted on providing safe escort back to England. Harriet deemed Carrington more dangerous than any band of brigands, but secretly relished matching wits with him. But after being taken in his arms for a tender kiss, she found herself wondering — *could* a lady find love with an irresistible rogue?

A SCANDALOUS PROPOSAL   (4504, $4.99)
by Teresa DesJardien

After only two weeks into the London season, Lady Pamela Premington has already received her first offer of marriage. If only it hadn't come from the *ton's* most notorious rake, Lord Marchmont. Pamela had already set her sights on the distinguished Lieutenant Penford, who had the heroism and honor that made him the ideal match. Now she had to keep from falling under the spell of the seductive Lord so she could pursue the man more worthy of her love. Or was he?

A LADY'S CHAMPION   (4535, $3.99)
by Janice Bennett

Miss Daphne, art mistress of the Selwood Academy for Young Ladies, greeted the notion of ghosts haunting the academy with skepticism. However, to avoid rumors frightening off students, she found herself turning to Mr. Adrian Carstairs, sent by her uncle to be her "protector" against the "ghosts." Although, Daphne would accept no interference in her life, she *would* accept aid in exposing any spectral spirits. What she never expected was for Adrian to expose the secret wishes of her hidden heart . . .

CHARITY'S GAMBIT   (4537, $3.99)
by Marcy Stewart

Charity Abercrombie reluctantly embarks on a London season in hopes of making a suitable match. However she cannot forget the mysterious Dominic Castille — and the kiss they shared — when he fell from a tree as she strolled through the woods. Charity does not know that the dark and dashing captain harbors a dangerous secret that will ensnare them both in its web — leaving Charity to risk certain ruin and losing the man she so passionately loves . . .